Collateral Lead

-A Novel-

Stephen Colcord

SCB

StephenColcordBooks.com

For information regarding scheduled events or to request the author appear live at your book club, library, classroom, or other events, please contact: colcordsteve@yahoo.com

StephenColcordBooks.com
SCB

For Steph, now you have a story.

And for all those that have been with me on one side of a closed door not knowing what awaited us on the other.

CHAPTER ONE

John Washington was frantic after the shooting. The ringing in his ears seemed to somehow intensify, even as time passed since the pull of the trigger that had initiated it. He struggled to catch his breath and found it difficult to get his bearings, while his peripheral vision mimicked a train tunnel through a mountain. With a hand full of money and some drugs that he had taken from Perez after he went down, Washington escaped the area on foot, with no real decisive reason for the direction he went. The pace of his feet hitting the pavement of the sidewalk indicated that they were moving faster than they ever had, while at the same time feeling as though he was running through unset concrete. As his ears rang deeper with each thumping stride, they also began radiating heat in the cool New Jersey night.

He wasn't sure if his counterpart, Keith, had been hurt or what his condition was. A few things had now become clear after his frantic flight from the scene. Once he had a chance to actually think about what had happened, it was obvious he had been set up to kill or at least harm the rival of another man. He raced toward the Delaware River on foot, the only landmark in the relatively unfamiliar city of Camden that allowed him to get a sense of where he was on the map.

The daylight was starting to fade as the darkening night began to dominate the sky. Washington looked down at his burnt orange jacket, the color of the recently departed sun, and knew that he stood out. His motor skills had diminished from the stress and adrenaline, so it took several times clawing at the zipper to get it loose, compounding as he got more frustrated with each attempt. He was finally able to remove his light jacket, his outermost layer, and hustled over to a dumpster next to the gas station on the corner. The fence surrounding the dumpster was locked, most likely put in place to prevent the type of dumping he was about to do. Washington simply heaved it over, unconcerned if it landed in or just near the garbage container. His upper half was now covered in a gray hooded sweatshirt, providing him with a slight sense of camouflaged protection and a quick sensation of cool air. He would no longer fit the description he did just a few minutes prior, while he traversed the streets of Camden.

The sounds of sirens pierced the otherwise quiet winter evening, bringing his racing mind back to the present. Washington understood those sirens were racing towards his bleeding victim. It was also understood that when the evening progressed, they might soon be racing to find him.

All of Washington's contacts in the area had been established through a man that had just set him up, and those contacts certainly owed him no loyalty. Unconnected friends of friends were less than ideal in the situation that Washington found himself in. Who could he turn to? In the panicked scurry, the answer wasn't easy to find.

Tia was the third contact listed in the cell phone that Keith got him when he was released from prison several months prior. The contact list was organized alphabetically, and her last name was Bixby, which determined her place. She was probably also the third person that he would call in such a situation. He had stolen from her the last time he saw her, but she was still the most likely to answer. Getting a chance to quiet his mind and control his breathing, if only slightly, he made his decision to call.

The still shaking index finger hit the dial button and he waited. One ring, two rings, three rings. He knew she'd answer. She always had a soft spot in her heart for him, mostly because she could see Washington in her own son's face and hear him in his voice.

"Hello?"

"Tia?"

"Yeah, what's going on with you? Why are you so out of breath?" It wasn't often that he called her, he usually texted. He would generally only call Tia to speak with his son, and that was in the instances when Washington's own mother wasn't around to facilitate such an interaction.

"I need your help, bad."

"Where are you?"

"I'm still down south. I need you to come down and pick me up and get me the hell out of here."

"I can't just take your mom's car and drive down there and get you, you know that." She was more than annoyed. Annoyed at his irresponsibility. Annoyed with herself that even though she had just said no, she was still entertaining the idea of going to get him.

"I can't really tell you what's going on, I just need some help right now." Washington was getting frustrated at his apparent lack of ability to get her sympathy, to get her assistance, to get her to blindly follow his directions. Did he not make it clear how much trouble he was in?

"What would I even tell your mother?"

"Don't say anything to her, do you fuckin' hear me?" It was too late, he thought. He hung up the phone without another word exchanged, like so many of his prison calls with her had been cut short. This couldn't go any further, he would need another avenue out of town, away from the cops. Away from the harm the victim's family and friends would no doubt bring upon him if they found him first.

He continued what felt like a full sprint all the way to the banks of the Delaware, to a park near the aquarium that he was familiar with. Washington came up to the benches on the edge of the grass. Seeing more people around, his jog morphed to walking as he did not desire any unneeded attention. Sitting down briefly

4

on the first cold, metal bench, he tried to catch his breath and organize his jumbled thoughts, while the heat of his heavy breathing fogged up the area in front of his face. From the seated position he could feel the cool metal of his gun pressing on the bare skin next to his right hipbone. For the first time it really set in; he may have killed a man, though he couldn't be sure.

Washington slowly walked to the cast iron railing beside the bank of the smooth flowing river. He faced the water and away from the street where there were potential on-lookers. As though he was trying to calmly slide a quarter in an arcade game, he let the gun go, waiting until he heard an assuring splash. The cell phone had to go next in case he was going to be tracked because of it, he thought. The phone numbers of his mother and Tia were memorized forever in his head anyway from his days using the prison phones, painfully dialing each number every time he called. The splash of the phone sounded similar to the gun but less dense, like the difference between a swan dive and a cannon ball. He looked around one more time to make sure no one had seen him, briefly second guessing his decision to give up his ability to contact everyone he knew. With the weapon gone and the phone immersed in the water, a subtle wave of relief washed over him, if only for an instant.

Free from the items that linked him to the shooting, he started back east through the city. Ironically, he passed the jail and the courthouse on his way. It was a stark reminder to him that he needed to do anything he could to never end up in either place.

CHAPTER TWO

He was no stranger to the inside of a Brother's Burgers chain. He was no stranger to most dining establishments if he was being honest with himself or if anyone that knew him even a little bit was asked. At well over six feet tall and north of an eighth of a ton on the scale, Deputy Sheriff Mark Pollard had more than a small love affair with food. Although he probably wouldn't be described as fat by those who saw him, his conquests at buffets were the stuff of legends amongst his team members.

Pollard wasn't patronizing this particular Brother's Burgers franchise that day, at least not yet. He was there on a mission, on a case, on a hunt. He was tracking a wanted man, and he was at the point in the investigation when all the hard work leading up to that moment was about to pay off, or alternatively, the whole thing would come to an end in a spectacular crash. After years of experience in this business of hunting fugitives, Pollard thought to himself that he should be more confident. After all of the years in the business, Pollard knew better than to grab at that feeling.

The assistant manager at Brother's Burgers couldn't have been any older than the college kids from the local university seated around the table in the corner booth behind him. Maybe he was a student there too. Those college kids might normally take some notice of a deputy sheriff walking through the doors. It was likely that the unassuming winter coat, plain clothes, and lowered voice asking to speak with the manager helped him blend. He probably appeared to them as a disgruntled customer, not a man looking for a murderer near their quaint, snow-blanketed, New England campus.

Aside from the normal room scan all cops perform when they walk through any door, uniformed or not, Pollard took little notice of the students. They appeared to take even less notice of him as the four boyish mugs were blocked from his view by the screens held out in front of their noses.

In his own circles, Pollard was the butt of a lot of jokes and good-natured ball busting for the outdated flip phone that he carried, commonly referred to by his peers as the "fossil." He never understood the draw of staring at a screen constantly like the kids at that table were doing, an occurrence so common it was almost as natural as breathing. Pollard lamented his constant observations that even his professional contemporaries had begun the same habit on a regular basis when the team would sit down for a meal like the kids were that day. He was certainly happy that his college years, unlike these young men, were during a time when a photograph had to be sent for developing at the local photo shop or pharmacy and not shared instantly with the whole world with a click of a button. His job had provided him with the smartphone that he was carrying,

8

and if it wasn't for work-related functions, Pollard would have been happy to let the ever-progressing technology pass him by completely.

Brother's Burgers wasn't really a fast-food joint, but it really wasn't a dining establishment with waitstaff or anything either. It was somewhere in between, and that elevated status above fast food had Pollard hopeful that the assistant manager wasn't a complete moron. Moron or not, Pollard would learn that there was no video of the purchase he was inquiring about, and this assistant manager was the one who made the sale on the day in question. His answer, therefore, was immensely important. The early inquiries posed by Pollard were mostly to jog the kid's memory, get him thinking about that day and time, to take him to that exact moment in his head. How the conversation was progressing determined when the questions were asked, but the important questions always came a little bit later when Pollard was doing an interview. The deputy made one last request from the young manager after trying to keep his initial information gathering as simple and as easy to follow as possible. He knew the timing wasn't going to be any better than it was right then, and after an anxious stroke of his thin beard, he went for it.

"Is this the guy?" he asked while gently placing the folded photo on the counter like a car salesman sliding a pricey figure across a desk in the showroom of an auto dealership. All of the interviews, search warrants, talks with detectives and parole officers, all of that time spent pouring over reports and records, was either worth it or not based on this kid's reply. Pollard was agitated that it had come to this, but the next steps in the investigation all hinged on the young man's answer, and just as important, the manner in which he answered it.

CHAPTER THREE

Pollard had been a lawman for more than fifteen years. Now well beyond the half-way point between thirty and forty years old, he certainly wasn't a kid anymore and had seemingly less in common with each batch of twenty somethings coming into the profession in waves. He also hadn't yet been accepted as part of the old guard either, because there were still plenty of coworkers that would tell stories about things that happened long before he had arrived. Graduating from the first New Hampshire Police Academy session after September 11, 2001, Pollard had initially worked as a patrol officer for the police department in the town of Windsor, one of the municipalities within the county where he was now a deputy sheriff.

He explained in his interview when he left Windsor's employ that his aquarium was getting a little small in the confines of one little town. He would drive his cruiser from one end of the town to the other, turn around and do it again. He returned to the same nooks and crannies between the town lines shift after shift. It was the same repetitive domestic disputes and drunks, delinquent kids, and sharp corners where the fatal accidents took place. The same tourists that came for the skiing and the ice fishing in the winter, the boating on those previously frozen lakes in the summer and as the seasons turned, what seemed like the same crowds gawking at the sight of leaves morphing to the varied color of fire.

To self-torture, he would sit outside the Windsor Fire Department in his cruiser at 3 a.m. and wonder why his father, now a retired firefighter from the town Pollard had grown up in, hadn't pushed him harder to follow in his footsteps. Not so much for the nostalgic tradition of a son following dear old dad, but more so he too could sleep at night and get paid. It was the jealous envy every cop in the history of time had towards all firefighters everywhere. As it was said so often, there were only two groups that got paid to be in bed, the professional firefighter and the oldest of all professions.

Maybe it wasn't Dad's fault at all, he had finally concluded after driving by the firehouse for what felt like the millionth time. Pollard would joke with those who asked why he hadn't followed the old man, that he still pissed his pants just a little bit every time he got up on the roof of his own house. Whether it was to fix a shingle or shovel the deep New Hampshire snow safely down to the ground to reduce the weight, activities up on the roof were more than just unappealing to him.

Pollard adapted to the fate of his trade and had worked enough overnight shifts to know exactly how to jam his large frame and cumbersome gear hitched to his waist into the front seat of a Ford Crown Victoria. On the real quiet nights, there was often just enough comfort to get some unsatisfying sleep, but not like his firefighting comrades, cozy in their bunks.

After years of repetitive overnight shifts, he could tell when a light was on in one of the businesses in town that wasn't normally illuminated during the night and early morning. It also had become obvious to him when one hadn't come on that should be. He knew what time the delivery trucks arrived at the local box stores and supermarkets and had come to know the first names of the cashiers that worked the graveyard shift at the handful of 24-hour service stations in town. Picking a different gas station each shift, he'd stop in after night had become morning to grab a copy of the Stanton Daily Sun, a free regional newspaper from the neighboring small city, fill up the gas tank of the cruiser, and say hello. It was a moment of respite for the cashiers. With an officer in the shop and a marked black and white out front, they could let their worries about a local drug addict coming in to rob the place go away for a bit. Such a meeting gave the cashiers a chance to converse about anything weird or out of the ordinary that they probably wouldn't call to report. The odd hours created some interesting people watching, with those who had not yet gone to bed mixing with those who had the discipline to get up early every day. Pollard knew the cashiers thought about their safety just as much as he did his own. He usually left with the folded paper under his arm and a mention of a blessing of a good day's sleep that only members of the overnight shift fraternity could understand.

13

Pollard was well aware of which cars were headed into the diners and restaurants to open for the breakfast shift along with the names of the faces serving him his omelet. He would get a glance at the headlines in the morning paper he had just picked up before heading in for breakfast. Pollard would grab his favorite table under a picture of John McCain campaigning with the owner during the 2000 first in the nation presidential primary. At another diner, he'd settle under the autographed pictures of a trio of native New Hampshire comics, Adam Sandler, Seth Meyers, and Sarah Silverman. He would intentionally place the daily rag on the table next to his coffee almost as bait. The news was printed in that paper, but the real story would often be relayed by a familiar waitress who had the chance to hear what everyone in town had to say about the current events. While the hairdresser might have the inside scoop on the affairs of her clients, the waitress at the breakfast shop hears the conversations of a diverse group of townsfolk every day, and Pollard considered those conversations his chance at a nuanced perspective of the daily happenings in town.

Pollard wasn't described by others as an aggressive cop, in demeanor or self-initiated activity. Part of it was the dynamic of the shift, part of it was the philosophical disagreement he had with quotas. But what he lacked in some of his quantifiable measures he made up for in his ability on the stand in court, to go toe-to-toe with defense lawyers. His usefulness came with his ability to speak with both victims and suspects alike, develop rapport with people

14

ranging from innocent children to evil domestic abusers, and write a lock tight report of the facts.

But some of these skills also made him persona non-grata with the Windsor Police brass who were less than impressed with a know-it-all college guy, as they saw it. The promotions he was passed over for in Windsor solidified his understanding of where he stood and set him on a course to become a deputy for the county. On his second application for the job, Pollard was chosen. The timing of his first rejection, though painful, worked to his advantage.

For nearly a year, Pollard did what was asked of him. He got the lay of the land outside his extensive knowledge of the minor details of everyone and everything in Windsor. Getting to know the other areas of the county felt like the release from the aquarium he had referenced in his interview. The work was new and different and the honeymoon phase from that newness hadn't yet worn off when he got a quick visit one afternoon from the elected high sheriff himself. In this small department, it wasn't uncommon for deputies to have a conversation with the sheriff as he was an approachable man that was never off limits personally for his staff or the public. Pollard had certainly shared a few laughs and lighthearted moments with the sheriff over the first few months of his employment, even being the new guy. Alone in his shared office before the boss invaded, Pollard could quickly see that this wasn't shaping up to be one of those lighthearted moments. The sheriff's initial tone indicated a seriousness Pollard hadn't seen up close in the man elected by the people to be his boss.

"Hey Mark, got a minute?" The sheriff had a way of making it seem like this was simply a question that Pollard could decline if he desired, and not a direct order to give him that minute.

"Of course, sir. What's going on?"

"Well, how do you think your time here is going?" the sheriff asked while getting comfortable in the vacant chair at the adjacent desk. The sheriff looked up from the floor and made eye contact with his deputy.

Pollard paused briefly before answering, trying to ascertain where the sheriff was taking this line of questioning. He was, after all, still on a probationary first year status with the department and could be let go with no union protection. But Pollard had no indication or reason to believe that would be the issue. Keep the answer short, he thought.

"Things are good. I mean they're good. Really, really, good. I'm enjoying myself here getting to know some of the other towns in the county other than Windsor. So... good." It wasn't quite the brief response that Pollard had hoped for, but he hadn't been able to shake the quick anxiety before he answered a leading question like that from his boss. But at least he hadn't gone too far.

"That's... good," the sheriff retorted slowly with tongue slightly in cheek both referencing and emphasizing the number of times Pollard had just said the word good, but not so slow that he was mocking him. "How would you like to take over for Sherrill? Now that he's been promoted to sergeant, the US Marshals are looking for his replacement from our county, and we think you are the guy for it." The sheriff always cut to the chase and was less inclined to delay the important questions during this informal interview. He also commonly used the pronoun "we," as Pollard had noticed early on in his interactions with the sheriff, when really it was just him asking. But it was mostly during the sheriff's attempts to be persuasive, as though the perception of consensus might help the sale.

The sheriff was inviting Pollard to join the US Marshals Joint Fugitive Task Force, a fairly new concept in New Hampshire that had taken off in other parts of the country. One of the primary jobs of the county sheriffs was to locate fugitives from and in their county, and the same was true of the United States Marshals service for the federal courts. A modern-day posse of sorts had been created out of need, efficiency, and common interests between agencies. Pollard's department had a member assigned to the team used to locate and apprehend fugitives all around the state and beyond.

Pollard, still happy to be out of his fish bowl in Windsor and enjoying the newness of his current role, initially stammered. He had never even given it a thought during his first few months at his new job to transition into fugitive work.

"There's a ton of overtime available from the Feds and it would be great for your career, and a new experience." The sheriff continued, intentionally selling some of the upside before he allowed an opportunity for Pollard to answer, hoping to frame his response.

"I would have to talk to Kelly about it and get a little more information before I give you an answer on this, Sheriff."

"Of course, Mark. I don't need an answer today, but by the end of the week. Talk to Sherrill about it when you get a chance and hear what his experience was like. I wouldn't let you say yes without Kelly's blessing either, but I really think this would be good for you and you'd be good at it, Mark."

"I'll let you know by Friday, if that works?" Pollard had found the succinct answer he was initially looking for while not addressing the compliment. The sheriff, not wanting to linger or oversell, nodded, stepped out of the room and down the hallway without another word. Pollard was left listening to the clank of the sheriff's boots fading further away while contemplating his offer.

Pollard couldn't quite believe it. There were certainly others in the department who would like this assignment. Why me? Who cares, he figured, talk to Sherrill about it, get Kelly on board, and see where it ends up.

CHAPTER FOUR

Like the pressed flags behind a President in the oval office, Pollard's wall art hanging behind his own chair had purpose. Hemingway's words accurately depicted the shift in his professional focus.

There is no hunting like the hunting of man. And those who have hunted armed men long enough and like it, never care for anything else thereafter. – Ernest Hemingway

It had now been a few years since the sheriff came to him about the assignment to the Fugitive Task Force and Pollard had almost taken on a new persona with the change in his law enforcement duties. Gone were his days of midnight patrol shifts, evicting tenants and transporting inmates. Pollard had been sworn in as a Special Deputy US Marshal for this assignment. Deputy US Marshal Rick Dorsey, Pollard's teammate and regional partner on the Task Force, called it his "out of state hunting license," referencing his newly expanded jurisdictional authority. Pollard's boundaries had grown from the town of Windsor to the entire state of New Hampshire and now nationwide in less than twelve months.

The first few years on assignment with the Fugitive Task Force had brought a lot of great arrests and fugitive hunts for some serious offenses and some bad dudes. Locating and arresting sexual offenders, domestic batterers, armed robbers, and dangerous drug dealers occupied most of the team's time. The group's assortment of deputy sheriffs on full time assignment like Pollard, and the Federal Marshals working on the team comprised a unique crew, an effective crew when called into action.

Officially, each member of the team had his own duties and strengths. Unofficially, as Pollard and Deputy Sheriff Tony Vatrano, team member from New Hampshire's most populated county would surmise, each person fit into one of two distinct categories: runners and holders. Runners had the speed and endurance, wearing full gear, to catch a fleeing fugitive who might spring from a house or vehicle trying to get the advantage to escape when approached. Holders were those large and strong enough to keep them from getting away once they were caught within a house, vehicle or out in public. As Vatrano would often ask, "If you're not a runner and you're not a holder, what good are you for the team?" It was a joke of course, but like any joke that could bring at least a crack of a smile, there was some truth to it. Pollard, Dorsey, and Vatrano were holders by nature's blessing, and by the numbers on the digital scale. Dressed in full gear, they would easily combine for almost nine hundred pounds of "man meat" as Dorsey described it.

But brawn wasn't everything with this team. Dorsey, having worked as a marshal in the nation's capital and in some of the larger cities in Connecticut, was a bronze star winning combat veteran from the Persian Gulf War. He was back home in New Hampshire where he was raised, having started his law enforcement days behind the walls of the New Hampshire State Prison as a corrections officer. His experiences fit well with Pollard, the college kid turned small town cop, turned sheriff's deputy, and Vatrano, a Bar certified attorney who gave up practicing law after September 11th to become a deputy sheriff.

All three men were sitting in Pollard's office at the Sheriff's Department when the call came from team leader Jeff Brown, Supervisory Deputy Marshal. Brown was a large, African American man with a head shaved consistently to a shine, a goatee starting to show some gray, and a commanding baritone voice that could get anyone's attention. It still got Pollard's attention even though he knew what was coming as he hit the answer button on his cell phone.

"Pollard?" Brown yelled through the phone, clearly driving in his car somewhere as the hum of the motor and space between his mouth and the microphone made him sound distant, like he was calling from the bottom of a well.

"What's going on Brownie?" Pollard asked earnestly as he really didn't have any reference as to why Brown was calling.

"Nothing good. We're gonna need your help on a new one. We just caught a collateral lead on a murder case out of southern New Jersey. They can't seem to find the guy in Camden. It sounds like his mom and his baby momma live up in your county."

"Okay," Pollard replied, expecting at least slightly more information or some indication of what the next step was going to be.

"I've got the file. I'm on my way up to your office with Matthews. Are Vatrano and Dorsey still up there?"

"Yep. We'll wait here for you."

"Great, sounds good. Love you." Brown always ended his calls with his counterparts with a "love you." It was his way of breaking tension, like a good team leader did. Eventually it just became habit, and really, at the heart of it, there was some true sentiment behind it for all of them.

John Washington killed a man in New Jersey. He shot him square in the chest, allegedly of course. The autopsy indicated that a single, 9-millimeter bullet entered the victim's body about an inch from the left nipple. The shot came from an extremely close range as evidenced by the gunpowder residue on the victim's shirt, estimated by the experts at about two feet away. The man later died in a hospital emergency room. It was learned that the bullet went through both of his lungs and exited his body on the right side of his back, below the right shoulder blade. The medically induced coma only stalled the inevitable. Surgical staff could not heal the wounds fast enough as the man's lungs filled with blood, like a boat taking on water faster than the hole could be patched and the water bailed out. He eventually suffocated and choked to death, like a man drowning in that same boat.

In strict legal terms, Washington was alleged to have committed this crime as he had not been tried by any court on the matter. In the world of fugitive arrest warrants, as Pollard had quickly realized years ago, innocence and guilt are irrelevant and rarely even discussed. The arrest warrant literally commanded the law enforcement officer to "Arrest the Body Of...," in this case a Mr. John Washington, a twenty-five-year-old New Hampshire man. The signature of a New Jersey judge on the bottom of the page wasn't legible, but it was there and to the Fugitive Task Force, none of the other details really mattered unless those details would help in the effort to locate the wanted party. It wasn't up to them to try the case.

Dorsey would often say, "The best part about fugitive work is that you can mess it up a bunch of times, but in the end, still get your guy." Pollard heard this often during his initial time on the team, and like much of the wisdom that Dorsey would impart, it was found to be true. They could show up an hour late to a house where a fugitive had been, and if he wasn't there, things just re-set and start again. The same was not true in the criminal investigation of a murder. Evidence lost is evidence lost. Cases are made and lost with no going back sometimes, without a chance at a do-over. A missed chance at a confession, a contaminated crime scene, a witness account or piece of evidence that was never found during a canvassing, were all critical to an investigation and often only available with just one shot. So, with that on the back burner of his mind, Pollard read the warrant and affidavit for Washington's arrest prepared by Detective Charles Luce of the Camden County Prosecutor's Office. The hard work and effort it took to solve this particular murder was laid out on paper for Pollard to read, and he was impressed and humbled by those investigative efforts.

The written narrative in the affidavit that accompanied the arrest warrant was a page turner. From what Pollard could gather in his initial reading, Washington, and a man that he was staying with in New Jersey named Robert Keith, set up a local food delivery driver to come to a home to be robbed. It appeared as though the victim, Pascal Perez, who died of a single gunshot wound to the chest from that 9 mm handgun, was not known to Washington. Mr. Keith, however, was quite familiar with the victim, as they had done time in jail together in New Jersey. Keith knew the man was delivering food for a local pizza place and had convinced Washington to help in the robbery. When a heated struggle ensued between the three men, Washington fired the shot directly into the chest of Perez from close range, ending the brief but intense skirmish. It was believed Washington took his delivery money, as Perez was able to talk to responding police to provide some details. In total, it was a little less than $100.

Perez had no problem identifying one of his assailants, Keith, as his white supremacist views were no secret to those behind the locked doors and concrete walls of New Jersey prisons. Though wounded and in a great deal of pain, Perez stated he tried to fight off his attackers the moment he realized he was being ambushed. He described Washington as best as he could under the conditions and indicated that Washington had fired the shot that eventually became fatal. The injured man failed to tell the police about the drugs that were taken from his pockets along with the cash, but in the end it really wasn't relevant.

Perez was a well-liked kid in his circles. He had been immensely popular in the jails in New Jersey and in his neighborhood in Camden. Revenge was on the mind of a lot of those friends and their known gang associates, and the Camden County Police were wary of it. Locating the murderer first, before any others, was going to prevent further violence and had become a high priority for the department.

It was believed by the investigating detectives that Washington took off out of Camden overnight, ditching the 9mm handgun and his cell phone in the Delaware River, after he figured that the police in Camden were looking to talk to him about the shooting.

Mr. Keith surprised investigators with his eagerness to cooperate surrendering to authorities. He spoke with an eye toward leniency for his involvement as Perez was dead before being able to give a detailed statement instead of a dying declaration. Washington was known to have pulled the trigger, now confirmed by the victim and Keith, thus allowing Keith to persuade the investigators with one of the three men involved dead and the other on the run. Keith's rival from the prison in New Jersey was now dead. Someone else was going to be pinned with the murder for it, in what was being called a botched robbery initially, at least until the white supremacy undertones were vetted by the New Jersey authorities. Washington's past had included a conviction for armed robbery back in New Hampshire and he was paroled from the charge. His old cellmate, Keith, knew that. He knew that he could use that information, and emphasize it, to convince the police that Washington had done it again, this time as the trigger man. He certainly wasn't willing to take the murder charge for Washington, a guy he had just met less than a year prior in the New Hampshire prison. In fact, it seemed that he put this whole series of events in place so that he would not need to be charged with the murder at all, while still accomplishing his end goal. Even an accomplice charge for Keith would be easy to plea out if he cooperated. Although working with the police would normally come with consequences in his circles, it would be no problem for his white supremacist gang friends this time, given the murder had been committed in the name of their cause.

According to the affidavit, Keith told the Camden County investigators that Washington was trying to join the white supremacy gang he was a member of, and that the whole thing was Washington's idea to make a name for himself. But it wasn't supposed to be a murder, just a robbery of a rival gang member who was out delivering food and probably drugs. The detective in Camden was familiar with Keith after reviewing some of the prison records from New Jersey identifying him as a white supremacist. Keith's account seemed logical to those same investigators, that the white kid that he had met in New Hampshire State Prison was also now a part of the gang, or at least hoping to be.

Cell phone records put Washington in the area of the murder at the time it was committed. The eyewitness accounts from his old cellmate, the victim and others on the block confirmed who the police would be looking for. The 9mm handgun was recovered by the New Jersey State Police Dive Team along with the cell phone in the river as the last known activity on the phone was right on the banks of the Delaware. When the Camden County Police were trying to locate Washington from the cell phone data, it was clear to them that it ended at the edge of the river. Locating the gun was a helpful bonus to the murder investigation, but the submerged cell phone next to it put a wrinkle in the effort to locate the alleged murderer, knowing that Washington was no longer attached to it.

While Pollard read the affidavit, he nearly laughed out loud thinking of how different this story of a guy named Washington and his brush with the Delaware River was being told. It was in contrast to the events further up the river in Trenton a couple hundred years prior during the Revolutionary War, something he vaguely remembered from his childhood history classes.

With Washington's cell phone located in close proximity to what turned out to be the murder weapon, the case was solid. Being that Washington had few connections to the local area that were his and not Keith's, who had now set him up and sold him out, he had no choice but to get out of town. The fugitive team in Camden knew that but still followed up on some leads in the area. Those local leads on the whereabouts of John Washington were now exhausted, with neither the police nor the fugitive team from the area having any success locating him. The fact that Washington's corpse hadn't been located in the river near his phone and weapon gave investigators a very strong reason to believe that the victim's friends and associates hadn't found him yet either.

"Pretty crazy, huh?" Brown said after he saw that Pollard had finished reading. Brown had arrived with Deputy Sheriff Dan Matthews from one of the other New Hampshire counties to the south of Pollard's.

"Yup. Sure is," Pollard replied.

"I got some possible family right here on Facebook," Matthews chimed in. As the resident millennial on the team, Matthews was a little younger than his counterparts. His long hair was pulled back behind his face by the constraints of his green Hartford Whalers hat worn backwards. From North Dakota, across the great lake states, up to the crown of Maine and throughout all of Canada, his look was commonly referred to as "hockey hair."

Though Matthews didn't possess the speed of a runner or brawn of a holder, he brought a social media and technology expertise that allowed Vatrano, the biggest ball buster of the group, to forgive his inability to fit nicely into one of the required categories. Really, if forced to admit it, the whole runners and holders thing was created by Vatrano and Pollard to tease the young deputy. He was certainly a repeated target of the light hazing that comes with the territory of being the new guy.

"All right, but let's get as much information as we can right now before we move on anything." Brown, usually one to push for aggressive action on a case, knew that they hadn't advanced to that phase yet.

Though raised in an era before attention deficit disorder was commonly understood, Brown would most definitely have fit that diagnosis to a clinical "T." The other members looked at him, almost confused by his wish for patience and research before blowing out of the door.

"I know. I know." He laughed deep from his belly, acknowledging the astonishment in the room. "But really, we've got some homework to do on this one, and this is a homicide. This guy's mom, girlfriend and child should be around, and the team from Philly hasn't found him yet and they don't think that they will. Good chance he'll be with 'em around here in Stanton if they're here. If not, he's from New Hampshire, he might be somewhere else around here." It was a call to investigate from Brown, not a call to action, as rare as an eclipse.

CHAPTER FIVE

The aged but imposingly sturdy brick facade outside of the public entrance to the New Hampshire State Prison for Men was only four stories high, but it felt bigger when the heavy metal doors slammed behind them. Dorsey had cut his teeth behind those walls in his initial break into the world of law enforcement. As a much younger man, he caught on as a State Corrections Officer when he got out of the military after combat in the Middle East and a peace keeping tour in the Balkans. To Dorsey, the place hadn't changed at all. The sounds and smells, a fair amount of the people working there, and even some of the residents were quite familiar to him. Pollard, however, had never really been past the receiving area where inmates were picked up and dropped off, so his experience differed greatly from Dorsey's impromptu homecoming.

The two men were on the grounds of the prison to see New Hampshire Parole Officer Rich Briggs. The team in Philadelphia had indicated in their collateral lead that a warrant for Washington's arrest from the New Hampshire Parole Board popped up when they started looking for him. It was issued about eight months prior to the murder with extradition limited to the six New England states.

That limitation was common for the garden variety offenders, so Washington would have been safe from the New Hampshire authorities in New Jersey. Such a detail was no doubt a selling point that Washington's former cellmate, Keith, had used in his pitch to convince him to go down there. Briggs was listed as the officer requesting the warrant through the Parole Board. Washington had been assigned to him upon release to the local halfway house located just a few blocks from that brick façade.

"I have never physically laid eyes on the man," Briggs started a little defensively as Dorsey, who had worked with him at the prison in what seemed like a lifetime before, smiled out of half of his mouth. It was hardly uncommon for parolees and probationers to never even appear at their initial meeting with their parole officer, to set up the terms of their pending release from transitional housing.

"Settle down Briggs, this isn't our first rodeo. We know," Dorsey assured him through tight lips behind his deep orange goatee. It wasn't the first time they had heard this from a parole officer when looking for a wanted person, and it probably wouldn't be the last.

Briggs nodded and turned towards Pollard's large silhouette, filling up the entire doorway to his office inside the guts of the prison. Dorsey made his introductions after observing the two strangers had made eye contact. Comfortable in his old stomping ground, he had initially forgotten that Briggs and Pollard would have little reason to know one another.

Chasing down a suspect who had violated parole or bail release was not a new experience for Dorsey and Pollard. Many of the fugitives that they found over the previous years had been let go over and over by judges and parole boards, a source of aggravation for so many of the members of the team. As he stood in the doorway of that office, Pollard gave some consideration to that pattern. In the nearly three years since Pollard had been with the task force, he couldn't recall a time that he was involved in the arrest of a fugitive who hadn't been in jail or prison previously and released. In this case, the man set adrift before his maximum sentence date, Washington, had now committed a murder. Allegedly, of course.

"Now we know that you have no first-hand knowledge of the guy, we're only here for whatever records you've got at the prison anyway." With Pollard and Briggs now acquainted, Dorsey settled the expectations of their visit to take some of the pressure off.

"Records I have. I pulled his files when you called," the parole officer retorted confidently.

Washington had done eighteen months of his three-year sentence on Conspiracy to Commit Armed Robbery when he was twenty-two years old. He was a suspected member of a white supremacist prison gang that had just started to take hold in New

Hampshire, spreading from the Ohio, Pennsylvania, and New Jersey area.

"I'm not sure where the white supremacist stuff comes from." That affiliation was not something that Briggs could substantiate in any recorded report, or photos of tattoos or writings, but he was still flagged generally as a member in the prison software system. "Maybe you guys can find it in the file. I couldn't," he lamented.

"My guess would be his association with Mr. Keith." Dorsey stated the obvious to the parole officer who hadn't been afforded the opportunity to read the reports from the New Jersey authorities.

Though he was not able to track Washington's whereabouts upon release, records from his incarceration were right at Briggs' fingertips on his computer. In the middle of digging around the records system at Dorsey's request, Briggs dropped a manila folder on the small round table in the corner of the room as though he had almost forgot about it. Pollard jumped at it like a feeding animal. Dorsey continued to stand over Briggs' shoulder as the parole officer looked up over his glasses and back down at his hands, stroking the keys through the various screens of the prison database entries. "Phone records, incoming and outgoing mail, visitation records, emergency contact info." Briggs acted as though he was making up for his lack of supervision of Washington. Dorsey, sensing the sentiment, put him at ease by overstating his gratitude, but only slightly.

"This will be great!" Dorsey chuckled. "Can't wait to dive in. It sure is different than when I was working here. All this stuff used to be kept in logbooks and triplicate carbon paper." He took his ballcap off and rubbed his forehead and short red hairs atop his head as if reminiscing on the time gone by.

Pollard was only about halfway through his examination of the hard copy file in the folder when he stuck his head up to get his partner's attention. "Hey Dorsey, it looks like we're going to need Vatrano on this one." The initial armed robbery a few years back that put Washington in prison took place in Vatrano's county, in the state's most populated city. "Looks like he's originally from the west side."

"But according to the visitation records that I can see, mom and baby momma and his four-year-old kid all live in your county now. And the outgoing mail log shows the same. The hole you came out of or the hole you get into." It was Dorsey's crude reminder that many of the fugitives on the run often end up located in the domicile of their mothers and girlfriends. The phrase had become so common over the years that it was now a cliché. Briggs' mouth opened in shock and then transitioned quickly to a hardy chuckle. He appeared amused by the phrase, and the ease with which it rolled off Dorsey's tongue.

Like a robber stuffing cash in a bag, Dorsey hastily jammed the freshly printed records in the manila folder, adding to what Pollard had already gone halfway through.

"Hey Briggsy, when we get this guy, can you make sure the fuckin' prison holds onto him this time please?" Dorsey joked, knowing full well that Briggs, with no say in such decisions whatsoever, had to just take his light-hearted abuse.

Briggs quietly nodded his head like a beaten man and escorted the two visitors out of the secured parole office area of the prison and back out to the parking lot. He knew he didn't have anything meaningful to offer to the case other than what he had provided on paper. "Always good to see you again, Dorsey. Nice to meet you, Pollard." His words were delivered with a slap on the back to each man, sealing the deal on their goodbyes as he retreated back toward his office.

"Likewise," Pollard replied.

Without saying anything, Dorsey cracked half a smile at his old coworker, equal parts apology for the gentle ribbing and demonstration of gratitude for the help. Replacing Dorsey's silence, the clang of the large metal doors added the final punctuation on a reunion with his old chum.

Dorsey was behind the wheel driving back to Pollard's office. They were quiet for some time as Pollard set out to finish perusing the file in his lap, now slightly thicker with the records that Dorsey had added. The numbers on the mile markers that they breezed past on the highway began ticking higher and higher as they traveled to the north.

"Perez, huh?" Pollard muttered, somewhere between speaking and thinking out loud.

"What?" Dorsey replied, a little lost and caught off guard as the silence had been broken without any conversational reference.

"The dead guy in all of this. His name is Perez. Makes you wonder about this white supremacy bullshit with Washington." Neither one had really even considered the victim of this crime yet. The killing had occurred hundreds of miles away in a place neither had ever been. They weren't tasked with notifying the family of his death or interviewing friends and witnesses from that neighborhood. They would never drive by the spot on the street where the murder took place or see the makeshift memorial of flowers and candles that had covered the area when the yellow crime scene tape came down. Perez was just the name of a victim on an affidavit for an arrest warrant for the target of their hunt, John Washington. It was just business at that point.

"It's different behind the walls, Mark. At least when I was there," Dorsey explained. "He may have been flagged as a gang member just for certain friendships and associations that he had. If he joined, it was most likely for self-protection, or to belong to a group, not necessarily because of his beliefs."

Pollard listened to Dorsey's explanation, as he respected his experience and expertise on the matter, but he wasn't quite sold.

"And really, he was there for eighteen months, how indoctrinated could that fucker have gotten?" Dorsey asked the question in the same fashion that a good attorney might give his closing argument. Pollard thought back to the narrative in the affidavit for the arrest warrant. "Or maybe he is a white supremacist," Dorsey continued, hedging against his previous statement. "What difference does that make to us?" Pollard tilted his head slightly as he pondered an answer to the question posed to him, but he ultimately offered no response. Dorsey wasn't actually expecting one anyway. "I mean really, who gives a shit?" Dorsey added rhetorically. Pollard then moved the conversation 180 degrees from the thought and brought up lunch.

"It's Tuesday, time for some tacos."

CHAPTER SIX

For almost fifteen years Pollard had been working in some capacity within his county, either as a Police Officer or now as a Deputy Sheriff. He had never even heard of John Washington. Being that it wasn't a big county, most of the requests he got for help locating wanted subjects were names that he had become accustomed to hearing. It would be odd to have no knowledge of an armed robber in his area, but not so odd if that armed robbery occurred three years prior and two counties away in the state's largest city. Vatrano had volunteered his efforts to get whatever he could for records in his county, after receiving a text message from Pollard when he and Dorsey left the prison. It was the county that Washington had spent his entire non-incarcerated life in, so Pollard was hoping for some connections.

"What do you have for me?" Pollard took Vatrano's incoming phone call without much concern for a customary greeting.

"I got nothing in the past few years down here. I mean nothing. Before that armed robbery charge, he's had police contact all over, but now, nothing." Vatrano seemed as surprised to be saying it as Pollard was to be hearing it.

"Guess he really got the fuck out of town when he left prison then, 'cause we don't have shit up here in our county records either. He's never been to our jail, never been transported by us, never had contact with any of the police departments we dispatch for. It's strange." With a collateral lead to his county, Pollard was expecting at least a trace of contact between local police and the suspect. But it just wasn't there. "I guess if he had made some contact with the law in New Hampshire recently, he would have been scooped up on the arrest warrant for the parole violation."

"Exactly. I'm on my way up to your office. Brownie and Matthews are coming too. I think Dorsey's running late, but we'll all be there soon."

"Good, we'll hit the streets up here on this. See you in a bit."

While initially waiting for Vatrano to get back to him, Pollard had been doing some of his own digging. Although text messaging was not his favored method of communication, it was preferred by the confidential informants he had developed over his years of hunting fugitives. Developing an informant wasn't always easy. Some were guys from town that often ended up with child support warrants from the local family court. Pollard would give them the benefit of a few extra weeks to come up with the cash before going to look for them. In exchange, they would sometimes be his eyes and ears throughout the county when a bigger fish needed frying. The trade-off had some moral implications, but Pollard worked it out in his own head. Eventually the child support obligation was paid and the wanted party didn't have to sit in jail. In return, some violent and dangerous criminals were apprehended safely and on the deputy's terms. It was a win all the way around. However, the victory required that he think less about those relying on that child support payment.

Informants were often his first contact when looking for someone in town, and many had been fugitives that Pollard had located himself. The relationship that develops between the hunter and the hunted creates a bond. When the hunted felt as though he or she was treated with respect, the hunter tended to gain from that new association.

The text message requests to his informants went out individually instead of in a group. Pollard held each person's confidence seriously. It was an annoying process sending out the same message six or seven different times, but it was a necessary one. Pollard would generally start each person off with a full name and any street or gang names that the target might have. If he got a bite from one of his informants indicating that they knew the person, he would follow up with photographs to confirm they were talking about the same individual. It all allowed for a more confident feeling when someone stated that they knew someone by name and then confirmed it by face. He had found through trial and error that more people would mistakenly identify a picture than a name and that created more dead leads and wasted valuable time and effort.

While the day dragged on, replies from the half dozen or so informants trickled through Pollard's phone. None had any knowledge of the name John Washington. He sent the photographs just in case Washington had used a different name here in Stanton, an area he probably wouldn't be too familiar with or well-known in. Usually someone had some sort of connection to a degree with a fugitive, some sort of information to put a puzzle piece in the mix. It was a small county and Pollard's fugitives were often from the same area. Washington's status as an outsider appeared to be having a negative effect on Pollard's success rate with his consistently reliable informants.

Though not a routine tactic, Pollard then took the time to send out a picture and name of Washington's mother and the mother of his child. The negative responses came back quickly, all except for one. She believed that she may have seen the two women a few times with a toddler in a nearby park. When pressed by Pollard, she was only about fifty percent confident in the identification. It was all basically useless information and much too long ago to act on or even try to expand on. Washington appeared to have no known connection to this county other than his mother and baby momma who, according to the prison records, lived in town. But even the women were anonymous to some of

Pollard's local regulars. Using his informants was an attempt at a quick resolution. Unsuccessful for now, he would need to delve into more records and reports.

Though Washington's mother had shared his last name, and that of his father, she went back to her maiden name and had been known as Anna Walsh for the last twenty something years. She was now forty-nine years old and, as Pollard was finding out while searching through records, had little history in his county. Her driver's license, vehicle registration and visitor and mail information from Washington's prison file all indicated that she lived on Elm Street in Stanton, New Hampshire.

Stanton was the county seat and where Pollard's office was located. A municipality of a little more than 20,000 people, it was just a small town in most of the world, but in New Hampshire was considered a city. It bordered the slightly less populated town of Windsor, where Pollard started with this whole idea of being a lawman.

Pollard had never heard of Walsh. Based on the most recent vehicle registration, it appeared she moved to the area while Washington was in prison. It also appeared that the mother of Washington's child, Tia Bixby, was living with Walsh. Bixby's information on the records Pollard had acquired was the same as Walsh, except she did not have any vehicles registered to her.

The address was the same one that Pollard had been given in the collateral lead sent up by the task force in Philadelphia when they ran out of places to look in the Camden, New Jersey area. The accuracy of the New Hampshire address was quickly found to be questionable. Pollard's department records indicated that Bixby and Walsh had been evicted four months prior from that Elm Street address. It was an action taken by a couple of his fellow deputies. Maybe Bixby and Walsh had moved back to Vatrano's county where Washington was raised. Maybe they moved along to New Jersey or Pennsylvania with Washington and weren't even in New Hampshire anymore. Pollard was quickly starting to question if this case was going to have a connection to his county or even his home state at all.

The group had assembled at Pollard's office, just like Vatrano had indicated that they would.

"So, here's what we've all got so far." Brown paused, took a breath, and pointed at Pollard. "We've got no good address on the mom or the baby momma right now. Believe it or not, they have not kept the Department of Motor Vehicles up to speed on their new address after getting evicted," Brown joked as it wasn't rare for the DMV records to be way behind. "But," Brown pointed to Matthews, "the millennial has some recent photos on social media of the women. They appear to be with Washington's child at the park down the street from this very office. It's probably from a few months ago based on the fact that the foliage was still on the trees. One of Pollard's informants thought they may have seen them at that same park a few times as well, but she wasn't really sure."

"We have no actual information as of right now that Washington is with them, except that the Philadelphia team appears to have hit a dead end with his associates down there. According to the team leader in Philly, it sounds like Washington isn't welcome back to a lot of the places in Camden and it is unlikely he's there at all. If he is, there are going to be some rival gang members looking for some fuckin' payback."

"We've got phone numbers for each woman from Washington's prison call log, but we can't just start calling and asking to come over to speak with them. If he is actually with them, he'd be in the wind before we hung up the damn phone," Pollard chimed in.

"For Christ's sake, they had warrants for the guy's arrest in the first 48 hours and we can't even figure out where the people who aren't even hiding are living!" Vatrano half joked. His faux rage saturated in sarcasm and frustration emanated from behind his dark eyes, the product of his nearly purebred Italian lineage.

Dorsey offered up his usual angle, "I'll check bennies." He had an in at the welfare office with the state. If Bixby, Walsh, or the child were receiving state benefits and using their loaded-up state debit card for cash or approved food items, he could get a track on the purchases and the locations. It might not give them the address they were looking for, but it could give them a neighborhood where they were shopping or getting gas. "Let me make a call." Dorsey stepped out, always avoiding an audience when making calls to the welfare office. His girl on the other end must have been cute, they often joked with him, something Dorsey never confirmed nor denied.

Matthews hadn't looked up from his phone the entire meeting. With his elbow on his knee and phone in hand, he continued to scroll with his fingers while his face was inches from the screen. He was practically a breathing replica of Rodin's *The Thinker* statue.

"Anything good?" Pollard inquired, kicking Matthews lightly in the shin to let him know the question was directed his way.

"No, I'm pretty deep into it. You know about the pictures from the park in Stanton, right?" He rattled off the response without looking up, maybe without blinking. He combed back a loose strand of hair between the top of his ear and the edge of his cap before continuing to scroll.

"Brownie just mentioned it. Were you even listening?"

"The only other thing I have is some pictures with what appears to be the car registered to Walsh," the millennial Matthews stated bluntly, intentionally ignoring the question about his involvement in listening.

"The VW?" Pollard said with his voice rising in pitch.

"Yeah, sweet fuckin' whip. Check out the blue hubcaps." "Spray paint job?"

Matthews held the phone out to Pollard's face. When he saw that Pollard had seen it, he pulled the phone back and resumed his position for scrolling.

"Shit! I know I've seen that exact car around, not sure how recently though!" The unique hubcaps couldn't be mistaken. Pollard fought back the feeling of confidence that had washed over him. He knew not to grab at it. "Shouldn't be too hard to find if it's around with those electric blue hubs."

"What's Stanton PD got with that car, anything?" Vatrano inquired specifically to Pollard.

"Not sure. Let's call over."

"I'll grab Dorsey and take a ride around town to see if we can't find that car."

"Alright."

Leslie, the dispatcher from the Stanton Police Department was as helpful as she could be. Neither Bixby nor Walsh had much contact with their department either. It made sense given that they weren't native to the area and Washington, the one most likely to have police contact of the group, had been in prison.

"It looks like they called about a year ago when Walsh's car was broken into. But other than that, just a couple of outstanding parking tickets," she said with no illusions that it was all that useful to him. "We have a phone number for Walsh if you want it."

"Sure, I'll take it." Pollard started to jot down the number while the dispatcher read it off to him, but he didn't finish, realizing almost immediately that it matched the one from the prison records that he already had.

"What car was it that was broken into?" he asked, hoping that the car might not have the same fate as the phone number he already knew about.

"It looks like a 2009 Volkswagen Jetta, registered to Walsh."

"And where was it broken into?" Pollard was aware it was his last chance to gain something new.

"Right on Elm Street." It was the address that they had been evicted from, the one from the prison and motor vehicle records. Pollard knew that they weren't going to be found there, and neither would Washington.

"And nothing else on either one, huh?"

"No, sorry Mark. Hey, my other line is ringing."

"Okay Leslie, thanks for your help as always."

Pollard took a little time to digest the information. It was the same phone number and same vehicle. Maybe Washington's mother had more stability in her life than he initially figured. Although she hadn't updated the Department of Motor Vehicles and was evicted from her last known address, she may have been squared away enough to have her mail forwarded. An investigation at the post office, a federal government agency, would be no problem for Federal Marshals Dorsey and Brown.

As though he could hear Pollard just thinking his name, Dorsey's number popped up on the phone. He had just left Pollard's office with Vatrano to go out looking around Stanton for a silver Jetta with spray painted blue hub caps. They didn't know what else to do at that point and they were yet to be successful with any leads.

"It should be a lot easier than this," Dorsey said, like a fisherman who hadn't even gotten a nibble.

"The car will pop up," Pollard assured him, but Dorsey didn't need any assurances. Pollard was mostly talking to himself and he knew it.

"My girl at the State just emailed me the info on the bennies. I forwarded it to you. Take a look."

"What the fuck am I going to see?" Pollard asked, a bit annoyed knowing full well that Dorsey was up to speed on the case and with his experience, would have known if there was anything useful. Pollard thought he was now just toying with him.

"Ha!" Dorsey let out a loud, obviously fake laugh. "The EBT card, which was issued to Bixby, has only been used in the New Jersey and Pennsylvania area in the last few months, up until a few weeks ago. There's no balance on it now, they'll have to wait until the next month to get a new balance. The address on the account is for Bixby on Elm Street, so no luck there with any hopes of a good address for the women."

"Well, hopefully we'll have him by then. If not, let's keep it on the back burner so when there is a new balance on the card, we'll know where it's being used."

"Yeah, I sent the info down to the Philly team too. They are going to do some digging at some of the stores it was used at. See if there's some video showing who the fuck has been using the card." Dorsey continued, "If it is all of them in Camden, the ball is back in their court, and I think New Hampshire may be out of play. Either way, my girl put a flag on the card, so if it gets used, we'll know as soon as she does."

"If it's just Washington down there using it, he's a piece of shit. Using the bennies that are for your kid for yourself hundreds of miles away!" Pollard shook his head slowly.

"Well, he did kill a guy." Dorsey made his statement bluntly, causing Pollard to realize how silly that was to even say.

"Where are you now?" Pollard asked quickly, without openly acknowledging that he had temporarily let the murder aspect of the investigation escape his mind.

"I'm over by the Dunks on School Street."

"Great, stop in over at the post office for a minute and see if by chance Bixby or Walsh had their mail forwarded. It's worth a shot. They would need to keep a New Hampshire address to keep those bennies, maybe you can find something."

"Gladly, I'll give you a buzz in a minute." Dorsey hung up without a farewell, a sign to Pollard that he was getting in his serious mode. The post office would also be closing in a few minutes as the late afternoon was quickly fading toward evening.

Dorsey walked into the post office taking note that there was no one waiting at the counter for any help, a bit of a gift from the fugitive hunting gods, he thought. He walked up to the first employee and asked to speak with the postmaster, placing his credentials and circled star United States Marshal badge flat on the counter for the employee to see. They were left there until the postmaster of the Stanton Post Office walked out from behind the counter to speak with him.

"What can I do for you, Marshal?" he said, acknowledging the obvious item placed on the counter with a head nod. Dorsey tucked his wallet and badge back in the left rear pocket of his jeans, taking out a piece of paper with the names Tia Bixby and Anna Walsh written on it. He had the Elm Street address written below it.

"Do you guys have a forwarding address for either of these two ladies? They were evicted from that address not that long ago," he asked while passing the paper across the counter.

"Hold on, I'll check for you." The postmaster took the small note and walked a few steps over to a computer to the right of the main counter. After just over a minute, the postmaster walked back shaking his head.

"Nothing forwarded for either," he stated while pursing his lips. He made brief eye contact with Dorsey confirming he got the message and shook his head slightly from side to side.

Dorsey took the piece of paper back, thanked the postmaster and walked back outside. Vatrano knew watching Dorsey approach the car what the result had been. Just to reinforce it, Dorsey put the vehicle in gear before saying anything. When the car started to move, he simply said, "Nothing," while looking in his rearview mirror, negotiating a reverse turn in the tight post office parking lot.

It had been about 48 hours since receiving the request from Philadelphia to try and locate John Washington in New Hampshire, and the team was no closer to finding his potential whereabouts than they were the morning it had been sent. It was under that cloud that Pollard, Matthews and Brown were still digging for information in Pollard's office. Dorsey and Vatrano had just arrived from the unfruitful visit to the post office and patrol around town looking for blue hubcaps. The normal joking and foolishness were at a minimum, a rarity for a group that normally kept things real light. Pollard was embarrassed in front of his peers, unable to locate two women and a four-year-old child who probably lived in his small county, and it was unlikely that they were even hiding.

"I'm assuming you would have called if you got something good. How'd it go over at the post office?" Pollard answered his own question and then asked it anyway. He knew what the response from Vatrano would be as soon as the question left his lips.

"Actually, the post office gave us the new address, so we went over to the house. We have Washington in fuckin' custody," snapped Vatrano, always going sarcastic when he was disgruntled. "He's out there in the back of the car cuffed up, we just came in here to let you all know in person." It had clearly been a long couple of days without any results. The frustration was now starting to manifest itself in their conversations.

They all knew it was slim chances at the post office based on the outdated information found with the State on the benefits, car registrations and licenses. "So, the women are probably evading bills, given that they got evicted from the last known address and Bixby is getting bennies from the State electronically," Dorsey lamented. "You don't want or need a corrected mailing address for any of that shit."

Brown, reading the mood of the room and sensing a dead end on actionable information, made the informal motion to call the mission off for the day and adjourn. "There's always tomorrow," he said half-heartedly to the group. "Back here at 0700 sounds good to me." It was as good as ordered.

Pollard planned to stay in his office just a few minutes longer, unwilling to give up for the day just yet. By now, his efforts were motivated out of guilt for his failure to produce a location for the women, an entire step removed from finding his target. The quiet instigated by the departure of his teammates struck him as calming, but also unnerving with the lack of satisfaction from the day's work.

He punched up Walsh's name in the Sheriff's Department records database again. The call for service documenting the eviction was sitting there. He was able to access the records from that legal action that the evicting deputies had undertaken. Listed as the customer placing the eviction request was the owner of the building over on Elm Street. It was worth a shot he figured, nothing else had worked out that day anyways. He grabbed his office phone and dialed the number.

"Hello?" The respondent's scratchy and weak voice sounded like an older man and a heavy smoker.

"Mr. Thompson, this is Deputy Pollard over at the Sheriff's Office, how are you tonight?" Pollard had turned the charm on in his voice, a difficult task given the mood he was in. He focused on the possibility of information gathering in order to keep up the nicety.

"What can I do for you, Deputy?" The man didn't deny he was Mr. Thompson, a good clue that he had the right man on the line. He did, however, sound hesitant, like he was expecting this to be a scam call.

"We did an eviction for you several months back at your place on Elm Street. I was hoping you might know where the tenant was living now."

"Ms. Walsh, her daughter, and grandson?" he asked, hoping to confirm they were talking about the same eviction. Pollard didn't bother correcting him on the small discrepancy regarding the nature of the relationship between the two women.

"Yeah, that's the one. Do you know where they moved to? Did they provide you with any sort of forwarding address?" Pollard was encouraged that at least the landlord knew exactly who he was talking about.

"No. They left here without paying the last two months' rent. Last I knew they were living over at the hotel down by the lake. She lost her job from there though, or at least that's what they told me. Something about the hotel gettin' sold off. That's why I haven't been paid any of the back rent. I never took her to court on it, figured I'd cut my losses and move on 'cause I haven't even seen them around town. The new tenant is rather good." The landlord sounded like he had taken a rational approach to his business, an approach founded in experience. The hotel was one more avenue that Pollard could take to try and find her though, both as an employer and maybe her residence.

"Alright, thanks anyways. Take it easy."

"You as well."

Pollard hung up. Weighing the pros and cons of going over to the hotel, Pollard settled on the fact that he could probably handle one more rejection that day. He promised himself it would be the last stop, grabbed his bag and headed to the parking lot, figuring it was on his way home anyways.

Pollard's eyes were drawn to the headlights beaming across the snow-covered lake a few hundred feet offshore from where the hotel was situated. It was likely an ice fisherman setting up his bob-house for the upcoming weekend, but the complete lack of light other than the vehicle in the middle of the dark lake caught his eye. In all his years in New Hampshire, it still didn't seem right seeing automobiles driving in the same location that boats were operating just a few months before.

Pollard had been to the hotel before. It had changed hands several times over the past few years, becoming a chain and then back to an owner-operated small business. Each new owner never seemed to get past its prevailing reputation as a drug den. Though down by the large lake in town, it wasn't somewhere Pollard could ever see himself staying, not with what he had learned about the place in a professional capacity. He approached the lobby of the single-story structure. The large neon vacancy sign hanging in the window caught his attention as it hummed like an insect on a muggy summer night. The door closing behind him served to squash the noise.

He could see the flickering lights of a television coming from the other side of the partially closed door adjacent to the front counter. There was a musty odor attacking Pollard's nostrils, emanating from the thick matted carpet as though it had gotten wet recently and not fully remediated. Pollard could tell that there had at least been some updates to the inside of the hotel since the last time he had been there looking for a fugitive, more than two years ago. It wasn't that this hotel was particularly bad, especially compared to some others, but fugitive hunting and hotels always seemed to pair with each other.

Pollard's presence was quickly detected. Though he fancied himself as somewhat worldly, Pollard couldn't discern through physical appearance or the accent, whether the middle-aged man coming out from the office to greet him was Pakistani or from India. To Pollard it didn't matter, but he knew enough about that region of the world to know that being confused for one or the other would probably be a big deal to the man he was about to talk with. So, he vowed not to guess, at least out loud.

There was no one else in the lobby and the parking lot seemed sparse. He deemed his usual discretion unnecessary, so Pollard took his credentials from his coat pocket and produced them immediately. By state law, the hotels and motels were required to produce a list of guests if requested by law enforcement. Pollard figured at worst, a guest list for the past few weeks would suffice if the interview didn't go the way he hoped.

"Hello, sir!" the man said, while eyeballing Pollard's credentials next to the florescent green sheet of paper displaying the updated check in and check out times. The proprietor gave a quick nod of acknowledgement and Pollard slipped his badge and identification back in his pocket.

"Hi, Mark Pollard from the Sheriff's Office."

"My name is Rajesh, but many people call me Roger. I own this hotel now. What can I do for you, sir?" The man seemed to have pride in his new acquisition.

"Rajesh, I'm looking for a woman by the name of Anna Walsh. Apparently, she used to work and possibly live here. Ever heard of her?"

"No, sir. I don't know that name. I have all new staff here. I only started operating here after the summer. She may have worked for the owner before me though?" He phrased his response to the deputy in the form of a question, mostly out of fear that it might not be an accurate conclusion. Pollard knew that Washington's family connection to the hotel was likely severed with the transfer of ownership, and he was probably wasting his time. In no mood to keep chasing dead leads, he cut his losses.

"Thanks for the help. Good luck with the place," Pollard said abruptly as he began his retreat toward the parking lot. Rajesh appeared a bit stunned at the abbreviated interaction with the deputy but mustered a confused wave goodbye.

Pollard stepped back out into the frigid evening, happy to have traded the moldy smell of the lobby for the cold air freezing the hair in his nose. With a goal of making it home with no more disappointment, he climbed back into the driver's seat of the truck.

On the commute home Pollard had plenty on his mind. He was reviewing the talk with the parole officer, the information on the lead from Philly, the prison records, the social media posts, the state welfare benefits, the local police contacts, the hotel, the post office, and the landlord. Something was missing, as all of those leads should have produced more than they had.

Dorsey and Vatrano had been unsuccessful in their search around the city looking for a vehicle that could not have been any more obvious with bright blue hub caps. Other than some social media pictures from a local park, there was nothing to lead Pollard to believe that Washington's family was still in the area. He couldn't tell how old the child in the picture was with enough accuracy to say if the photo was from this year or last. At this point, it seemed fifty-fifty if he was able to rule out New Hampshire for the Philadelphia team, or whether he would actually put handcuffs on their man.

Pollard pulled into his driveway, put his truck in park, and ran his right hand through his hair, while letting out the deep breath that he had just taken in. Greeting him at the side door into the kitchen was Boomer, with his tail wagging impatiently. The sight of the dog was just what Pollard needed. Kelly poked her head around the corner too. Normally, the face of his wife looking back at him would have snapped him out of his work mindset, but it wasn't shaping up that way on this night.

"Hey, hun," Kelly said, sensing almost immediately that although her husband had arrived home, his brain was still elsewhere.

"Hi," Pollard mumbled, petting the dog all the way into the living room while walking awkwardly to avoid stepping on a paw. He leaned into a kiss from his bride.

"The dinner leftovers are on the counter if you're hungry."

"Thanks, I'll grab some."

This had become the routine dance. He used to apologize for getting home after dinner, but that had faded after a few months of missing hot meals time and again. The sheriff had partly sold the assignment to him as overtime, and Pollard had sold it to Kelly from the angle of increased financial stability. But overtime pay really meant more hours, and those hours were from all parts of the day, including dinner.

Pollard fixed a plate full of cooled food for himself in silence. He ate from the coffee table in the living room where his wife and dog were, fending off the latter trying to procure scraps, while carrying on something that resembled a meaningful conversation with Kelly.

The regular small talk ensued between the bites of food from a couple that had been married for more than a decade. Included in the conversation were a few anecdotes from the day, the updated office gossip, the check engine light coming on in the car, and how Boomer met a new friend on their walk. After he finished the dinner leftovers, Pollard advised Kelly that he was moving to the shower and then on to bed. It was still early, but he was tired from the day, mostly from the lack of results of the effort he and the rest of the team had given. He took the dog out to relieve himself and trudged up the stairs to the shower. Kelly was making her way to the bedroom as well, the dog right at her feet making the same migration.

Pollard put his arm through the space between the shower curtain and the tiles to check the temperature of the flowing water. Finding the water suitable, he stepped into the tub and ran his hand down the curtain to seal it against the wall. The warm shower rained down on Pollard, leaning down a few inches to get his large upper body under the nozzle to be fully immersed.

His thoughts, now in the quiet confines of his bathroom, were jumping from each piece of new information that he had consumed over the past two days. He knew that clearing his mind was not an option. Pollard looked for his shampoo and saw the row of bottles lined up along the shower tub, labels all facing out. The configuration was a sure sign of Kelly's OCD tendencies. There was his body wash, shampoo and what appeared to be an entire salon's worth of other products that Kelly used, that he had never taken much notice of. Tonight, what caught his attention was that they looked like a perfect row of cars parked parallel on a narrow street. That image was all it took.

"The parking tickets!" he exclaimed out loud.

Stanton didn't have metered parking in the downtown area, as the struggling business district didn't need any more obstacles preventing people from visiting. There were only a few two-hour parking areas, but that wasn't strictly enforced. On-street parking between midnight and 5 a.m. was a much more common problem, because such an act could inhibit snow removal. It was forbidden from November first to April first, a full five months of New Hampshire's long, brutal and snowy winter season. The most likely place someone would park during those hours would be close to home, and Pollard knew it.

Pollard put the shampoo bottle down without removing any of its contents, shut the water off and jumped out of the shower a little earlier than he had originally expected. Only kind of dry from a brief pat down and his feet still wet, he went for his phone laying on top of the nightstand on his side of the bed. Kelly watched all of this unfold from the doorway of her closet, a curious look on her face.

"Stanton Police Department, Dispatcher Harris," the voice on the other end of the call answered.

"Emily, it's Pollard from the Sheriff's Department."

"Hey Mark, what are you up to?" she said, familiar with her colleague from the county.

"Listen, I called earlier today during dayshift about a woman named Anna Walsh. Leslie said she had a couple of unpaid parking tickets. Could you tell me, when are they from and where were the tickets written?"

"Can I put you on hold for a moment?"

"Sure."

It felt like longer than a moment to him, but Pollard knew how busy a police dispatcher could be at any given time. Though anxious for information, it was no emergency.

His eyes caught a quick glance of Kelly and then looked away when the dispatcher on the other end of the phone broke the silence, "Mark?"

"Still here!" he said expectantly.

"So, one was written on December 21st and the other on January 4th. The first one was written on High Street and the other on Depot Street. According to the records, she hasn't paid either one."

Pollard knew those streets intersected in that area of the city and it was almost all residential and multi-family homes. "Are both for overnight, snow ban parking?"

"They sure are. Is this lady wanted?" the dispatcher asked, familiar with Pollard's duties and why he might have queried.

"No, someone she may be with. Thanks for the information, Emily." Pollard sounded a bit short, and the young dispatcher noted his urgency.

"Anytime."

Pollard felt that this could be a substantial step in locating the women who might be quartering his fugitive. That familiar sense of confidence rushed over him. He let it linger and went to bed after returning to finish his shower, knowing that he would have the information that would turn the 0700 meeting of the team on its head. At last, a breakthrough. Kelly, now looking at him with a wry smile, didn't even ask, she could tell by his new demeanor that it was good. The dog must have sensed the same, leaping onto their bed like only the powerful legs of a Jack Russel Terrier could. He landed gracefully between his two humans. Pollard didn't even care, the dog could spend the night.

CHAPTER SEVEN

The life and times of John Washington through his first quarter century on Earth wasn't an unfamiliar or unique story to many Americans. He was born to a father that he never knew but carried his last name as a reminder of the man for his entire life. Before his first birthday, his dad was gone. Given the violence and drug abuse that his father brought to the family, many figured it was best for the young boy, and openly said so to his mother, Anna Walsh. While his dad may show up with a gift for him before Christmas, and might call every couple of years, he really shouldn't have bothered. Washington's young mother did the best she knew how to raise him as he transitioned from infant to toddler. Though there was no silver spoon in her son's mouth, he always had a spoon, and she made sure that there was food on it.

Washington's mother had a reputation as a hard worker and loyal employee. She was a long-time staff member of a state-wide hotel chain that was well known throughout several parts of New Hampshire from the Canadian border to the Atlantic Ocean. It included a location on the west side of the state's largest city where she settled on raising her young son by herself. The job stability provided more than just a paycheck each week as childcare duty was swapped between fellow employees working opposite shifts. Along with his mother, an entire hotel staff pitched in to help raise John Washington as a toddler.

A few years after John's birth, Anna Walsh's younger sister moved in with a baby boy of her own. There were about three and a half years between Washington and his younger cousin, a big difference early in life, but an age gap that somehow seemed to tighten as they grew up. Together, the single mothers and their children shared a three-bedroom apartment on the third floor of an old triple decker. The blocks of similar buildings that surrounded them were full of old charm, and the people that occupied them had just as much character.

Their neighbors on all sides spoke French fluently and primarily. It wasn't the language of the Riviera, but more likely spoken by the descendants of asbestos miners of southern Quebec, who had come to live and work in New Hampshire. It was a true working-class neighborhood; they all worked, and they worked hard. There was also certainly a criminal element to the neighborhood and even in the high schools, but Walsh gave her best effort for as long as she could to keep her son, her sister, and her nephew safe.

Looking for a fresh start, Anna's sister started working at the hotel with her shortly after her arrival in town, starting in the housekeeping department. They would alternate shifts and childcare duties. Other than to pass the kids back and forth, they really didn't see all that much of each other, either at work or home. The system worked well for several years and as the kids started school, some of the responsibilities lessened. Washington and his cousin were twelve and sixteen years old when the man that his aunt would eventually marry started coming around the apartment. He was a good enough man and helped Washington and his younger cousin learn the ins and outs of athletics, football in particular. It was the first time in his young life that Washington had a strong male role model. Almost four years older, Washington would beat on his cousin regularly in the confines of a football scrimmage. He would protect him with even more vigor out on the streets of a neighborhood that was shifting its working-class image to one of crime and violence.

In less than a year, the man took Washington's aunt and his cousin, though more like a brother to him now, out of state to get married and start a new career with an opportunity in upstate New York. While Anna initially contemplated going with them and keeping them all together, she ultimately decided to stay back on the third floor of that old triple decker, worried in the down economy that she might not get another job in New York. The hotel had continued to treat her well, and she didn't want to uproot John from his high school, all factors that led to her staying put. The decision to stay would weigh heavy on her in the years to come, beating herself up with the "what ifs" as her son struggled with the departure of his cousin, aunt, and positive adult male example.

As a seventeen-year-old, Washington became reckless and obstinate, more so than most teenagers. He had quit the football team, something he seemed to love so much before, not wanting to take direction from anyone, especially some old white-haired coach. That same attitude was now commonly given to his mother and her directions. He no longer felt the need to be a good example to his younger cousin who had been taken out of sight two states away. It might as well have been across the country to a seventeen-year-old with no car.

It wasn't long before he was mixing it up with the local police, though initially it was mostly petty thefts and vandalism type issues. He even got in a few scraps with some of the newer residents in the neighborhood that he felt weren't giving the proper respect to him and his crew. A couple of simple assault charges for fighting in the streets and alleys around his high school followed, along with the corresponding trips to Juvenile Court for him and his mother.

Anna dragged her son through his remaining high school years. The spring he turned eighteen, she pulled him just far enough to get his diploma and cross the stage in a cap and gown. It was the last real accomplishment that she and her son had the occasion to celebrate.

Once out of high school he took on a few different jobs, none of which excited him. He worked at a car wash, grocery store and, for a brief time, as an assistant to a tow truck driver. But Washington was never responsible enough to stay employed, usually because of his attitude, his lack of work ethic and his constant absences without notice or legitimate explanation for his bosses. His mother was long past being able to control him, or even offer guidance that he would listen to. Just after his twentieth birthday was when he told his mother that he had gotten his former high school girlfriend, Tia, pregnant after they had briefly reunited.

When Tia got kicked out of her parents' home, Anna Walsh brought her in. Though she barely knew her, Anna didn't want her to face the same realities she did by losing her man when Washington was an infant. She was trying to force a relationship between her son and the mother of his child by keeping them in close proximity, though there was no foundation to build on. It only served to push Washington further away as he didn't even want to acknowledge his responsibility, much like his father hadn't.

The lack of steady employment and the expanded influence of some of Washington's neighborhood crew had him more desperate than ever for funds. Young men need money for status, for the right clothes, for the right intoxicants and Washington was no longer willing to bust his ass at a job to get it. What he lacked in money, he had in an old car that he got for free from the tow company before he left their payroll. Not wanting to continue storing the old clunker, Washington took advantage of their offer to get it off their hands. That free car would end up as the catalyst in putting Washington in a situation where prison was his new reality.

Most of John's friends didn't have regular access to a vehicle. He was quickly volunteered to deliver "packages" for people he didn't even know. It put fuel in his gas tank and maybe a few pairs of new sneakers on his feet, but it was also that lure of quick cash that ushered in his eventual downward spiral.

Washington was convinced by a friend to drive him to an all-night quick mart gas station to rob the clerk, drive away and split half the proceeds evenly. The simple plan that night was interrupted by the sound of a single gunshot and his friend running to the passenger side of the vehicle, while Washington waited just down the street. His friend vehemently claimed that the gun went off by accident in the rush of the moment. When Washington saw the security video footage at his trial for his role as accomplice, he knew better.

The young father was unwilling to cooperate with the police or prosecution in the case. His stubborn attitude caused him to butt heads with his public defender, much like he wouldn't listen to the wisdom of his old football coach, teachers, or his own mother. Washington was sent to the New Hampshire State Prison to spend a minimum of one and a half years and a maximum of three years for the accomplice to armed robbery charge. It was a fairly harsh sentence for such a charge, but there was a clerk that was shot and injured, and Washington was unwilling to plea out, instead taking it all the way to trial. The prosecution had dropped the accomplice to attempted murder charge, so the judge felt that he wasn't left with much discretion at sentencing after the jury found him guilty.

With her son now in prison and taken away from his child, Anna saw the cycle of life that had been put in motion. It was the same cycle she had seen before, just new actors a generation removed. Not wanting her grandson, Lucas, to see the same fate as her own son, she took Tia and the child out of town with her. Her employer offered to set her up with a job at a hotel that they had just purchased a little farther north near the big lake, in the small city of Stanton. The cost of living would be a little lower, and the negatively changing neighborhood dynamics around her place on the west side was the straw that broke the camel's proverbial back. She was no longer getting rent help from her sister, lost the not-so-steady income from the child support checks that ended with Washington's eighteenth birthday, and was now helping support Lucas. These factors forced her to skip out on the last month's rent a few times as she moved around, but now she held presumably realistic hopes that her life could improve up in Stanton.

While doing his prison time, Washington would get letters and visits from his family. He would hang the crayon drawings that Lucas had made for him next to his bunk along with some photos. The child, though his, was basically a foreign soul to him. A letter from his father, who was just as foreign, was certainly a surprise a few months into his sentence. The old man had no doubt spoken with his mother about it or read it in the papers. Washington never did write back or call the number his father wrote in bold letters next to his signature.

He would phone his mother and talk regularly, but the situation with Tia was a little more complicated, with each of them getting upset given the circumstances. Many of their conversations from the prison phones ended with a premature and intentional disconnection of the call. The occasional hang-in-there letter came signed from his aunt, uncle, and cousin with a return address in New York that he had never gotten around to visiting.

Washington's cellmate during the final months of his stay in prison was a few years older than him. He appeared to the impressionable Washington as though he had the world figured out. Robert Keith had been transferred to the prison in New Hampshire from a facility in southern New Jersey due to some gang affiliations and incidents with a rival Hispanic group housed there. Officials in New Jersey surmised that Keith would have less opportunity to do damage in snow white New Hampshire as a white supremacist than he would among a lot of the Black and Latino gangs that dominated their facilities. After some skirmishes in the New Jersey prisons, he was sent out of state for his own safety, but also by prison management hoping to avoid the potential dangers that come with racial tensions inside the walls.

Washington had confided in Keith in a way that he hadn't with any of his other fellow prisoners, retelling the story of his armed robbery charge that ended with him in jail and an innocent convenience store clerk with a bullet lodged in him. Many inmates would embellish their story about how they ended up in prison for a multitude of reasons. Washington didn't feel the need with the older, seemingly wiser Keith, who had gained his trust. It was something Washington hadn't felt since part of the family left for upstate New York years before.

Keith's offer to Washington to come to New Jersey to make easy money was met with optimism. Washington wasn't real keen on going up to Stanton anyways, a place he didn't know, to be with his mom and raise a child with a girl he really didn't even like anymore. Other than Lucas, there wasn't any depth to the connection between the two, aside from some juvenile high school hormones that spilled over into adulthood. He also thought a new environment in a new state would make more sense. The logic was further reinforced by the way his conversations would go with his cellmate contrasted against the slamming of the phone when talking to Tia. When Keith learned that his parole date was about a month apart from Washington's, it made the deal a reality.

The two met up again following their assignment to the same halfway house after being paroled. Washington was relieved that Keith had waited for him like they planned, before heading back to New Jersey, an act that showed loyalty that he was all too quick to reciprocate. They decided to leave together the following day in violation of the parole they had each been granted recently. It was Washington's first and only night spent at the halfway house.

CHAPTER EIGHT

After an evening filled with utter chaos, Washington had managed to formulate a scrappy and hasty plan of escape, but one that just might work. He needed to get immediately out of Camden for his own safety. From there, he would be able to figure out a permanent solution more calmly.

Trekking another mile or so from the Delaware River, he had found himself at the Camden bus station. It was a local landmark that he could remember as he had arrived there with Keith several months prior and been there a few times to meet with others. Washington was pleased with his ability, under such stress, to find his way around a city that he hadn't spent too much time in. He clutched at the cash and drugs in his pocket. The few bucks that he had from before the robbery, combined with what he took from the victim, was not enough to give him any comfort. The electronic benefits card from New Hampshire was no good to him until next month, so it sat in his wallet just waiting. He knew without actually taking it out and counting it that he wasn't going to have enough money to make it all the way home using public transportation, wherever home was.

By the time he crossed the lobby towards the ticket counter, he had pulled together a semblance of calm. His hands were shaking, partly from the adrenaline, partly from the cool and damp night. Somehow, even during the chilly evening, he had worked up a bit of a sweat that had now made him shiver, with a sharpness that ran from his toes to his forehead. His sneakers, moist on the soles, squeaked lightly as he walked across the tile floor of the nearly empty lobby. He inhaled deeply and let out a sigh before he turned and approached the ticket counter.

"How much for a ticket to Newark?" he asked.

"It's $19 dollars one way." The clerk at the counter didn't even look up from filing her nails. She had clearly worked there long enough to know the price to Newark and wasn't going to be overly bothered as her night shift was coming to an end.

"I'll get a ticket for the next bus that leaves." He didn't need to hear any other options. If he got to Newark, he might be able to make it to anywhere, he figured.

"I'll need a photo identification as well," she said. The young woman took possession of the crumpled-up cash that he had laid on the counter like she was working a blackjack table in nearby Atlantic City. The folded bills had dampened slightly from the heat of his front hip pocket, while he was running through the cool Camden streets.

All he had to offer was a non-driver New Hampshire identification that he received when he was released from the prison to the halfway house. It was common practice to provide one to inmates headed for work release and other endeavors, so they could have a valid, government issued identification, much like a driver's license. He knew it was an avenue the police might find him through, but he didn't have another choice. It was too late to try and fake his identity. Mustering up a lie and telling her that he didn't have one didn't seem wise and might prevent him from boarding a bus. Washington also worried that such a move would make him more memorable to the woman behind the counter, and he didn't need any extra attention. He was unsure if she had even looked at him yet. The plastic of the identification made a smack, as it too hit the cracked laminate counter where the money had been laying a few moments prior. Washington looked up moving only his eyes, attempting to keep his face from view. He had noticed the security camera directly above the ticket agent, no doubt capturing his transaction.

"One dollar is your change and here's the ticket. Bus leaves from terminal dock number three in about twenty minutes, 9:45 p.m." She handed him a crisp dollar bill from her register, not like the sloppy pile of five dollar bills he had just handed her. Still without looking up at Washington, she slid the ticket and his identification across the counter, through the hole at the bottom of the plexiglass. He took the items and went towards terminal dock three, where he found just a few passengers starting to board, roughly fifteen minutes before departure. The hum of the idling

77

bus engine was noticeable, not because of the volume, but because his ears had finally stopped ringing.

Washington made as little eye contact as possible with the sparse group of people on the bus and the driver waiting outside the door as he entered. He had no luggage to check. For the first time he thought about what he was going to do for a long-term plan, with no clothing or other essentials, and just a few more dollars left to get by.

The pasty white boy from New Hampshire created a stark contrast to the dark bus seats in the middle of the night in Camden. The route had been scheduled to make a stop in both the cities of Trenton and Elizabeth before it would continue to Newark. Newark was about as far north as he thought he would make it, at least for tonight before he would assess his options again.

The ride felt especially slow to Washington, after everything leading up to it that day had felt like a blur. He turned the overhead light off above his seat, again, hoping to blend into the scenery on the bus as best he could, to remain inconspicuous. The motion of the large bus tires on the highway initially had a soothing effect on Washington, much like an infant could be lulled to sleep by a ride in the car. The bus crossed the Delaware River toward the on-ramp to Interstate 95. Washington looked back to the riverfront where he had ditched his phone, along with what he feared was a murder weapon. He lamented his current situation, but as the highway miles began to drag on, Washington had a jolting thought.

If the police went looking at the bus station for a suspect trying to skip town, they would know his destination from the combination of his ticket and identification.   The information was easily attainable.

By the time they reached the brief stop in Trenton to drop off and pick up new passengers, he had made his decision. When the bus eventually came to a stop in Elizabeth, Washington hustled off discreetly. He found himself in a completely unfamiliar part of a city he knew he had never even been to in his young life. It wasn't ideal, but at this point, he was safe. Or at least he hoped he was. If authorities went looking for him based on the destination of his ticket, they would most likely start in Newark, several miles away. Even more comforting, there was little chance that any friends of Perez would find him there.

CHAPTER NINE

With a thick layer of ice coating all over it, Pollard scraped heartily at the windshield of his truck in the predawn darkness. Boomer had peed and pooped and hustled back to the house in condensed time, the near record cold February morning temperature freezing the pads of his paws as he scampered. His lack of sleep from the night before had him a little sluggish, but he didn't care, because it had been interrupted by excitement for the new lead, not angst. Pollard had a side trip to take care of before his regular commute into the office and it was going to take him to the spot where High and Depot Street crossed in the small but densely populated neighborhood in Stanton.

The corner onto High Street was a bit slick under the tires due to the refreeze of moisture on the road. Enough light started to emerge from the impending sunrise that Pollard could see adequately. If there was one thing that Pollard had missed about those overnight patrol shifts in Windsor, it was the sunrise every morning. He would catch it whenever possible in the most picturesque parts of town, provided his radio was free of calls for service.

The sky remained cloaked in a wispy light cloud cover unlike the deeper shades of blue later in the day. A flash of bright blue was what caught Pollard's eye in the parking lot behind the duplex on the corner of High Street and Depot Street. The two hubcaps exposed to the road were all he needed to see on the silver Volkswagen. It too was covered in the frozen dew, just as Pollard's truck had been in his own driveway. He pulled past the lot and took a sharp left turn into a larger apartment complex directly across the street. There was only one way out of the duplex where Walsh's car was parked, so he was certain it wouldn't leave without him seeing it move.

The silver Volkswagen had parked front bumper to rear bumper with the other car deeper in the narrow driveway, probably the reason for the on-street parking violations that brought him there. That parking configuration ensured that there was little chance of anyone leaving the residence in a vehicle that wasn't the one he had come to look for. With his fingers trembling slightly at the excitement of locating the vehicle, he immediately sent out a group text requesting Brown meet him at the apartment complex, and the others gather down at his office as planned. Although the request and directions were obvious, the intrigue was just too much for most of the group traveling into town. Within what felt like only seconds, Pollard's phone lit up like the Las Vegas strip. Brown was the quickest on the cell phone draw and got through first.

"What the hell is going on?" He bypassed the customary good morning greetings.

"I've got the car. It's parked at a duplex at the corner of High and Depot in Stanton. It's covered in ice. I don't want to let my fuckin' eyes off it."

"How'd you find that?"

"The parking tickets from Stanton. They were issued to her for overnight on-street parking at this intersection."

"Ahhh," Brown verbalized like the fading sound of a patient with a tongue depressor doing as the doctor had ordered. He was impressed but also a little perturbed that neither he nor anyone else in the group had made that connection the day before. It was one of those things that had become obvious to him immediately after hearing it.

"Let's get the rest of the team geared up at my office. If you can come relieve me once you're ready, I'll go to the office and brief them. We can sit on it for a little bit and see what sort of shit happens today. I just don't want to lose that car." Pollard was protecting his find like it was a treasure.

"Sounds good, I'll gear up and meet you over there. I'll be on TacB," Brown said, referencing the encrypted radio frequency they could use without fear of public scanning.

"Roger that." Pollard hung up and accepted Vatrano's incoming call when Brown completed his standard "love you" salutation.

"What's up man?" Vatrano inquired. The rasp in his voice sounded to Pollard like Vatrano hadn't yet spoken aloud to anyone that morning due to the early start.

"I've got the car. I'll be at my office as soon as Brown comes to sit on it for me."

"Nice!"

"I'll see you at my office in a few. Dorsey's calling."

Pollard would go through a similar exercise for each inquisitive member of the team. After Brown relieved him to watch the car, he went directly to his office where he met Dorsey, Vatrano, and Matthews in the parking lot by the marked Sheriff's cruisers.

The mood had decidedly changed from when they were all last together about twelve hours before. It had become real. Dorsey reported some information that would solidify their belief that Washington would be in Stanton.

"All of the EBT benefit purchases in Camden from a few weeks back were made by Washington, by himself. The Philly team is saying that there's no sign of the women or child on any of the videos they watched." The likelihood that Washington would be found in New Hampshire had grown substantially. They had found the car belonging to Washington's mother in town. The purchases made in New Jersey on the EBT card had been Washington himself, and the Philly team had exhausted all the leads they had in a city that Washington had no connection to. It had each member of the team believing that Washington was among them in

Stanton. It wasn't a lock yet, but experience would tell them time and again that hunches by a multitude of investigators that matched often yielded the results that those same hunches had predicted.

Pollard went on to explain the parking tickets and his first-hand knowledge that the car was sitting there, along with the regrettable fact that they still didn't have the address, as it could be either door of the duplex. With a surveillance operation of an unknown duration ahead of them, each member set out to get their gear on, use the restroom and grab some snacks. A good cop will always use the bathroom when he has the chance, and he should never be hungry. That was a standing rule for this team. They split into pairs and deployed in two vehicles out to High Street.

Vatrano and Dorsey took the back corner on Depot Street where they could see the rear doors of the duplex and had sight lines on the car that had been so difficult to locate. Matthews and Pollard deployed to the High Street side, unable to see the vehicle, but not so close that they would be made by people in the neighborhood. They remained close enough that if the car left the lot, they would still see it when coming out to the street. Brown left his spot briefly to take care of his morning rituals that he had been denied while waiting for the others. When the task was complete, he returned with a triumphant announcement over the radio in his baritone voice, that he was back.

It wasn't quite 0800 hours, and each member of the team knew that "bandit time" was often delayed. It was usually 11 a.m.

or later before they had seen activity at a lot of places on previous cases. The same would be true in this case. The morning dragged on for several hours with nothing to report from the duplex. Though the first few hours of surveillance like this were usually mingled with some excited anticipation, that feeling was beginning to fade for each of the men.

At just past 11 a.m. Vatrano put the first call over the radio, "We have a female going to the car, looks like Bixby maybe. Hard to say with the hood on. Dark coat, blue pants, probably jeans." After three hours of sitting and watching nothing, all the men sat up in their respective vehicles with a renewed attention. Vatrano had the best visual on what was happening. Unable to hide his excitement, he rattled off a play-by-play as if describing a close horse race, not a young woman completing the mundane task of heading to the car for the first time that day. "She's unlocking it and getting in. Quite sure she's alone. I don't see anyone else. Car just started up."

Brown, taking his team leader responsibility seriously, interjected into Vatrano's blow-by-blow. "If the car goes up High Street, I'm following. If it goes down Depot in either direction, Vatrano and Dorsey, you guys follow. Pollard, you two keep eyes on the house regardless."

Vatrano picked right up with the call over the radio as Brown's directions finished with a final squelch. "Not sure which door of the duplex she came out of, but she's in reverse now headed to the road." With the car backing out towards the street, Brown, Pollard and Matthews got their first good look at the vehicle. It came into their view away from the obstructions of trees, fences, and buildings. They all concluded that she was definitely by herself.

The Volkswagen headed down Depot Street showing off the distinctive spin of the hubcaps, morphing into what looked like a solid blue circle in the wheels. Vatrano and Dorsey followed from a reasonable distance to make sure that Bixby, if it was her, did not think she was being stalked. Any family member hiding out a murder suspect would most certainly be observant for such things.

"Not sure if this is a heat run, but she's by herself," Brown stated. He was referring to the practice of fugitives sending someone out other than themselves to see if the police were in the neighborhood, a form of counter-surveillance. "So, stay far enough back while you're behind the car so you don't get fuckin' made. Call it out over the radio and I'll be even further behind." Brown wasn't one to want to sit any longer than was absolutely necessary and thus volunteered himself for the action.

Matthews and Pollard were now alone watching the residence. It wouldn't be the first time that a fugitive, thinking no one was left watching the house, attempted to flee during the opportunity. The two deputies readied themselves, hoping to see a man fitting Washington's description come out of the house so they could wrap this case up.

Brown made the decision to also follow so that they could change out the vehicles closest behind Bixby to remain less noticeable. It would also allow for one vehicle to get stuck in traffic or behind a red light while the other continued on, should that happen.

Matthews and Pollard had their ears stuck to the radio like a couple of guys listening for the lottery numbers, while holding what they believed was the winning ticket. All the while, their eyes were watching the duplex waiting for the slightest indication of movement inside or out. The radio crackled when the group following Bixby got further away. Eventually, the message was relayed back to them that the vehicle had pulled into the McDonald's on Broadway, near the city line with Windsor. There was still no movement from the home that Pollard and Matthews could detect.

After a few minutes, Vatrano got back on the radio advising that the vehicle was leaving and headed back on Broadway towards the Depot Street area. Matthews saw the vehicle coming back towards the neighborhood and let Vatrano know, so that they would not follow the car in and give up their operation. The vehicle proceeded to park in the same spot it had left about twenty minutes before. Pollard and Matthews were in position to see Bixby step out. She exited the vehicle carrying the food and two large drinks, stepping on the front porch to open the door of 28A Depot Street.

87

Bixby successfully balanced the fast food all tucked in one arm and hand, while placing the key in the knob and pushing the door open.

"She's going into 28A. The door on the left," Pollard said over the radio to everyone. They now had an address that Bixby was staying at. "It also looks like she's not feeding more than two adults and possibly a child."

"Is that two regular adults, or two of you?" Vatrano rhetorically radioed back, deploying his standard degree of sarcastic wit.

"No, just based on the amount of drinks and food. Is it her and Walsh, or her and Washington? I don't think there are more than two adults in there if she's buying for everyone." Pollard intentionally ignored Vatrano's light dig, choosing instead to play out the possible scenarios.

"Either is possible. Maybe Walsh is staying somewhere else with the kid? Can anyone put eyes on a car seat?" Brown had brought up a good point that would give them some sort of indication.

"I think we've got the best look from over here. We can't see one, but I'm not sure that a four-year-old would have a car seat that was visible from this distance. He would more likely be in a booster seat." Matthews, though he didn't have kids, brought up an even better point, something that his teammates weren't going to allow to go to his head.

"You would know," Dorsey jokingly chimed in, the mood of the group improving with the increase in activity at the duplex. "You just got out of yours last year, right?" The youthful deputy was used to it; he offered no retort, more an act of self-control than a sign of defeat. There wasn't much he was going to be able to say that wouldn't come right back at him anyways.

It was clearly feeding time for those residing at 28A Depot Street. As morning turned to afternoon, they had not seen any further movement from the house since Bixby had returned. Tardy for their own lunch schedule, the team decided food and bathrooms were necessary. They would break off vehicle by vehicle, maintaining constant surveillance on the house. When one vehicle returned, another would leave. Matthews, though recently insulted by Dorsey, deferred to him to go relieve himself first. "You probably ought to go now Dorsey, given your age, we don't want any accidents." While more often the brunt of age jokes, Matthews couldn't let the opportunity pass without reminding his older counterparts just how old they were to him. The urinary frequency of his elders was a consistent arrow in his quiver.

Surveillance is never a preferred activity among men of action. It certainly was not favorable to Brown who had a nearly insatiable itch to press on. He did what he could to remain calm for most of the afternoon. The team was able to determine who was in the neighboring side of the duplex, 28B Depot Street. They observed an older male and female leave the residence around 2 p.m. and obtained a license plate number from the vehicle they left in. Pollard, looking to learn even more, made a phone call. On the other end was one of his associates at the Stanton Police Department, a narcotics detective, well known for his drug work in the small city that unfortunately had piles of it.

"Hey, Mark!" Pollard was greeted with the enthusiasm he had expected.

"Hey, Chris. Just wanted to give you guys the heads up that we're sitting on a house over on Depot Street. What do you have for activity at 28A?"

"Is that the duplex right at the corner with High Street?" As Pollard had been shown in the past and again with the answer to that question, the detective knew the small city well.

"Correct, the duplex."

"Nothing comes to mind right off hand but let me check some of my informant files. I know we haven't made any buys on that block for quite some time." Pollard gave him a few minutes. In the pause Pollard threw all three names at him: Bixby, Walsh, and Washington. The detective, who had a near encyclopedic knowledge of the drug players in the small city of Stanton, was not familiar with any of them or anyone at the address.

"Do you want me to put the names out to some of my informants or do you want to keep it quiet?" The detective asked, not wanting to overstep but also remain helpful. Pollard knew that most of the detective's informants were drug related. He thought for a moment that it was possible that he and the detective from Stanton could be reaching out to the same informants. The worlds of fugitive hunting and drug investigations were so overlapped that sometimes Pollard wasn't able to discern any difference between the two related genres of law enforcement.

"I don't think Washington has any connection to this area, so don't throw his name out. Walsh and Bixby have been around for about a year or more, maybe see what kinda shit you can come up with on them. I'm mostly trying to see if anyone resembling Washington has been seen with either woman. I'll email you a photo and descriptors. In the meantime, let your watch commander know we're out here and let your crew know who Washington is, just in case someone sees or hears anything."

"Sounds good, I'll keep my eyes out for that email. Let me know if anything else comes up."

"Chris, it's a murder warrant out of New Jersey. Make sure everyone uses caution and keeps a lid on the fact we're out here looking. It's unknown if Washington is aware he's wanted or that we're even looking for him in New Hampshire." Pollard was a little nervous about putting the information into more hands, but at the same time, wanted the extra police eyes and ears in the hunt.

"Murder, huh? Well, we'll see what we can do."

Pollard felt good about how he left it with the detective and turned his attention back to the duplex.

Surveillance was not fruitful through the rest of the afternoon. The streetlights came on in the early evening as they did in New Hampshire that time of winter, while the team grew increasingly antsy. Neither Bixby nor anyone else in 28A Depot Street had left the residence other than for the trip to McDonald's. When the darkness thickened, the interior of the residence was aglow, but with shades drawn, the chance of seeing Washington was slim.

At around 8 p.m. the group sat in complete darkness. The team had spent the better part of thirteen hours on the same street, watching nearly nothing, and it had taken its toll. Unable to substantiate any evidence of Washington's presence, Brown made the call over the radio that the team was going to rally back at Pollard's office. Each car left in ten to fifteen-minute intervals in an effort to avoid the look of a coordinated group to anyone that might be watching.

After a long day, the confines of Pollard's office felt even smaller than normal with all of the team members crammed in it and spilling out into the empty hallway. The Sheriff's Office where Pollard was located was a converted wing of the old county nursing home. They had moved in when they outgrew the basement of the county courthouse. Each office was roughly the size of a single nursing home bedroom. Regardless of the amount of space that was being taken up physically by the team, the ideas, scenarios, and conjectures started to fly out into the tiny spaces that were left to occupy.

"He's in there, let's just go get him." Brown sounded confident but had nothing more than a hunch to back it up. He was mostly looking for a reason for some action on the case.

"But if we blow up this house and he's not there, he certainly won't be back if he has been coming around, and we've missed our shot. Right now, all we've got is the vehicle and probably the mother of his child at a residence right here in town. We have absolutely nothing that says he's there right now," Dorsey replied, with a less optimistic but also more measured tone that his experience and personality tended to lean towards.

Pollard tried to find some middle ground. "Philadelphia sent us the lead to check out the baby momma and momma. If we go in, we can either confirm or dispel that he's here and send that information back to them. If he's not here, it shuts this down as a place to hide and might push him back to Camden or somewhere else. It could get him moving and making mistakes to stay on the run, and that will get him caught."

"As far as the Philly team is concerned, New Hampshire is the only place they think he might be. If he's not there when we go, I don't think they have a second place to try to look. They would be starting at zero again with no leads to follow up on or send out," Dorsey retorted, again trying to sell patience.

"That's exactly why we need to check it out, at the very least it might generate some new information that we could pass along. Worst case scenario is that he isn't there and we throw an interview at some people who know him really well." Brown was hinting that the inside of the house was the next logical stop, and it wasn't really subtle to the rest of the team in the close quarters of Pollard's office.

The team decided as a group that they would go to the duplex the following morning, early. If Washington was staying there, he'd be there at a time of day when most of the world, even on "bandit time," was sleeping. It was to be a 0500 briefing and operation, nearly eight hours away. They remained at the office that evening, gathering up as much information as they could about 28A Depot Street. Tax maps, city assessing records and even online real estate rental and sales listings were reviewed to get the best idea of the layout of the home. Washington had killed a man and may kill again. Mitigating potential missteps now in anticipation of their search the following morning could literally be a life saver, and each team member knew without saying it.

Pollard had not heard anything back from the Stanton narcotics detective, so he sent him a quick text. No bites from any of his informants on Washington being around, but he was still waiting to hear from a few. It pulled another block out of Pollard's confidence like a tipsy Jenga formation ready to topple. Pollard rationalized that it didn't really matter at that point. They would be at the door of the duplex in the morning regardless.

CHAPTER TEN

0500 hours on a mid-winter morning in New Hampshire is certainly no time for a picnic, at least not a comfortable one. It's not really ideal for anything, except catching people at home, or wherever they're laying their head, staying warm under the covers. Pollard took a peek at the thermometer outside the window above his kitchen sink. The plummeted temperature was expected, the fresh inch and a half of snow that fell overnight was not. As luck would have it, there was not so much snow that it caused problems on the roads, but enough to see the footprints of those who left the house early. Pollard's own fresh footprints out to the truck at that hour would soon be proof.

He was able to leave the house without disturbing Kelly or the dog. Preventing Kelly from waking wasn't usually a problem, but Boomer rarely let him leave without arising as well. Once outside, the squeak of fresh snow under the room temperature treads of insulated boots echoed in the muffled darkness, on the otherwise silent morning. Pollard imagined that the same silence would be broken at 28A Depot Street not too long from then. When he slung himself into the truck, he performed a "Dorothy," a maneuver that he had named and now mastered. He grabbed the steering wheel with his right hand and the driver's side head rest with his left. With his ass firmly in the driver's seat, he held both feet out of the door and clicked his heels together in a quick succession of three, before placing his boots on the floor mat. With the snow on his treads now sloughed off, he turned the key and headed up the driveway. Whether the early bird got the worm that morning was still to be decided.

The entire team and a few other Marshals from headquarters had accumulated at Pollard's office, trickling in one-by-one. Some warrant services were sure things. Search warrants of primary residences of known wanted persons were always preferable and were commonly referred to as "ground balls." This morning's operation would be a little different as there was no search warrant. It would require a blend of consent on the part of the residents and the ability of the crew to gain that consent. Or, in the alternative, they would need to develop enough information to legally push their way through any resistance. The operation would then transition into a tactical building search for a wanted murderer. If located, it would be game over. If not, it would morph from a tactical takedown of the home to an information gathering interview with the individuals residing there.

Pollard and Brown briefed the assembled team on the information they had at the time. It was viewed as a refresher for those that had been there the day before, and to catch up those in the group that hadn't.

"It's presumed that there are at least two adults in there and possibly a young child. You all have your assignments on the operational plan in front of you. In the event of an emergency, Matthews' truck will be the ambulance." Matthews held his hand up and nodded to everyone, acknowledging his own possible role in the worst-case scenario. He pointed to the place on his vest where he clipped his car keys in case that worst-case scenario rendered him incapable of driving.

The ambiance in the room full of normally jovial men was uncharacteristically serious and without a sarcastic comment or giggle.

"Just a reminder about the footing on that front porch. The snow will most likely not have been shoveled at all. First man to the door, that's you Dorsey, make sure we check the ramp to see if anyone has come or gone with the tracks in the fresh snow."

The briefing was abruptly interrupted by an incoming phone call to Brown. It was Vatrano. He had been sitting surveillance near the home on Depot Street while the rest of the team was going over the plan at Pollard's office. Vatrano relayed the new information that had been gathered on site.

"Brownie, had a light come on for about a minute and then go right back out." The quiet room allowed everyone to hear what was being said without the call even being placed on speaker phone.

Vatrano wanted to make sure the group knew that someone in the home may be awake on their arrival, possibly thwarting the element of surprise.

"Well, that's good," Brown replied. "At least we know someone's fuckin' home," he jested while trying to remain positive.

"The VW is still sitting there, covered in snow. I'm guessing it hasn't moved since yesterday when we saw it come back from McDonald's. It looks like it's in the exact same spot, parked facing in."

"Got ya. Vatrano, when we roll in, you grab front perimeter on Depot Street like we talked about." Brown was now doubling his efforts to make sure the assignments were clear, even though they were already defined on the written operational plan.

"Okay."

"We'll be there in about ten minutes. We'll hit you up on the radio on our way out of the office to let you know."

Brown hung up the phone without his standard "love you" salutation, an overt omission that indicated the seriousness of his intentions.

"Any questions from the group? Any questions on assignments and vehicles?" Each of Brown's inquiries was met with a meaningful silence from the rest of the crew. "Then let's gear up and go."

Almost in unison, the members of the assembled team got up and began putting on gear that was resting in small piles in the dimly lit hallway just outside Pollard's office. It was all done with a lack of any conversation aside from a few "radio checks" muttered in the microphones, and the confirmations of receipt returned. To Pollard, the quietness was expected. The Velcro of the large flack vests scratched. The lights on the ends of rifles and handguns were checked for proper function, creating a strobe effect as it was still dark outside, and the lights in the corridor were dull.

Each member of the team left Pollard's office and loaded into one of four vehicles, fully confident that they were ready. A total of eight deputies left the office and would meet up with Vatrano down on Depot Street, where he would jump in the mix to make nine. Three would watch the perimeter of the house while six would hopefully make entry. The target was a two-bedroom home with two stories, so the level of manpower felt appropriate.

Four large American-made trucks and sport utility vehicles made their way down Depot Street in Stanton just before 0530. The lack of traffic indicated that they were making the primary tracks down the snow-covered street, like the first skier off the chairlift on a morning run down the slopes. Other than Vatrano's tire tracks that led directly to his position parked on the side of the road, the white powder appeared untouched. After being prompted by Brown's radio message that they were thirty seconds away, Vatrano stepped out of his vehicle onto that same fresh snow, while witnessing the low-profile parade coming his direction from the top of Depot

99

Street. Two of the vehicles veered left into the parking lot of the duplex. The remaining pair traveled up to the intersection with High Street and came to a stop. There were no other cars parked on the High Street side, making the final positioning the driver's choice.

While witnessing the snow blanketed roads that hadn't yet been cleared, Pollard thought briefly about the intent of the parking tickets that provided the information that got them all to that location. He then flashed back quickly to the two drinks from the previous day's fast-food takeout pick up by Bixby. Pollard could see for himself in the dimly lit area that there were no footprints in the snow on or off the property, he didn't need Dorsey's report as first man up. If one of those drinks was for Washington, he was on the other side of that door. If not, well, Pollard didn't want to explore that option, at least not until he had to.

Dorsey was the initial deputy to the door as designed in the plan, with a stack of five more deputies behind him. It did not appear that anyone had awoken in either unit at 28 Depot Street due to the near silent approach of the team. There was no indication that anyone in the neighborhood had started the day yet: no dogs out for a walk, no cars parked and running to warm up, and very few interior lights on. Dorsey's first knocks on the door echoed around the neighborhood, cutting through the cold and quiet created by the fresh coat of muffling mid-winter snow. After the initial knocks, the howling of what sounded like a beagle, clearly coming from

28B Depot Street, pierced through the dearth of noise. Through their earpieces each team member could hear Vatrano's voice between the barks, "Light on upstairs! Light on upstairs!" He could see the second-floor window, above the stack of deputies, clearly from the street where he was watching the front side of the home.

The old duplex shook just a little, and the movement from inside the house was felt in each of the deputies' boots firmly planted on the floorboards of the front decking. Clicking of deadbolts and chains was followed by the door swinging open slowly. It was Anna Walsh, Washington's mother, standing in the open doorway in her pink robe. She clutched it closed at her chest as the blast of cold air rushed toward her from the outside like a breached levee. Pollard immediately thought about the second soda from the day before and that she might have received it from Bixby. He discarded his disappointment quickly, knowing he still had a job that needed to be done safely.

"We're here with an arrest warrant for John Washington. What room is he in?" Dorsey asked demandingly, only a few feet from the woman.

"That's my son. He's not here!" the woman replied in a high pitch, clearly shocked at the presence of the heavily armed men at her door at that early hour.

"He's not in this house right now?" Pollard posed the statement as a question from over Dorsey's shoulder, specifically hoping for the inviting response that he got back from her.

"No! Go ahead and look, he's not in here. Tia and my grandson are upstairs, let me get them." She granted the consent that they needed, lacking any further evidence that Washington was actually inside the residence.

Walsh retreated through the doorway towards the stairs. Dorsey and the rest of the team followed and secured the downstairs living room and kitchen area with a quick sweep. The entire first floor was void of any other occupants. Dorsey, Brown, and Matthews followed Walsh to the stairway. Bixby came out of a bedroom at the top of the stairs as the team looked up to her from ten steps below. Seeing the three large men at the bottom of the stairs, she shot back into the bedroom, causing movement among the team members. She emerged holding her young son, closed the door behind her, and came down the stairs toward the team in a scurry. Passing by the deputies halfway between the first and second floors, she successfully avoided eye contact while flattening herself against the wall on the stairwell. Holding Lucas tightly and descending to the first floor, Bixby was clearly still in the midst of the stupor of waking up. When she passed by Pollard, he broke his concentration briefly to shake the thought just below his conscience, that he was part of an occupying force in the sanctuary that is the home of another.

Walsh beckoned Bixby and her grandson out to the front porch, away from the armed men. Vatrano came closer to the house with the hope of catching anything the women were saying on the porch, all while keeping a visual on the exterior of the building, especially the second-floor windows. Though the probability had dropped, he was fully prepared for Washington to emerge from any number of egress points, looking for an opportunity to flee.

The three doors at the top of the stairway posed a twist for the deputies, though one that they had trained for. It appeared likely there was a bedroom door on each side of a central bathroom, as they had seen in their research the previous night. That knowledge of the layout didn't alleviate the feeling that this situation was like a big game of three card monte, with a murderer possibly behind each closed door.

"We need a man up!" Brown called over the radio for a fourth deputy to help clear the second floor safely.

While one pair of deputies cleared a room, the other two remained by each closed door. With unknown occupants, they focused on preventing escape or attack from the blindside with the concentration of offensive linemen protecting an all-star quarterback. "Clear, coming out," was followed again by "clear coming out," and then again. All three upstairs rooms had no other human beings inside.

Dorsey was mindful of his previous experiences with the team. They had found people on past cases hiding in washing machines, clothes dryers, cupboards, plastic storage bins, insulation in the attic and even behind false walls. With this in mind, he put out the request for a secondary and more thorough search of the home. The five deputies were able to accomplish this second search in just a couple of minutes, due to the small size and layout of this half of the duplex.

Pollard knew there hadn't been too much time between first contact with Walsh at the front door and the completion of the initial search. An elaborate scheme to hide Washington probably didn't happen at 0530, when everyone in the house showed evidence of being asleep.

During the secondary search there was extra time and the safety from possible threats to give more notice to clothing and other property. Not a single item was observed by anyone from the team that would indicate an adult male lived at the residence or was even staying there. Not a single piece of men's clothing out in the open or in a laundry basket. No boots or sneakers fitting an average sized man. No men's body wash or shampoo in the shower. There were only two adult toothbrushes and one child brush next to the sink in the upstairs bathroom, presumably for the residents now anxiously waiting on the porch for the team to finish their search.

"Collapse the perimeter and clear," Pollard put out over the radio and followed up with a more dejected tone, "He's not in here." This operation was now morphing to an interview phase, the consolation prize for not making an apprehension. Five of the deputies got back to their vehicles and completely left the neighborhood to prevent drawing any more attention than they already had. The serious action on Depot Street had lasted just under ten minutes and was done.

Before leaving, an older male neighbor in the duplex had poked his head out after hearing the commotion. Matthews quickly showed him a picture of Washington. Not having seen him there at all, the man just shook his head. The neighbor shared a common wall and parking lot with the two women, so his reaction was further confirmation that Washington had not been around.

Vatrano, Dorsey, and Pollard stayed behind while the rest of the deputies started back to the office. Vatrano and Pollard had developed an ability to work an interview well together and planned on completing this one. While Walsh and Lucas went into the living room, Bixby, Vatrano, and Pollard went to the adjacent kitchen at Pollard's request.

The home was in good shape relative to many of the homes that they had been in on previous cases. Walsh's mature presence was the cause of this, Pollard thought, or maybe her hotel experience. Either way, a sit down in the kitchen was not vomit inducing, and that was to be celebrated. Bixby appeared annoyed to have been awoken to the sight of heavily equipped and armed officers at her home.

"What the hell is all of this about? I'm going to get evicted for this," she protested before even starting a conversation, setting the expectation for her level of cooperation. Pollard knew she was speaking from experience regarding the eviction, but decided against addressing it, at least initially.

"Listen, we have a warrant for John Washington-" Pollard couldn't quite get the whole statement off his lips before being cut off by the young woman.

"Well, he ain't here!" Her voice had gotten slightly louder, indicating to Pollard a lack of cooperation, and most likely a lack of honesty in what was about to be said. In Pollard's experience, noise was a common side effect of fear, and was often a tell of dishonesty. Had they not already searched the house to see for themselves, statements made in such a way would have Pollard believing that their suspect was inside.

"We know that now." Recognizing that she was amped up, Pollard began speaking in a lower, softer volume, hoping to get Bixby to do the same, to calm her down and help develop some rapport with her. Agreeing with her like he just had might help too, but that remained to be seen.

"We need to locate him as soon as possible." Vatrano jumped into the conversation, "How can we do that?"

Bixby had a child with a man who had done his time in prison. She wasn't about to give him up whether she loved him or not. "All this over a parole violation? Don't you guys have better things to be doing?" She was fishing now, trying to elicit information from the deputies. Neither Pollard nor Vatrano was going take that bait. They also made note that she hadn't actually addressed Vatrano's inquiry.

"We need to find him and get him into custody, safely." Vatrano started down the same road with a slightly different technique. He would give her information like she was fishing for, just not exactly what she was looking for. Vatrano played it straight by displaying some of their cards, showing her what an outsider's view of the situation looked like. "You are the mother of his child. His own mother is living here with you along with that child. Where else would he be if not with you three?" It was a logical question that would require a quick and ineffective lie to try and prevent the deputies from getting what they wanted. Pollard and Vatrano knew that and got what they expected.

"I really don't know where he's been staying since he got out of prison. He doesn't come around here though."

Pollard knew about the Electronic Benefits Card issued by the State, in her name, being used in New Jersey with video proof it was Washington using it. He knew about the prison visits and the phone calls. He didn't need to call Bixby on her probable lies just yet though. He had to give her some credit, what she was saying might be true given the lack of local police contact with Washington in the months since he was paroled.

"How do we get in contact with him then? If something happened to his child and you had to find him, how would you do it?" It was a great question, getting away from Washington's culpability and transferring to the responsibility he had as a parent. Vatrano expected another false answer and he got it.

"I don't know how to get in touch with him."

The conversation went on for a bit longer. It became clear to Pollard and Vatrano that Bixby knew about the murder, or at least some sort of incident, as she slipped up and told them she knew nothing about what happened "down there." They both took it to mean New Jersey, and if she didn't know about the murder, she at least knew that he had been staying there after his parole to the halfway house.

Pollard wasn't going to push it any further with Bixby. There was no reason to force the issue given her initial attitude and lack of any indication that she was going to cooperate. For all Pollard knew, she was most likely a victim of Washington's selfish lifestyle. Pollard knew that being a complete stranger to her was reason enough to understand that she owed him no loyalty.

"Can I just get your phone number in case we have follow up questions? We don't want to keep coming over here like this. We certainly don't need you getting evicted over it." Pollard smirked at her knowingly and she smiled back, though probably for a different reason. He was hoping to leave it on a positive note, give her the idea that they were somewhat concerned about what effect their actions that morning would have for her. The impression was that they wanted what was best for her, almost an apology or making amends. It worked well enough to get a phone number anyways.

Feeling as though she had outsmarted them, and they had believed all of her lies, she confidently rattled off her phone number. There was a sense of security in the knowledge that she would have no problem lying to them over the phone just as well, if not better than she had in person.

Pollard reached for the front of his large tactical vest for a pen and into his pocket for something to write on. He jotted down her name and number on his note pad. Bixby retrieved Lucas from Walsh, and they went upstairs to her room, leaving the door slightly ajar behind her. That gave Pollard and Vatrano a chance to talk to Walsh in the living room before clearing out.

Experience would continue to show these men that a mother's love is always different. Or as Dorsey would put it, the hole you came out of is always different. Walsh appeared to actually be concerned for her son. Unlike Bixby, it didn't seem like Walsh knew about the murder, or maybe she was in denial, afraid to admit it even to herself. She went on and on about Washington going back to prison on his parole violation and how that might be good for him in the long run. It would provide a lesson that had clearly not been learned yet. She only went so far with her cooperation though.

"So how would you get in touch with him if you had to?" The script was nearly the same, the delivery was slightly modified given Walsh's level of cooperation and calmness.

"To be honest, I haven't heard from him in quite some time. I really wish he would see Lucas and be a part of his life. I know that my grandson wants that and so does John. He just can't seem to get around to doing it." Again, the question wasn't really answered. It was subtle, but not hearing from someone was different than finding a manner in which to contact them if necessary.

Vatrano hated any statement that started with a disclaimer like, "to be honest" or "in all honesty." It was a glaring tell for most people. Like a billboard advertising that the next words that would be coming from that person's mouth were guaranteed to be untruthful, or that the words before had been as well.

"The only person that might take him in would be Ronnie." She seemed to offer this new information with quite a bit of ease, and it again was not an answer to how she would get in contact with her son. "He was his only friend from back on the west side that even came to visit him or write to him while he was in prison." Pollard recalled a Ronald on the visitor list from the prison records. She was telling a partial truth, as aside from Bixby, Walsh, and the child, he remembered him being the only other name on the list.

"Where does Ronnie live now?" Vatrano stepped in for the question as he was more familiar with the neighborhood on the west side of the city.

"I'm not sure. He used to live on Poirier Street. But that was a couple of years ago now." It seemed that she was trying to give the appearance of being cooperative while at the same time providing them with nothing really useful.

After a few minutes it was obvious that although her tact was different, Walsh was going to be about as good for workable information as Bixby. Bixby was also within ear shot upstairs, so they didn't want to push it, but they also didn't want to leave without giving her the opportunity to provide information in the future. Maybe when she had a little more privacy, things might change. It was worth a shot, they figured.

"Here's my card. If you can think of anything else that might help us find him, please let us know. We really do want to get him into custody and safely." Pollard again wanted to leave the conversation on a positive note, to keep the bridge intact instead of burnt to a crisp.

"I do too," was all she had left to say. Pollard scribbled his cell phone number on the back of the card and laid it on the kitchen counter next to where he was standing. Hearing the concern in Anna's voice, genuine or not, only served to humanize the man they would continuously refer to as a "target" in a "hunt." Seeing his child that morning had the same effect. With the thought that

111

Washington had a mother and a child, and maybe an ex-girlfriend, that loved him, Pollard finished their intrusion with one final question.

"Could I grab your contact information Ms. Walsh?" Pollard asked, matching Walsh's own polite demeanor.

"Of course." She began to spout off the number. Pollard immediately recognized it as one that he had written down from the prison records and was confirmed by the police dispatcher when he had inquired. He found it interesting that she had the same number all through the years. Pollard had seen so many people change phones and plans in this line of work that the level of consistency stood out to him. It matched the level of stability that Walsh appeared to be trying to give to Lucas and Bixby.

Having completed the interviews, Dorsey, Vatrano, and Pollard hopped up into the truck to start towards Pollard's office on the other side of town. Vatrano was the first to bring it up, but it was quickly confirmed that each man had caught the same vibe from Walsh.

"She's hiding something, but it isn't her son," Vatrano said plainly.

"I was thinking the same thing. It's like she's covering up something or someone other than her son. It was a little strange." Pollard chalked it up to the fact that maybe she knew her son had committed this murder, and she hadn't heard a single law enforcement officer in her home mention it, not even once. Maybe she was trying to prevent being the one to bring it up for fear of exposing her son, or even admitting it to herself. "I almost believed her when she said that she thought going back to prison to learn a lesson might be a good thing for him." Pollard bounced the idea off the other two. "But she just didn't want to give him up for some reason."

Knowing that the answer to those mysteries could only be answered with conjecture and guesses, the group cleared from that area of Stanton and rallied back at Pollard's office with the rest of the team. Pollard felt even further away from Washington now and was hoping that Brown would be the bearer of bad news to the Philadelphia team.

After a brief conversation between Brown and Pollard, Brown invited him to call the other team with him. The fact that Washington was clearly not in New Hampshire with the family could be useful knowledge to the group looking in Camden. It was Pollard and Brown's belief that this may be the end of their involvement, at least for now, after they checked into the unlikely possibility that Washington might be with his old friend Ronnie.

Brown had kept the Philly team in the loop the previous evening about the intention to go to the house on Depot Street that morning. Deputy McKay, the lead Marshal on the case in Camden, was expectedly disappointed with the results, but they were all happy with the assurance that Washington would be shut out from the residence on Depot Street for respite. Certainly, if Bixby and Walsh were in touch with Washington, the news of the team's visit would keep him from coming around and may cut off another avenue for evading capture. It was small solace for both groups that were hoping to have handcuffs on him that morning, but Pollard had one last ditch idea and was willing to present it without fully vetting it to anyone else or even himself first.

"Who was able to go up on Washington's last known phone number, you know, the one that ended up in the river next to the murder weapon?" Pollard asked to his counterpart down in Camden.

"I know that Detective Luce from the Camden County Prosecutor's Office did right after the murder. I would need to reach out to him if you need those records." Marshal McKay had a slight hesitance in his voice, as if trying to figure out Pollard's angle.

"Can you send him my contact information and have him forward a copy of any of the records he might have?" Pollard had quickly changed his demeanor from disappointment with the results of the morning activities to hope that there may be a new avenue for locating Washington. It would involve a level of technology that he was not comfortable with, but he knew he would have plenty of help.

"I'll get Luce on the phone right now and either he or I will call you back in a few, sound good?"

"Sounds good."

Neither McKay on the other end of the call, nor Brown were quite sure where Pollard was taking this, but Brown figured he'd let him run with it.

"Hey Mark, I've got to head down to the seacoast on another warrant. I got a call on it while you guys were doing your interviews." Following up on a call about another fugitive case waiting in the wings for the team to tackle, something about a wanted sex offender, Brown took off for the southern part of the state, along with Matthews, to get the details from the local police down there.

Pollard, Vatrano, and Dorsey decided they were going to grab some breakfast at a local diner that Pollard used to haunt when he worked the overnight patrol shifts in Windsor. The waitstaff and cooks were still used to seeing Pollard come by in uniform before the 8 a.m. shift change, even though it had been years since he worked that beat. When he came in now on his new gig, in plain clothes and at different times, it still seemed foreign to them. He would always be considered a "regular," just not at his regular time anymore.

"Barely recognized you with the beard there, Mark." The buxom young waitress shot him a chop-busting smile, part hello, part playful dig at the lack of thickness in his facial hair. Pollard stroked the thin hair on his face and just smiled back as she walked past with a tray of eggs and pancakes over her right shoulder enroute to the corner table. The familiar flirtation caused him to forget momentarily about the team's lack of success that morning.

The three men had all exchanged niceties with the waitress and had just completed their breakfast orders under the watchful eyes of John McCain and the restaurant owner when Pollard's phone rang out. He stepped into the parking lot and sat in his truck to avoid talking about such sensitive information in public, and of course, to stay out of the biting winter air. He presumed it was Detective Luce on the other end of the call based on the screen of his smart phone reading "Camden County."

"Hello."

"Hey man, Chuck Luce, how are you doing?"

"Doing alright, I'm guessing they told you we didn't get much up here this morning, huh?" It was an honest assessment of the end result of the morning's work.

"Yeah. Oh well. McKay was saying that you guys were interested in some phone records I got on Washington after the murder. The phone itself is a little waterlogged, you know we found it in the river, so he won't be with it?"

"Yeah, I know, I read the affidavit on the murder warrant. Nice work by the way." Complimenting the detective on the handling of the murder case when he couldn't find his wanted party for him was the least Pollard could do. The detective had solved his case; the fugitive team, and Pollard, had not solved their own.

"Thanks," he said plainly, probably because he was a homicide detective, and such work was routine to him. The murders in Camden in any given year were about the same or more than in the entire state of New Hampshire, a fact that Pollard had glossed over at the time of this conversation.

"So, we have confirmed phone numbers for his baby momma and mother," Pollard got back on track. "Just looking to see if he had much historical contact with them."

"We have an open search warrant on the phone, so although the murder was a couple of weeks ago now, we still would be notified of activity if there is any. Unfortunately, the day after the murder, the activity on the phone, both incoming and outgoing, completely stopped around the same time it landed in the river. The last cell tower it hit was here in Camden and we thought it was near the house of one of his associates, but we came up empty on that. One of the guys suggested Washington's body might be nearby, in the Delaware. We found the gun first, and we weren't even looking for it, a nice little bonus. We kept looking for a body, and the diver found the phone in the same area as the gun."

"Crazy! Do you guys have the call history on the phone too, or just the locations from the towers?"

"It goes back a few weeks before the murder on the historicals, we were trying to see who he might have been talking with."

"You want to send those records up to me? I have an idea that might help us find him." It was a simple request, complicated only by the fact that the records were evidence in a murder case that hadn't been tried yet.

"Will do," Luce replied plainly. Pollard was more than excited with Luce's level of cooperation, something he wasn't totally expecting from the homicide detective, probably unfairly.

After finishing the call, Pollard hustled back into the diner expecting his omelet would be waiting for him. As he had predicted, Dorsey and Vatrano already had a few bites missing from their respective plates, giving Pollard an indication as to how long his had been sitting on the table getting cool. His first bite gave him a perfect gauge that it had sat just the right amount of time, as the cheese was still hot but hadn't burned the roof of his mouth.

Pollard had received the records from the Camden County Prosecutor's Office via email before he had finished his sizeable breakfast. Not wanting to discuss the sensitive details of the documents in public, he invited Dorsey and Vatrano back to his office. They seemed a bit surprised by the offer as they thought the trail appeared to end a couple of hours earlier on Depot Street, at least for the day. Pollard needed to review the documents from Luce and run his idea by his trusted coworkers. Vatrano was also going to check on what he could find out about the old friend, Ronnie.

CHAPTER ELEVEN

With a belly full of breakfast food and back at his office with Vatrano and Dorsey, Pollard was able to open and review the documents that the homicide detective had sent him from the investigation in Camden County. The records that Pollard had received regarding Washington's cell phone usage during the days leading up to the murder confirmed what he had already been told by the investigator. Washington's phone had been pinging off cell phone towers in the Philadelphia and Camden area for weeks leading up to the murder. It quickly went silent that night. Logical, he figured, as it was later located on the bottom of the river. Pollard pulled his notepad from his pocket and located the two phone numbers he had jotted down in the kitchen at the duplex on Depot Street earlier that morning.

With just a quick glance he was able to recognize that Washington had texted or called each number multiple times in the weeks leading up to the murder, enough to show a steady and consistent pattern of contact. Although the phone records did not provide the actual wording in the messages, he was able to ascertain the cell towers that the phone was activating from and a direction and approximate distance from each tower. Along with that information, the date and time of the messages was easily visible. As Pollard had suspected, Washington had regular contact with his mother and the mother of his child right up to the day of the murder when the phone went for a swim.

Unless Washington had completely stopped communicating with both women, he would have found a new way to contact them now. Pollard knew the women weren't square with the team while being interviewed in their home earlier in the day, and this new information further confirmed his belief. The records indicated that he had even contacted Bixby right around the time of the homicide, based on the timeline of events that Pollard had come to understand. The call to Bixby was Washington's last outgoing call from that phone.

"So, hear me out," Pollard started with Vatrano and Dorsey as if hoping they would at least give his idea a chance. "If he's been in contact with these two women this much, he's still in contact now, just not with this phone that he clearly decided he couldn't keep on him while escaping. The question is, can we get the records on whatever new number he's using? And with that, can we get the information on which cell towers it's activating from and try and figure out where the hell he might be now?" Pollard was setting up his own sort of presentation with the questions he felt he might already have the answer to.

"How do you figure we could get our hands on this new number, if he even has one? The women aren't going to give it to us. They made that pretty fuckin' clear." Dorsey asked and partially answered the obvious question.

"Maybe we will be able to get it from them and they just won't know it. Can we get enough for a search warrant for the cell phone numbers belonging to Bixby and Walsh? They each just personally gave us their phone numbers to reach them at, and Washington was contacting them at those numbers from the old phone until it went in the river." Pollard held up the paper records where he learned that information, like an attorney showing a jury an exhibit of evidence. "That would give us the recent contacts to both women. There would be a new phone number that would have most likely started contacting both of them sometime after the time of the murder up to today. We would then have a reasonable belief that the new number common to both women's phones would be Washington." He stopped briefly to get a sense if they were following his logic. "We would have to get a warrant for that new, common number to get the cell tower information and it would give us a fairly good direction to start looking in." Pollard looked at both men, waiting for some type of response, positive or negative.

Vatrano, with his legal background, was skeptical but intrigued, "I don't know that you'd have probable cause to get search warrants on people who haven't committed a crime and *then* get a search warrant for a phone number that you can't even prove belongs to our murderer."

"That's what you're here for, Tony Vatrano, esquire," Pollard replied, both jokingly and also hoping to stroke Vatrano's legal ego into a more positive endorsement for the idea.

"I think we can get it done." Dorsey jumped in to add his two cents on the matter. "If nothing else, if the cell tower data is any good, we could narrow our search down to a confined area or get an idea where he may be or who he's with. Shit, he might be using a friend's phone that actually has a phone subscription with an address attached and we would be right there."

"We're a long way from that point." Vatrano brought the group back down to reality. "Let's work this out and see if we can't get it in front of a judge. We're not searching for evidence of the crime, so there's nothing to suppress in a court hearing about the murder. It's worth a shot, but we've got to get everything we can going into this." Vatrano was playing the role of the devil's advocate as he often did, but also seemed up for the challenge.

Pollard turned to his computer and pulled up a template for an affidavit in support of a search warrant. They would have a long afternoon ahead of them preparing a presentation for a judge that had to be perfect in every aspect, or else it would be dead-on-arrival. Vatrano's inquiries into Washington's friend, Ronnie, back in his home county, would have to wait for now.

CHAPTER TWELVE

Washington had successfully made his way out of Camden and into the city of Elizabeth, a small victory, but a victory for him nonetheless. His only immediate plan was to hunker down, stay below the detection of anyone that might deem him suspicious and avoid the law. He knew he was far enough removed from the friends and family of the man he might have just killed, and the police who might also be even closer behind. It would be some time before he could get past that feeling of being set up by a man he thought of as a friend, even a mentor. That he had been taken advantage of and used for someone else's gain, and someone else's demise. He hadn't fully wrapped his head around that betrayal yet, still focused on the process of gaining his own safety.

There were only so many people in his world that would take him in and help him at a time like this. His mother and Tia both knew that he had violated his parole. When he was done at the halfway house, he was supposed to be living in Stanton with them while on supervision, but he had never even met his parole officer.

Washington had only been to his mother's new place in Stanton for a little less than a full day before heading off to Camden, for what he hoped was a big opportunity. After visiting with Lucas for a little while and catching up on some of his mom's home cooking, he left with whatever cash was in his mother's purse and the electronic benefits card that had been issued to Tia. He knew he could purchase certain food items with it anywhere in the country and it could be used like an ATM card for up to $200 in cash each month. Best of all, the card balance would be refilled after each flip of the calendar.

Even with the thefts, Tia and his mother both wanted him to come back, demonstrating a fluid line between love, forgiveness and enabling. Although victimized by his actions, they would still entertain his phone calls and have him talk to his son. The women were motivated by their desire for the child to get what Washington hadn't in a father. Washington was willing to play the game and pretend that he cared so that he could continue on without confrontation, to perpetuate his bad deeds and poor life decisions.

After the murder, going back to mom's house wasn't an option. It was certainly a place where the law would be looking for him. He had been in touch with the women and his son while staying in New Jersey, but he wasn't really specific with what was going on. They could tell he was in trouble, as he seemed to be since he was seventeen years old. He wouldn't tell them where he was or where he was going. On this night, he needed a phone number from his mother as his contact list was now, he believed, at the bottom of the Delaware River by the banking on the New Jersey side.

Although getting close to midnight, he knew his mother would answer the call for him even though the number he was reaching out from was a pay phone. She always answered, just like any mother holding the anxiety of her child being in distress, or the fear of being notified that he had met his demise. The latter was the reason she answered the call on that evening. After briefly exchanging pleasantries, Washington pushed for what he was looking for.

"His number is right here, let me get it."

He waited about as long as it took her to grab her little black book that stored all of her numbers, not trusting that she could locate it in her contacts in the phone while still talking. She gave him the number willingly and without a lot of question. Washington had once been in possession of the digits, but never committed them to memory. Clearly, she had not spoken to Tia, Washington surmised, as his last phone call to her a few hours earlier was far more dramatic.

"Now I don't know what's going on but be real careful calling him. And don't you be dragging him into whatever mess you're gettin' into." Her mother's intuition was focused in a plausible direction. "It's been a while since you've seen him, things are going well for him now, and you know I still love him."

"He's not going to be in any trouble, mom. I swear it." With that sworn falsification, he was able to get the phone number at the price of another false promise to the woman who had given him life. "And mom, I'm calling from a pay phone, I lost my phone. I'll call you when I get a new one in a couple days, okay?" He felt like giving her that information would put her at ease when she tried to call him and didn't get an answer. It wasn't a warning so much for her sake as it was to his advantage when he might need something later down the road.

Much like he had been duped by Robert Keith, Washington knew he had to do the same to someone else for his own survival. His mom had given him that phone number without much questioning, even though it was getting close to changing from night to morning. And although it had been some time since they had spoken, he summoned the courage, hoping that guilt or sympathy or even empathy would prevail. He was able to call him from the same bus station pay phone after making it to Elizabeth with the $109 he had taken from the man he had shot. It took three consecutive calls answered by the outgoing voicemail. Washington declined to leave a message each time but did need to pay for each new attempt. The time of day and strange number were clearly working against him. On the fourth attempt, the voice answered on the other side, somehow sounding both familiar and foreign.

"Man, I need you right now. More than I ever have." It was a bold opening statement to someone he hadn't talked to for quite some time.

"What'd you get yourself in to? I can't be driving all the way to New Jersey to pick you up in the middle of the damn night." He sounded both annoyed and concerned; Washington would need to take advantage of and magnify that latter emotion to get what he would need.

"Listen, They. Are. Going. To. Kill. Me." It was non-specific, with emphasis on the word kill, but it was certainly a statement he had never made to anyone before. It caused some alarm, but by design, created even more concern.

The voice on the other end didn't need to hear much more. The car was at his disposal, and he had the time to go and pick up Washington. "I'm coming, right now. The bus station in Elizabeth you said, right?" He punched the bus station into a quick search on his phone and got the address to confirm they were talking about the same place.

A few miles from home, he stopped to fill up the gas tank that he had left nearly empty after using it that day, not expecting any impromptu trips to New Jersey to pick up Washington. It was going to be a long drive and he had come to grips with that. Before heading out on the interstate on his way to Elizabeth, he simply plugged the address into his phone GPS and began following the prompts from the lady's voice on the app. It was the only voice he would hear for hours that early morning.

He couldn't even call Washington to tell him he wasn't coming if he decided to change his mind. It was partly why he continued down the road and didn't turn back like his instinct was telling him, even screaming at him, to do. Guilt and loyalty overlapped as they fought to be the overarching emotion of the night.

Washington knew it would be hours until the arrival of his ride, but it was the best that he could do given the circumstances, his only real hope. Meanwhile, he needed to stay away from any unneeded attention, nearly alone in that bus terminal in the middle of the night. He walked casually over to the trash cans in the center of the lobby and dropped his New Hampshire Non-Driver Identification into one, much like he had his gun and phone in the river several hours before. The smack of the swinging lid mimicked the sound of a splash that had given him some relief on the banks of the Delaware.

Now if confronted by law enforcement while hanging around the bus station, he could at least give a fake name without the chance of verification of his true identity by being searched. All he could do now was wait and watch for his ride out of town, hoping that he had been convincing enough on that phone call to a man he hadn't seen in so long, and that he wouldn't be let down.

CHAPTER THIRTEEN

The outside of a judge's chambers always brought Pollard back to his school days and the reminiscent feeling of being sent out in the hallway or to the principal's office. It was just after 8 a.m. and the court day had just started. For Vatrano and Pollard, the previous afternoon had turned into evening getting the search warrant completed. They had planned with the Clerk of the Court to get in first thing, before the judge's robe even touched down on the bench. Pollard had Vatrano with him because he had done so much to help him prepare the warrant. There was some security in numbers to lower the anxiety, but just a touch.

Judge O'Brien had a reputation in Stanton and beyond. It was a reputation that was earned by spending years being a hard ass on the criminal defendants that came before him, but also on the prosecutors, defense attorneys and cops that would go in front of him as well.

Lucky for Pollard, he and the judge had some history that he hoped would help in this matter. Before being appointed as a justice, O'Brien had previously been the County Attorney and had worked with Pollard on some cases early in his career as a prosecutor. More importantly than the teamwork that led to the successful prosecutions, Pollard had also never stretched the truth or massaged some of his testimony to try to make a charge stick. He knew that O'Brien would remember the instances when they lost, when the verdict was not guilty. That he would be cognizant of those times when Pollard was honest even when it hurt their case. Recalling that history still didn't do much for the feeling in Pollard's gut, seemingly a mixture of first date anxiety and job interview jitters.

Judge O'Brien's clerk picked up the phone after just one ring as she could see who was calling on the other end.

"Okay, I'll tell them." The phone was hung back on the receiver. She then set her eyes on the two men standing in her office and caught their attention. "The judge is ready for you. Go on in," she said, while motioning with her head towards the heavy hardwood door behind her chair that led to the judge's chambers. Pollard had been before a judge with less and gotten a search warrant signed. He had also been to a judge with more and been denied. Not quite sure where to set his expectations, he breeched the threshold into the office with Vatrano right behind him.

"Good morning, Your Honor," Pollard opened. "Judge, this is Deputy Tony Vatrano, I don't think you have probably ever met." Pollard was sure they hadn't met. Vatrano's home office was two counties away and Vatrano already told him that they hadn't. But

Pollard had always found it was wise not to speak to judges with absolutes or assumptions.

"Good morning, gents." The old judge greeted them with a head nod to the newly introduced deputy. "So, what has you here in my chambers so early this morning?" Ruling on the search warrant they had brought in would no doubt be the judge's first official act of his legal day, possibly before he even had a chance at a hot cup of coffee.

"Well, Your Honor, I have a search warrant that I'd like for you to review and hopefully approve. If I might, I'd like to give you a little background on this case, this one is a homicide." Pollard didn't get a chance to continue.

"Let me just stop you right there. How about I review your affidavit in support of this request and if I grant it, we'll have saved all of us a great deal of time, right?"

Pollard wasn't sure if the question was rhetorical or not. He answered anyways, "Right, Your Honor," not wanting to argue with that logic or disrespect his valued time. Especially when he was hoping to gain favor.

"Have a seat," the judge said, motioning with his open left hand toward the old wooden chairs positioned stage right and stage left from his desk. Both men followed the request, or order, while the judge sat back in his chair, simultaneously swiveling, and reclining slightly.

Pollard figured either one of two things was happening. The judge was in a hurry and would make a quick decision on the warrant to get Pollard out of his chambers. Or his hard-ass tendencies were on full display within the first thirty seconds of their meeting, and this was going to be an uphill battle. Pollard and Vatrano sat in silence while waiting to see which scenario might become reality.

Judge O'Brien laid the papers out in front of him after removing the paperclip. Holding his pen in his right hand, he scratched his brow, careful not to touch the ink to his head. He braced his arm by placing his elbow on the edge of the shiny, dark, hardwood edge of his executive style desk.

With his gun, bullets, handcuffs, and other items concealed on his waist under his slightly oversized shirt, Pollard had a hard time fitting his large frame into the confines of the arms on the chair in front of the judge. It looked to Vatrano as though Pollard was squirming, and maybe he was, due to his size and possibly the anxiety.

Both men were trying to get a read on the judge's facial expressions as though they could follow him through the paragraphs. Judge O'Brien looked down at his desk through his bifocals and then up at Pollard. Pollard managed a nervous smile, clearly demonstrating to the judge he had no idea how he was going to rule on the warrant. Not wanting to appear cocky but also not wanting to give the impression he lacked confidence, Pollard just remained quiet.

"So, if I understand this correctly, you guys are looking for a search warrant for an invasion into the privacy of two women who you don't suspect have committed any crime?" Knowing that the way he had phrased that was somewhat inflammatory, the judge put his hand up, while still holding the pen. He was hoping to prevent Pollard from interrupting, as the judge saw him shift his weight like he was preparing to interject. "Furthermore, you don't believe that evidence of a crime will be located on the phone records, only that those phone records will provide you with another completely different phone number that you would then need another warrant on, all to locate a subject wanted for a crime. Not necessarily that you would find evidence of a crime on that new phone either." The judge paused. "This break in my synopsis is my way of telling you that I would like some of that background you were wanting to give me just a few short moments ago."

Vatrano, with his legal background that was unknown to the judge, offered up his best defense of Pollard's request as though he was representing him as his own personal counsel. It was also his own work that he was motivated to defend. "Your Honor, you clearly have a good grasp on what it is we are hoping to do." Vatrano started with a gentle stroke of the judge's ego, never a bad move. "This is certainly a different type of warrant than you are probably used to seeing in that the end result is not solving a crime,

133

it's finding the criminal." The judge sat back in his reclining leather chair as if indicating with his body language that he was ready to receive more of Vatrano's oral arguments. Vatrano astutely observed the non-verbal cue from the judge and continued. "We are not looking for evidence of a crime. None of the records would be presented before a jury as evidence. No other judge would be ruling on the validity of this warrant at a trial. We are simply looking to find a human being and arrest him on a crime that he is alleged to have committed several states away. When that person is found, he would be returned to New Jersey authorities and none of the records we gather here would have any bearing on that case at all. It would have no bearing on any case anywhere. Once we have arrested the body of Mr. Washington, our involvement is over. You can't suppress a human being. He's not evidence, he's the defendant." Vatrano, like any good lawyer had played devil's advocate in Pollard's office the day before, only to improve his ability to make their case in front of the judge an even stronger one.

The judge tilted his head back more than just a little. It looked to Pollard like he was considering things a bit differently than he had just moments before. Without prompting, Pollard started in to keep the momentum growing. "Your Honor, this is certainly a minimal invasion. We would not be seizing property, only records. There would be no disclosure of any of these records at any trial. We would not be tracking the location of these women going forward, only a historical record of towers that their phones were hitting off. And these aren't just two women, these are his mother and the mother of his child. We have records from the prison as you can see. We have the phone records from Camden showing his calls to the numbers that each woman has personally stated to me is their personal phone number. We know his old phone was found in the Delaware river and is inoperable. The pattern of his contact with these women over the past years, we think, combined with the minimal intrusion to the women and the lack of presentation of any of this at any trial, is enough to get it granted."

The room went eerily quiet for a few seconds that felt more like minutes. Vatrano knew he had nothing to add and assessed that this judge, that he wasn't as familiar with, wouldn't put up with much repetition. Pollard thought at that point he had made his best case and continuing might push the judge to think he was lobbying too hard. The judge, after giving it one last long ponder, cradled his pen, and signed his name to the bottom of the paper in a swift swooping motion.

"I don't usually like being lobbied so hard," he said as if Pollard's forehead was a plate glass window, and the judge could see into his thoughts. "I see where you guys are with this, though. If you get the number that you believe is Mr. Washington's, please come back to me with the warrant for that." It was a strange request. Pollard figured the judge didn't want him going to another judge that might see what he had granted, and O'Brien knew no trial judge ever would. Or maybe he was just curious how it would turn out. Pollard didn't really know and didn't much care at that point, the warrant was signed. "Now get on out of here, I have a full a docket today," the judge exclaimed with a nod to the door.

"Thank you, sir," Pollard said calmly, trying to hold off on celebrating in the judge's chambers for fear it would give the impression that they had pulled one over on the justice.

Pollard and Vatrano skipped half of the courthouse steps out the front door and hopped into the truck to head back to the office. It was time to get the search warrant off to the phone companies so they could start getting the data as soon as possible, often a daunting task itself. Knowing the next task was a one-man job, Vatrano left Pollard's office. He had some digging to do in his own county to see if Washington's old friend Ronnie might be around.

Later that afternoon, Vatrano's name flashed on the caller identification of Pollard's vibrating phone as he pulled it from the pocket of his carpenter style jeans. He was hoping to hear from Vatrano regarding Washington's friend "Ronnie," who they had identified as Ronald Barton from the prison visitation records. If the phone records they hoped to get matched a location that Barton may be, they'd have their starting point. Vatrano knew Pollard would be waiting for the information and sought to take full advantage of his captive audience of one.

"Marco!" Vatrano always gave Pollard an Italian alter ego when he was giving him good, and often comical news. It got Pollard's spirits up and instantly raised his expectations.

"What did you find out about our friend Ronnie down there on the west side?" Pollard asked with heavy anticipation. He didn't even give Vatrano a chance to talk about anything else by asking that familiar important question first.

"Got some lock-tight good news on his current whereabouts," Vatrano beamed with great confidence, almost sarcastically so. It took Pollard a minute to realize he was being set up for a laugh as he couldn't see Vatrano's facial expression through the phone.

"So, where is he?" Pollard asked before realizing, as he should have, that Vatrano wasn't going to let him off the hook quite so easily.

"Well, my sheriff's office had contact with him about three weeks ago down here." Vatrano paused as if waiting for Pollard to play along and ask. Pollard obliged along with an eye roll from the other side of the phone.

"Aaannnddd?" Pollard elongated the word as though the single question was a full sentence.

"Well, that contact we had was for a transport from county lock-up over to our superior court. He was taken over on a probation violation for a charge from last summer."

"So, he's on probation? Did his probation officer give you his address?" Pollard was now guessing where the story was going. He knew he had guessed wrong by the tone of the response.

"Hell, no! I told you my information is lock tight! He's still sitting over at the county fuckin' jail. I just got off the phone with the booking sergeant. He's been there almost four weeks now, since before the murder!" The lead up to the news seemed a little excessive given the end outcome, although it would prevent the team from wasting any time chasing down the lead on Ronald Barton. Pollard chuckled at Vatrano's use of the phrasing, lock tight, now getting the joke.

"So, I guess he's not staying with old friend Ronnie then." Pollard stated the obvious as though he was thinking out loud.

"Well, if he was staying with him, we'd be done with this case now!" Vatrano laughed at the thought of the fugitive murderer already in jail hiding out with his high school friend.

"Who knew? They actually kept a probation violator in jail on a cash bail, huh?" Pollard asked, as though excusing his lack of following along.

"First time for everything."

"Talk to you later on man, thanks for the info." Pollard hung up with a grin on his face. It wasn't information that was going to lead them to Washington, but it still felt like a small success, as crossing off a potential lead had felt at least a little bit productive. It was only a minor distraction from his efforts to contact and serve the cellular phone companies. Worth the laugh, he figured, as he dove back into his recently interrupted duties.

CHAPTER FOURTEEN

It took nearly two days after he had contacted the cell phone company, but Pollard received Walsh's phone records in his email late on that Sunday evening. Kelly had already gone up to bed with Boomer while Pollard had remained in the living room as the Bruins game had gone into overtime. The opposing team was the Canadiens, therefore he was obligated to stay up for the end result, being a true fan. He could see from the email that the file was too large to open on his department issued cell phone. It was no use opening the documents at that point anyway, he rationalized to himself, because he didn't have Bixby's records yet to do a side-by-side comparison to find a common number.

The excitement of the announcer's voice from the game on the television broke his concentration. 3-2 was the final as the Bruins had just scored the winning, sudden-death overtime goal. Secure in the knowledge that his Bruins had beaten the hated team from Montreal, he started up the stairs for bed and dragged a toothbrush across his teeth before getting in. The excitement of the hockey game wasn't what would keep him up that night. Pollard could not stop thinking about the unopened file on his phone sitting on its charger plugged into the outlet in the kitchen. With any luck, he would have Bixby's records the following morning as well.

After taking the dog for his morning routine, Pollard went out the side door early and without breakfast, a rare occurrence for him. Kelly was off to start her work week as well on the cold Monday morning.

He hadn't shared any of the case with her. It wasn't a security or confidentiality issue with Pollard, he was just never in the habit of sharing much of his work with her, or anyone else for that matter. Even during his days working night patrols in Windsor, his shifts were mostly boring, interrupted by moments of terror, sadness, and aggravation. He never felt it useful to go through those moments twice, once in real time and then again with his wife. It just wasn't something that he found helpful for himself. Admittedly, he had never really considered if it would have been helpful for her.

Pollard took a peek at the email on his phone again before getting up into the truck, mostly to confirm that he hadn't been imagining that Walsh's phone records had come the night before. They were still sitting there, safely in his inbox. He headed into the office like he was a child on the way to open a surprise Christmas present.

The drive into work passed in a blur. Pollard went right past the dispatchers and gave a quick wave. He muttered a few brief "good mornings" to some of them waiting to go home after the overnight shift, while he hurried into his office and sat at his old desk chair. After he clicked print on the document attached to his email, the hum of the printer in the hallway beckoned him. With the pages still a little warm in his hands, Pollard sat down at his desk to begin his examination of the records.

Pollard started with the cell towers that were associated with Walsh's phone activity over the past couple of months. He could see that almost all the tower hits were in Stanton or from the local hilltop towers in some of the other towns, including Windsor, that surrounded the small city. Although he would have liked to see a pattern of cell towers somewhere else that would give him an indication that Walsh may have been visiting Washington, it wasn't to be. Based on cell phone usage, it didn't look like Walsh had spent much time at all outside of the Stanton area.

Pollard pulled out the records that the homicide detective had sent him on Washington's phone that they found in the Delaware River. He could cross reference the outgoing calls and text messages from Washington's old phone to Walsh's incoming calls and texts and vice versa. It was plain to see that the last communication from Washington's phone to Walsh was the day before the murder. He could also see that Walsh's last outgoing text to that number was the actual day of the homicide.

Pollard could understand why Washington would have destroyed his phone by throwing it in the river to prevent authorities from locating him, much like Pollard was trying to do now. But for Walsh to stop texting and calling the number on the same day that Washington's phone went dead in the river meant only one thing to Pollard. Walsh somehow knew to stop contacting Washington on that number on the exact day it was destroyed. She had to have been made aware that the phone was useless, most likely by Washington himself.

The key now would be to find the number that Washington would have used to begin contacting Walsh sometime after the murder, a number that did not appear prior to the murder date on her incoming calls and texts. If such a number existed on those records, Pollard thought, it would have to be Washington on the other end.

Pollard reached for a marker in the mug on his desk that held his pens. Scanning down the document he found the murder date listed with all the dates of the calls and texts on the left column. He drew a red line through the middle of the page creating a delineation between the contacts from before the murder and the contacts that had occurred after the murder. Finding similar numbers on each side of that demarcation became like a game. For the sake of efficiency, he decided to open an Excel spreadsheet on his computer.

He began placing each of the numbers that he could see Walsh had contact with between that newly drawn red line and today's date. There were several, but one of the numbers had to be

Washington, he figured. He could feel the confidence rushing over him as his hasty plan was being put into action. Pollard pushed that feeling away and began to double check that he had recorded each number in the spreadsheet. Organizing the list so that the numbers were in sequence would allow him to compare each new number with the older contact numbers.

A second column was starting to fill with the numbers preceding the red line that he had drawn. Pollard was observing as the numbers would match from one column to the next, allowing him to eliminate those numbers that occurred both before and after the red line.

As he began to delete all the numbers that met his imposed criteria for elimination, a sudden realization had Pollard stop dead in his task. What if Washington was staying with a friend or family member that would have been in contact with Walsh both before and after the murder? What if he was with Bixby's family? What if he was borrowing that person's phone to contact his mother? The number he was using to contact her could just as easily be in both the before and after column on his newly created spreadsheet. He dismissed the insecurity and anxiety of that scenario being reality and pledged to cross that bridge when and if it came. He then took some solace that Judge O'Brien hadn't asked the same questions when reviewing the search warrant.

Pollard continued to plug away at entering the numbers in each column of the spreadsheet. When he was done, it was clear that there was only one number that appeared on the records after the murder date that didn't also appear before the murder date.

"Holy shit!" Pollard exclaimed out loud to no one, as he was alone in his office. He looked down at the records and saw that number had been used several times on incoming and outgoing calls to and from Walsh's cell phone over the past several days. Each time the number was contacted, Walsh's phone would have been in Stanton as indicated by the towers it was hitting and the direction between towers. If this was Washington, it was almost certain that he wasn't going to be found in Stanton at his mother's place, something they had already confirmed in person a few days before.

Pollard stared intently at those ten digits and could almost visualize Washington's face within the numbers. He wrote the phone number in big block letters on his desk calendar so that there would be no mistake.

When Pollard looked again at the number now written in his own writing, something else struck him. New Hampshire had only one area code throughout the entire state, and the six, zero and three that was freshly inked on his desk calendar brought another pause. It was as though he was so used to that area code that it didn't stand out at first. If Washington had purchased a new cell phone that was now being used, and this was his number, he would have likely purchased it in New Hampshire. It was also possible that he was now using the phone of someone from his home state that he could be staying with. With his friend Ronnie locked up and almost certain that Washington was not with his mother or Tia, Pollard started to think that there was someone in New Hampshire that they had not yet known about. It was also just as likely that Walsh had made a new connection in New Hampshire that had this new phone number and it had nothing to do with her son at all.

Having served its purpose, Pollard minimized the newly created spreadsheet on his computer. After closing the document, his eyes were immediately drawn to the notification that he had an unopened email waiting. The email was from an address he had never seen, the carrier for Bixby's cell phone that he had sent the search warrant for. The records on her phone that he requested were now prepared for him to view as well, and with impeccable timing.

With Bixby's records now open on his computer, Pollard took the suspected number that he had just written in giant script on his calendar and held it up to the screen. He could see almost immediately that there was a great deal of contact over the last ten days or so between Bixby's phone and that new number he got from Walsh's records. As he scrolled down the page, he found the murder date. There were no contacts to or from that number on that date. He became more confident as he manipulated the mouse and continued to scroll past number after number, that was not the one he was holding in his hands. No contacts before the murder with that number at all. The number only appeared on Bixby's phone records after the date of the murder. In the Venn diagram of phone contact, Walsh and Bixby had the number in common and each only had contact with the number from the day after the murder up to the most recent record. It was him. It had to be.

He needed to share in his jubilation. Sitting alone with such a victory didn't seem appropriate given the magnitude of the situation in this case. Pollard's first call was to Vatrano, who had just started his day from his home county.

"It fuckin' worked man!" he said as Vatrano answered the call while driving in his car.

"What worked?" Vatrano asked with no context to even try to figure out what Pollard was referring to.

"The phone records. I have one new number that appears only after the murder on each of the two women's phones. It has to be him."

"Holy shit, that's awesome! We've clearly got a little more work to do then. I'll come up later today and we can hammer out the next search warrant."

"We sure do. Wait, hold on, Brownie is calling, I'll talk to you in a little bit." Pollard clicked over to Brown's incoming call. He picked it up thinking Brown was looking for some updates, like he knew Pollard had just made a big discovery. In a pleasant surprise, Brown had an update for Pollard.

"Just got off the phone with the guys down in Philadelphia," Brown said, not sounding overly excited. "I'm not sure where this leaves us, but they got some information on Washington's whereabouts and activities on the day of the murder."

"Okay, what is it?" Pollard was intrigued and was almost expecting Brown to tell him that they weren't going to be needed in the hunt after all.

"He got on a bus in Camden later in the night after the murder. They got the information from the guys at Transportation that he had purchased a bus ticket using his New Hampshire identification. For some reason there was a delay in getting that information confirmed from the records. According to the video that they got, he made it all the way to Elizabeth, New Jersey even though his ticket that he had purchased was for Newark. Because of that, they don't think Elizabeth was his destination. He didn't purchase another ticket from Elizabeth, so they went up there to go check it out." Pollard was now anticipating a successful resolution in that part of New Jersey, but he guessed wrong again. "The video at the terminal in Elizabeth shows him in the fuckin' lobby and eventually getting picked up in the parking lot by a small, dark colored car. They think a Honda or Toyota." Brown had slowed down a little bit, trying to make sure he was passing along all of the pertinent details as accurately as possible.

"His girl and mom are using a silver VW, no way it was them." Pollard confirmed what Brown had already known. He also knew it couldn't have been them as he had just seen all of the cell phone towers their phones had used over the past few weeks, and it didn't appear either woman went anywhere near New Jersey.

"I know, they think the car had yellow plates. New York would be the likeliest guess, but it could also be New Jersey, if the plates were a little lighter yellow. They couldn't make out a plate number or get any look at a driver. It was about five in the morning and dark out and the video was pretty grainy."

"So, a small black car. Yellow would definitely not be New Hampshire plates. It wouldn't be any of the New England states even." Pollard was again thinking out loud and telling Brown what he already knew.

"Right," Brown acknowledged. "Not sure if we are chasing a shitty lead up here now. They wanted us to have the information on the car in case it meant anything to us as we move along. They're going to keep working it up to check turnpike tolls around that time and a few other avenues to maybe see where the car may have been headed. It's also possible it was a car working for a rideshare app, they are going to look into that. I'll keep you updated if anything else is discovered, especially if they can figure out who owns that car."

"Well, I don't think New Hampshire is out of the question yet, even if the car picking him up was from New York or New Jersey." Pollard was being intentionally provocative.

"What makes you say that?" Brown bit.

"The phone records for the two women came in." Pollard still wanted to maintain some suspense, just for fun, as Brown seemed a bit dreary when he first called.

"Did you get a new number in common?"

"Sure did. And it's a fuckin' 603 number too. He's not far, this is where he's from after all. Or at the very least, someone from up here is helping him out and sent him a new phone or is letting him use theirs."

"Definitely run with it then. We'll keep doing our side of things until it's reached an end. Even if he's not in New Hampshire, a ping on this new phone number may be exactly what they need down there." Brown realized that he had rained on Pollard's parade a little bit having called with the information about the New York or New Jersey registered vehicle picking up Washington in New Jersey. Especially when Pollard had just found what he believed to be the phone number. Brown changed his tone quickly and remained supportive.

"That's the plan." Pollard had come too far. Brown was done with the updating he needed to do and wanted to let Pollard have his moment. "I'll be going back before the judge with a search warrant for the new number with Vatrano, we've got to get after that this afternoon."

"Awesome man, love you."

Another trip to the judge's chambers scheduled for the next day already had Pollard a little anxious, but not like his previous trip.

CHAPTER FIFTEEN

Kelly was trying to cook healthy on a more regular basis. It was a futile effort, Pollard thought to himself, given his undisciplined dietary choices during the day. He certainly didn't make such statements out loud to her though.

There were times when Pollard felt he had gotten too far into a fugitive hunt to take the time to load up all the details and tell Kelly what was happening. He saw it as a conversational annoyance, like trying to catch someone up to the plot of a movie they had started watching half-way through. If he told her about the phone number, he'd have to tell her about the judge, and the cell phone companies, and the interviews with the women, and not finding Washington that day. The plot was already developed to a story that he didn't yet have an ending to. Historically speaking, the early stages of some of those same hunts were also often boring and uneventful. Those initial activities weren't worthy of a story and there was no plot yet. And with that dichotomy facing Pollard, Kelly was rarely the recipient of any story at all.

Pollard ate the salmon and broccoli that Kelly had prepared while he considered telling her about the phone number that he had uncovered earlier that day. But how do you make finding a phone number into a story, and did he really want to tell her about the interviews and record searches it took to get there? The conclusion he came to was that it wasn't the time. Pollard's standard procedure in such situations was to ask Kelly about her day, to deflect away, and let her run with it.

As Kelly filled him in with the happenings of her day, Pollard could not get his mind off the date with the judge the following morning. Unhappy that he had again been consumed by such details from work, Pollard tried to distract himself. In the end, he went to bed presenting his new request to the grizzly old justice in his head, his eagerness to avoid the expected wrath being the cause for such extensive mental preparations.

Vatrano had arrived back at Pollard's office early the next morning. Though the bulk of the work had been done the afternoon prior, there were still some things that needed to be buttoned up. Both men thought that this search warrant would be a breeze compared to the last one, but Judge O'Brien was always a wild card, which prevented the ease they were looking for.

"We can't screw this up at this point. I think we've got 'em," Pollard said confidently to Vatrano as they put the finishing touches on the search warrant on the new phone number that was found in common contact with both women after the murder.

"We won't screw this up. And we don't got 'em. We might, and I mean might, have his phone number to ping." He threw Pollard's own words back at him for emphasis. Vatrano wasn't about to go charging into the judge's chambers full of bravado and high expectations. It just wasn't part of his style.

"I know, I hate phone pings just as much as you do." Pollard was an easy counterpart to reign back to reality, especially for Vatrano. A phone ping was just that, a phone ping. It wasn't a suspect in custody. There were no guarantees in this business, both men knew it and they couldn't lose track of that. With the search warrant completed to a standard that they agreed on, a trip back to the courthouse was the only thing left on the itinerary. No sense going to see the judge on an empty stomach though, so lunch would have to be consumed first.

The outside of Judge O'Brien's chambers had a different feel to it that day as compared to their initial visit. Pollard and Vatrano were now catching the judge towards the end of his workday. They took a peek at the docket posted just past the security checkpoint in the lobby, indicating what looked like a light day in O'Brien's courtroom. It gave them a sense that the judge might be in a good mood, though it was a shaky sentiment at best. They were basically prepared to place the old search warrant in front of the judge with the updated information that they had now received regarding the new phone number believed to be tied to

Washington.   Pollard felt more like an experimental scientist reporting his findings to the financial backers of his grant while looking for funding to continue, than a salesman trying to get the judge to purchase his end product.

"He's all yours, gentlemen," the clerk said with a big smile directed at the deputies hovering in her doorway. "He's been waiting for you since you called on the way over."

"Good afternoon, Your Honor." Pollard surprised himself a little by speaking first and with such authority. To the casual observer though, it wouldn't have been considered forward.

"Well lads, I was hoping you'd make it back in here at some point. I'm guessing you got the results you were looking for?" The judge also didn't like to speak in absolutes, but he knew they had found the results that they wanted from the original warrants he had signed off on. Otherwise, he had surmised, they wouldn't be standing there in front of him.

"We did, sir." Pollard, more confident this time than at their previous meeting, didn't even hand the warrant packet to the judge. He began to explain. "Both Bixby and Walsh's phone each had received…"

The judge put out his hand and beckoned with it like a toddler saying "gimme." Pollard handed over the folder with the new information and search warrant request in it, this time for the phone they believed was being used by Washington. The judge cracked open the file and began reading with a slight smirk on his wrinkled face. Pollard just looked at Vatrano and shrugged his shoulders. Though his hand gesture initially demonstrated otherwise, the judge didn't want to be fed the document like a child. He would read the documents and ask questions if needed, just like last time.

Closing the folder on the warrant and affidavit for the new phone number without signing it, the judge initiated the follow-up conversation, one Pollard was hoping was just for clarification.

"The first two numbers that you were granted warrants for, the individuals presented those numbers to you as their own. Their relation to a suspected murderer is clearly established. Now I have a case where you have brought me a phone number that no one has claimed. These women have not claimed it to be either one of their own nor have they identified Washington as the person on the other end of this number. How can I grant a search warrant for a phone number that has no known owner?" The judge raised his bushy white eyebrows after completing his question as though maybe he had stumped the deputies. He waited for a response before going further.

Pollard was initially miffed, given that the judge specifically requested that they return directly to him with the new warrant. Had he set them up to fail? Judge O'Brien knew when he signed the originals what was coming if the first warrants were successful. Here they were in front of him with exactly what was expected, and he was acting as though he wouldn't be endorsing the new warrant.

Vatrano didn't give Pollard a chance to answer. "Judge, we've established that Walsh and Bixby own their phones. We've established their relationship to Washington, like you just said. We've now established that each woman has begun to receive phone calls from a new phone number that neither had any previous contact with, on the exact same day, that just so happened to be the day after the murder. The Camden County Prosecutor's Office has arrest warrants, signed by a judge in New Jersey, because they have established probable cause that Washington committed this homicide. We now, humbly, put before you that we believe that there is probable cause to believe that the phone belongs to, or is being used by, a wanted murderer. And also, that the information obtained from the phone, to include the towers that it is currently and historically hitting off of, and the other phone numbers that this phone may be contacting, will lead us directly to him." Vatrano hadn't stopped for any duration, even to take in air.

"Go on," the judge said with a touch of amusement across his face as he could tell that Vatrano wanted to keep presenting to him.

"We will learn quickly enough if this phone doesn't belong to our guy. If it doesn't, we no longer have use for it and the slight invasion into the phone owner's privacy will be all done and again, just like the last warrant, the findings will not be needed in open court. If there is something on the phone that interests the Camden County officials in regard to the crime of murder, they would then need to apply for their own search warrant to use at the murder trial in New Jersey, through their own courts. This warrant will not be used at trial down there. We only want the suspect, Your Honor, no evidence coming from this warrant will make it into open court." Vatrano took a half step back from the judge's desk while shifting his weight to his other foot as though signaling that he was done speaking.

The judge reached across his desk and grabbed a gold pen from the holder attached to his gold name plate. He opened the folder and flipped through the pages of the warrant as he moistened his fingers on his tongue to keep the papers separate. He glided the pen swiftly across the signature line, dated it, closed the folder, and handed it back across his desk to the awaiting Pollard.

"Good luck gentlemen." The judge then looked over to his computer screen on his immediate left and placed his hands on the keyboard after dropping the pen down next to it. The judge clearly had nothing more to say. Vatrano and Pollard received the not-so-subtle hint and backed out through the door to the clerk's office. They hustled back out to the parking lot.

"Let's go get this thing served and find out where this fuckin' guy is!" Pollard exclaimed to Vatrano as they descended the courthouse steps again. They were feeling that familiar sense of victory and anticipation of what was to come, while still trying to maintain a sense that anything was still possible, both good and bad.

CHAPTER SIXTEEN

"He's getting all Jason Bourne on us," Pollard said into the phone from the rotating chair at his desk, referring to the fugitive's success in throwing off his hunters. Brown and Dorsey were on the other end of the phone call.

"So, you can't get the information?" Brown asked with a level of serious concern that he didn't often exhibit.

"I can get it, it's just harder and going to take a little more time. There are no phone contracts or subscribers, you just pay for the phone and get the minutes and texts that you prepay for at like, a Walmart. It's not the same as the other phones that we did this on, so it may take a little bit." It was bad news for Brown, who had hopes in calling Pollard to get something to stir up some action. Brown had other fugitive files that the team needed to be working on, but he was giving the Washington case priority. Prolonged search warrant service and administrative wrangling on the cell phone data was not what he had in mind. It also wasn't exactly building excitement with Pollard. He hadn't anticipated this headache, especially after the other two search warrants went so smoothly.

"I'll call you back after I figure out exactly how to get it served and we have some information to go on." Pollard and Vatrano looked at each other with a disbelieving head shake at Brown's perceived impatience. After all the phone records, warrants, research, and presentations to the judges, they were hoping for a little more appreciation. They understood that Brown wasn't upset with them but frustrated with a lull in the action, especially given the promise that this case was starting to show. They had come to expect it from Brown, but it was still bothersome, and just a little bit comical.

"Love you," Brown exclaimed as always to end the phone call. It only slightly softened the aggravation.

After jousting with several different telephone entities operating in the United States and around the world, Vatrano and Pollard finally achieved some success in getting the warrant in the correct hands for the results they were looking for. They were anxiously awaiting the live, up-to-date, phone "pings" that would be sent electronically to start filling up Pollard's email inbox in real time. The cell tower information would be coming first and the phone records coming later, hopefully that afternoon according to the person he just hung up the phone with. With his email open on his computer screen, Pollard and Vatrano sat and watched a blank screen with the anticipation of an avid gambler, waiting on his horse to get out of the gates. The chime of the email notification cut through the air before either one saw the icon notification of a new message. Pollard clicked the attachment on the new email that had arrived.

The information contained in the first live message simply listed the phone number, two tower locations and an approximate distance and direction from each tower. It only gave a rough estimate of the coordinates the phone was near. According to the explanation Pollard had received from the man he had just spoken to, the towers pinging a location was not necessarily due to phone calls or texts incoming or outgoing from that phone, but simply by an activated and powered on phone hitting off the two towers as it was giving and getting information. The contemporaneous hit that had just come in was due to the phone being currently on and searching for two towers for a signal, not a phone call or text.

Pollard scanned his eyes down the attached document, almost giggling with excited anticipation. It simply stated 2.2 miles west/southwest of the tower on Mt. Kennison and 600 yards northwest of a tower on Piper Hill. Both towers were located within the limits of the city of Kennison, New Hampshire. The projected accuracy of that ping was given a 300-yard radius that the phone would be in, not exactly a direct location like a GPS coordinate.

The small city of Kennison, New Hampshire was almost a hundred miles away from Pollard's office where they were currently seated digesting this potential new clue. It was also that far from Walsh's duplex, also in Stanton.

"I was hoping for something somewhat closer to Stanton." Pollard was a little taken aback by the randomness of the cell tower locations. Kennison was not what he had expected nor was it a place that Washington had any connection to, at least not that they had uncovered. After giving it some brief thought, Pollard rephrased, "I guess I don't really know what I was expecting."

"Or somewhere in Jersey or near Philly. That would have made sense. Or even down in my neck of the woods on the west side." Vatrano refined Pollard's thought, referencing the area of New Hampshire where Washington had been raised, went to high school, and would probably consider his "home."

Kennison on the other hand, was a small college town near the border of New Hampshire and Maine in the northern tier of the Granite State. Some referred to the area as "not quite Canada" due to the city's close proximity to the 45th parallel, halfway between the equator and the north pole. The city was roughly the size of Stanton, so it was a New Hampshire "city" but was also home to Kennison State College, with a student body of about 5,000 undergraduates. It was where Pollard's wife Kelly had attended college a few years before they had met, so Pollard was somewhat familiar with the area, having visited on a few occasions with her.

"How far to the nearest border crossing from Kennison?" Pollard was thinking out loud to Vatrano.

Given the nickname of the area near the international boundary, Pollard had the brief thought that maybe Washington was headed for the border.

"I'm not worried about him getting into Canada, if anything, he's going to need a passport and he'll be identified by Customs and Border Patrol. The warrant is active, and even if he had the right documents, he would be a fool to drive right into a line to greet law enforcement." It was sound logic and put Pollard quickly at ease.

"Sounds like we need to figure out who he's with up in Kennison then." Pollard looked at Vatrano somewhat apologetically for the obvious nature of his statement.

"I don't think his mom or Tia would be any help in telling us who he knows up there, and even giving them the idea we are looking there would probably chase him out." Vatrano returned the favor, one obvious statement for another. Both men knew exactly who they needed for help on this. Pollard pulled out his phone.

"Hey man, what's up?" It was Matthews, always answering as though he was annoyed to have to speak into the phone instead of punching out the words of a text message.

"Got a task for you, man. We need some help. We've got to figure out who Washington might know up in Kennison." Pollard wasn't about to start putting up with his annoyed tone, so he hit him with the expected duty right off.

"Kennison? What the hell would he be doing up there, that doesn't fit with anything so far, right?" Matthews seemed just as confused with the seemingly random location as Vatrano and Pollard had moments before. He didn't get an answer from either, to what they assumed wasn't really a question. After the brief pause that he had granted the men for an answer, he continued along. "All right, I'll see what I can do. I'll let you know if I find anything."

Matthews hung up without getting an answer to his question but with a task he felt confidently prepared for. Methodical searches of social media platforms that lasted for hours, looking for links between Washington, Bixby, Walsh, and the small college town across the state was right in his wheelhouse. Though they were reluctant to tell the young deputy, Vatrano and Pollard had just as much confidence in his ability to get it done.

"You know we need to call Brown, right?" Pollard could tell Vatrano didn't even want to bring it up. They each shared the same fear, with Pollard sharing it out loud.

"He's going to want to head out to Kennison tonight based on a single phone ping and a direction from two towers within a three-hundred-yard radius." Pollard was again stating the obvious to Vatrano.

"That's not happening. It can't. We need the call history from that phone before we go anywhere. For all we know, he could be anywhere around there, or just traveling through Kennison right now while hitting those towers. We need the historicals on the phone, man. And really, we need Matthews to come up with who the asshole is that he might be with and figure out where that person is living." Vatrano was right and Pollard knew it, but it still didn't alleviate the issue. Most fugitive hunts came down to one thing: not finding the suspect as would seem so obvious, but rather, finding the person the suspect would be with.

"Why don't you call Brown then?"

"We both will." It was a fair compromise. They figured if Brown really did want to charge out to the area of Kennison, the two of them would do a better job of calming his A.D.D. tendencies than one of them trying to do the convincing alone. The strategy was to use the pronoun "we," much like the sheriff had done to Pollard all those years ago to convince him to start on this wild ride.

CHAPTER SEVENTEEN

The bus station in the city of Elizabeth was not hard to find, even for someone who had never been there before. Figuring out the exact location of Washington, who was without a cell phone to call as he approached, contained a greater degree of difficulty. When he pulled his car near the edge of the bus terminal, he could see who he believed to be Washington sitting behind the large window. Washington's head was down as though sleeping but jerked up quickly as the headlights of the Honda Civic splashed against the dirty glass. It had been years, but the driver could make out Washington's profile clear enough to believe he had found him.

Being the only car that had approached for hours during the early morning, Washington assumed it was his ride arriving, so he walked slowly toward the door to check. His approach got him closer to the vehicle where he could see into the car and confirm it was the face from his past, but also his present ride out of town. Stepping out of the bus terminal into the cool morning air, he continued around to the passenger door with each step increasing in pace ever so slightly. He opened the door with a creak of metal on metal from a hinge that needed some lubrication. The jump into the passenger seat of the vehicle was without hesitation, feeling the warmth of the heat blowing softly from the vent, and for the first time in hours, a sense of relief.

"Thank you so much. This is huge." Although Washington hadn't seen him in so long, he skipped the greetings to express his thanks. He also didn't suggest parking and using the bathroom for a guy who had been in the car for hours, as getting out of town was his only objective. With that goal in mind, the car started north, several hours behind the bus that had dropped him in Elizabeth on its continued route to Newark.

"Sounded pretty serious on the phone. What the hell are you doing down here anyways?" It was a rhetorical question. It was the type of question that could set up an entire inquiry, or an airing of grievances. In the end, each man did his best to avoid such a situation.

Washington knew he had several hours in the car to discuss what had happened. It was an unavoidable topic. The two men hadn't seen one another since well before Washington had started his prison sentence in New Hampshire. The confines of a vehicle made the avoidance of so many topics that they had never ventured toward seem extremely obvious. Neither really knew where to start the conversation, which kept them from starting at all.

The dialogue, almost by design, kept him from going into detail. Washington made it known on several occasions that he was being saved from great danger, from a group of people that would kill him if given the chance. It was all so dramatic that not much thought had been given about how Washington had even gotten himself in this situation. There was no mention of shootings or murders and certainly no mention that he had done anything felonious. Washington knew if he was going to continue to get the help he needed, he would have to lie and lie well. It was paramount to make himself out to be the victim, something he had practiced his whole life as he learned how to manipulate those around him to enable his lifestyle.

The major four lane highways eventually dwindled to two lane state roads and then surface streets. They had taken turns on and off with driving duty even though only one of them held a valid driver's license. Washington was still on a rush from the day's events, or what was now yesterday's events, and his desire to get away.

They each eventually caught a little nap while the other one drove, both having had a long day with no sleep. Washington had the most hectic day of his life and his now sleeping passenger had already spent hours driving to pick him up. It was better that way, Washington thought, let him sleep and the hard topics would be successfully avoided. They stopped for gas a couple of times and Washington got a pack of cigarettes as they left New Jersey, but other than that, it was just the two of them in the small car.

There was a familiar feeling about pulling up to that house even though it was the first time that Washington had even seen it. It felt to Washington as though they were somehow transported back in time, to a memory that never actually existed.

The ride from Elizabeth had them chasing the sunrise as it came up to the east. It was now a new day, a fresh day, without a cloud in the sky. It was all so surreal to Washington as he walked through the doors of the house with nothing but the clothing he had on and the items in his pockets. The air was considerably cooler than he had remembered, certainly a drop from the day before in southern New Jersey.

"The guys I'm living with are good, just stay out of the way a little bit though. I'm kinda new around here. It's cool if you crash, though," he quickly clarified to reassure his house guest. "There's an old mattress in the basement, I'll get you set up with some blankets."

"I really do appreciate it. You have no idea. I knew I could count on you." Washington was shoveling on the praise; manipulative, but effective in getting what he needed. "Hey, I do need one thing though."

"What's that?" he asked, thinking what more could John even ask for except for maybe a change of clothes?

"I need to get a phone. Mine was stolen from me yesterday by those people down in Camden." It was all a lie to show his fictitious victimization, deflect responsibility for what had happened and ultimately get someone, anyone, to help him again. It worked.

"Let's eat and crash first, then we can go to Walmart and get you a phone. Does that work?" He would have gone then and there, but getting some serious rest was really on his mind after driving throughout the entire night and morning.

"Thanks a lot. I've got enough money to get one of the cheap flip and dial ones." Washington didn't want to push the accommodating nature that had been displayed by insinuating in any way that he would need the phone purchased for him.

"I've got meetings a couple nights this week with the rest of the guys in the house, but nothing today. So, this afternoon should work fine to grab a phone. Get some sleep."

Laying low sounded ideal to Washington. In Camden, he was anonymous, but in the tight knit surroundings of this new neighborhood he might stick out, at least as foreign to the area. Necessity to be unseen trumped his desire to be out. He spent most of the next few days in the basement, coming out only to smoke the occasional cigarette and chat with a few of the housemates. Washington would eventually get that new flip phone, not ideal for sending texts, but he could still have contact with the outside world. The phone was a safety net if things got hairy in the house and the necessity to make a quick exit occurred.

CHAPTER EIGHTEEN

Secure in the knowledge that they had nothing to do in the investigation at that point but wait on the historical phone records and a report back from Matthews on the social media connections, Vatrano, Dorsey, and Pollard met up for a couple of draft beers at a bar near Dorsey's house that evening. It wasn't their favorite haunt, but it was centrally located between Vatrano's county and Pollard's office, so it had become a popular spot to gather, purely out of convenience.

Pollard desired to keep the conversation light and hoped to steer it in that direction. Dorsey talked about his skiing trips that he had gone on over the winter and how he was looking forward to a day off to head out and hit the slopes again. Pollard had returned from Florida a few weeks prior on a visit to Kelly's parents and they caught up on the details of that trip. But then predictably, the conversation turned to the job. Although there was no stated understanding, each of the men knew it would when they agreed to have these drinks.

Mid-case drinks were different than the celebratory, caught-their-guy drinks that were usually more jovial, more self-deprecating, and full of anecdotes of some of the silly or strange things that happened before the handcuffs landed on the suspect. Celebratory drinks were the preferred time for Monday morning quarterbacking, with each describing when they just "knew" they would catch their fugitive. In the middle of the case however, it was never quite as humorous and far more challenging to find the lighter moments.

"I'm hoping those records are what we think they are going to be." Vatrano was the first to bring the conversation back to the ongoing fugitive hunt. Someone had to be, so there was no real social consequence for being first. As if he was only waiting for someone else to break that ice, Dorsey quickly pounced on the opportunity to get involved.

"They will be. And if they aren't, we'll find another way." Dorsey's years of experience often showed in his confident words. Some, who didn't know any better, would call it bravado, but it wasn't. He acted like he had been there before because he had, and he knew time and time again they had come up with their man. Pollard, never one to want to jinx himself, was less confident than his peers, but still upbeat.

"I just don't know at this point. I think we've got him, and it will only be a matter of time whether we confirm or dispel that this is actually his phone that we're up on right now." Pollard, almost as though he had forgotten, pulled his own phone from his pocket to check his email for new pings from the suspected phone number. He had received only one more activation, again coming from the Kennison area, just during the time that had passed while they were sitting in the bar. It was nothing to get overly excited about, but he showed it to Dorsey and Vatrano anyways. They nodded softly with approval at the location as the feeling that an impending trip to the Kennison area was becoming more of a probability.

Dorsey, keeping his positive momentum on a roll, stated out loud, "It's only a matter of time." Confident words from a confident guy, and it was starting to bring Pollard around to the idea of the whole thing getting wrapped up sooner than later.

With tabs paid up and an adjournment of the informal meeting, Pollard gave a final wave goodnight across the parking lot. His comrades drifted towards their vehicles on the street and Pollard made a line towards his own. He could see his breath in the cold evening air as he approached the driver's side window. The reflection of that white cloud coming from his mouth, giving the appearance that he was smoking a cigarette, caught his eye. As the cold engine cranked over in his car, he watched as Dorsey and Vatrano pulled out of their spots on the street almost simultaneously.

It was common experiences that had sparked and sustained most of the relationships that had formed in his life, Pollard thought to himself. As he gave some consideration about his relationship with his teammates, for the first time, in the parking lot of that bar, he thought about the relationships he had formed with those on the other side. The objects of all of the fugitive hunts were, after all, just people. The experience of those chases was shared, as though each were on the other side of the glass reflecting back at themselves, not really considering the other man.

Pollard had sprouted a relationship with John Washington, having never met him, having never spoken with him, having never laid eyes upon anything other than a photograph of him. It was an unexplainable connection that he could not recall experiencing with any of the other hundreds of wanted persons he and the team had tracked down over the years.

As he put the car in gear and made for the road home, he wondered exactly what John Washington was doing that night, and more importantly, where he was doing it. The answers he could find to those questions at that moment could only be filled with conjecture and possibility. He pondered if Washington had ever considered those who were out looking for him. If he had the time and frame of mind to reflect, or if Washington was frantic in his path of escape, full of fear and desperation. The deputy questioned if Washington would even understand the efforts of the men who left the bar that night when he would eventually be taken into custody. Pollard figured that his thoughts of the shared experience were a luxury that he had that his fleeing counterpart probably didn't. He shook the thoughts away as quickly as they had come and shifted his focus on the drive home.

Brown had been in surprising agreement with Vatrano and Pollard on needing more than just locational pings from the phone before moving forward. The records of the numbers in contact with the phone were an important piece of the puzzle. Even with his penchant for pushing the action, Brown knew there was no need to rush something and lose their man due to impatience. The historical records from the phone company were in Pollard's email inbox the following morning. Along with the records came an entire night's worth of cell tower pings on the phone, with each activation represented in its own separate email. The overnight pings on the phone were hitting off of the same towers and within a few hundred yards of each other in Kennison.

Now in the comfort of his office and with his computer in front of him, Pollard was able to review each of the actual locations. He printed out a hard copy of the cell phone tower pings and had each one in his hand. Using a mapping website, he was able to place the coordinates and directions of each of the pings from just over a twenty-four-hour period. Though each ping had a little bit of a distance difference, they were clustered together in a condensed area of the city, as the plotted dots started to look like the target of a marksman from the shooting range. It appeared as though each plotted point was located in a densely populated area on the edge of Kennison State College where the campus bled into the downtown. The cell pings varied only slightly in distance and direction that would either indicate that the phone was moving only in the neighborhood or that the accuracy of the phone pings was not as exact as Pollard had hoped. He figured it was about a three to five-hundred-yard radius inside which the phone could be located based solely on the multiple points he had dotted the map with. But with so many single-family homes, apartments, and college dorms in the area, picking which building that Washington might be located in would be a needle in a haystack scenario and entirely unworkable.

This specific scenario unfolding was exactly why Pollard hated chasing phone pings. It only got an investigator near enough to the suspect that it was excruciatingly annoying to be so close and not know where to go to. If Matthews came through with any potential ties to the area through social media, the situation could change dramatically. If that person was established in the general area of the phone ping, a reasonable surveillance operation or search and interview could be done to try to locate the fugitive. The investigation had boiled down to finding that unknown connection, as it was unlikely Washington strolled into Kennison, New Hampshire and threw down a first and last month's rent and security deposit. The new person that they were searching for had pivoted the investigation from the fugitive to who the fugitive was with, as such inquiries often did. Pollard was hoping that Matthews would come through on who that person was, and that he wouldn't be hard to find, especially if he wasn't hiding.

With the phone pings as they stood now, and with no one tied to Kennison to be looking for, surveilling literally dozens of buildings for Washington would be impossible. Going to Kennison and just hoping to see a twenty-five-year-old guy of average build walking around a college town in the frozen New Hampshire winter, all bundled up with hoods and hats was a losing plan also, and Pollard knew it. The human intelligence piece was missing from the puzzle, there was no information to match with what the technology had given them, which made the technology limited in its usefulness.

Getting away from the phone ping mapping that was now increasingly frustrating Pollard, he was able to open up the historical phone calls from the number over the past few weeks, hoping to see who was being contacted from it. That was a second avenue that Pollard hoped could shed some light on where his fugitive was, who he may be contacting, and when.

Pollard could plainly see the numbers for Bixby and Walsh all over the records. More importantly though, Pollard could now see the towers that were used to complete the phone contacts. It provided him with a sense of where the phone had been, and in turn, where the person who held that phone had been. Call after call continued to come up on Mount Kennison and Piper Hill, the two main towers on the outskirts of the small city of Kennison. In fact, the phone number had not hit off of any other towers in its brief existence, leading Pollard to believe that the phone itself may have been purchased in or near Kennison. It was also now less likely that this was an established phone number that Washington was borrowing. Instead, it was now most likely that it was a newly activated phone, with records going back less than a month.

If this was his man on the other end of that phone number, Pollard was certain he was staying in Kennison and had been there for at least several days. If it really was Washington and he had bought the phone on his way out of Camden, or somewhere along his way up to New Hampshire, the cell phone tower activity would have hit in other parts of the northeast, and they didn't. The phone also wouldn't have the New Hampshire area code. While this information made Pollard feel good about his odds, it also increased his doubt. If Washington had made it to Kennison from New Jersey, no cell activity on the way up might be a sign they had the wrong phone, and maybe the wrong person. Pollard would have felt better seeing the phone active among the towers along the route from Camden to Kennison.

Pollard had gotten ahead of himself; caught in a place he didn't like. He was thinking in absolutes, as though he was certain that this phone was Washington's. He checked himself and recaptured the skepticism that most lawmen need to succeed. Maybe the phone was purchased there by some kid who knows Bixby and Walsh and maybe just started the semester at the college.

It was always important to play out the scenario where the intelligence is wrong. As he told the judge, they felt they had "probable cause" to believe the phone belonged to Washington, not that he possessed the knowledge "beyond a reasonable doubt." Pollard was still anxious about the situation unfolding. He wondered why there were no phone calls made back to Camden or Philadelphia. Calls to those area codes would have solidified his belief that the number was Washington's, but the records were unwilling to give him that satisfaction.

Pollard continued down through the page of the phone records and observed a number that stood out to him because it didn't match either Bixby or Walsh, the only two numbers the phone really had much contact with. He scribbled the ten digits down on the corner of his desk calendar, hoping to match that number to later calls, or research it further when he was done perusing the records.

Putting his eyes back onto the document, he continued on down the list of calls and found only one more number that was not attributed to Bixby or Walsh. He jotted that number down next to the other on his calendar. Pollard noted immediately that both of the numbers he had just written down were outgoing phone calls, and both were to the 603 New Hampshire area code. For a brief moment he almost thought that he had written down the same number twice, as the three digits following the area code were also the same for each of the outgoing calls, indicating that the prefix number was probably from the same city or town.

Pollard minimized the phone records on his computer screen and pulled up his internet browser. He knew that search warrants for those two numbers were out of the question as they were too many degrees separated. Hoping to get some type of public listing or clue as to who or what the phone numbers belonged to, he typed the ten digits of the first number into his search. He was in luck. As he hit enter after putting in the first number, it came up on multiple restaurant review websites along with a home webpage for King's Garden Chinese in Kennison. He jotted down the address and moved his attention onto the second number, replacing just the last four digits in his saved search. It, too, was also found to have a public listing as Brother's Burgers in Kennison, so Pollard jotted that address down next to the other one. The calls brought Pollard back to his own college days and the ordering of late-night food, as the person making the calls seemed to have the palate of a college kid and the phone call to the Chinese restaurant was just before 10 p.m.

Pollard pulled up the map of Kennison on his computer screen again. He put the address of each dining establishment into the address finder, plotting the points with the others. The burger place was within the 300-yard radius that he believed the phone contact was coming from, but the Asian restaurant was not. He refused to be sure, but of the four numbers on the outgoing contacts of this phone he had researched, two were to local restaurants in Kennison. The other two numbers belonged to Washington's mother, and the mother of his child. He pushed back on that familiar feeling of certainty. A trip to Kennison was going to have to settle this. He reached for the phone to call Brown to give him an update, this time, a call for action.

It wasn't long after he got off the call with Brown to update him on what he had learned through the historical records that Pollard's phone started vibrating in his pocket. Looking at the caller identification before answering, Pollard had to check twice to make sure he was reading it right.

"Hey, what's going on?" Pollard asked inquisitively, knowing that the specifics were hopefully coming next.

"Hey, man," Matthews said with a touch of excitement in his voice.

"What, no text message? You must have some pretty big fuckin' news that you would even make a phone call," Pollard jabbed, but not too hard, knowing Matthews might just have what he was looking for.

"I sure do. It looks like there is a male that has social media associations with both Bixby and Walsh. They're friends and have multiple friends listed in common. I'm not sure what the relation is, different last names anyways. Could be family, could be a close family friend. Based on his Facebook and Instagram page, it looks like he just started at Kennison State College this semester. He's rockin' a Kennison Football sweatshirt in a recent photo with a bunch of other guys in Kennison Athletics Department gear. I sent you a screen shot of his Instagram page with a couple of the pictures." Pollard could hear Matthews beaming with a little bit of pride that he was able to find the possible connection to Kennison, hopefully making the randomness of the location make some sense.

"That's fantastic. I knew you'd get this shit done." Heaping praise on the millennial after a job well done was a must and Pollard did so genuinely in this instance.

"Well, don't get too far ahead of yourself, I can only find him on social media. He must be from out of state, because there is absolutely no record of him ever holding a valid New Hampshire driver's license and he looks to be about twenty years old. His name is Adam Hamel, at least, it is if he's using his real name on his pages."

At that exact moment, in the excitement, it dawned on Pollard. If it was Washington in Kennison, he was most likely with this Hamel guy if he knew Washington's baby momma and mother. They now had the human intelligence to go with the phone ping. It had to be the link to where he would be staying, a coincidence was out of the question. In a split second, the joy became frustration as Matthews asked the obvious question that Pollard didn't even want to consider.

"So, do you think our fugitive is staying with this kid? Or do you think this kid is the one with the new phone and Washington just isn't calling anyone at all right now? Maybe he hasn't changed phones at all? I mean, it looks like this Hamel kid just started at Kennison State and isn't from New Hampshire apparently. Maybe Walsh and Bixby are the only people he knows around here. What are the odds he picked up the new phone when he got to school to start this semester? Maybe the Athletics Department gives them phones if they can't afford one. I don't know."

"I just don't know either, man. I just don't. Maybe Washington is even using this guy's phone if that's the case. I've got to call Brownie and get the team headed over to Kennison. It's the next logical move right now. We have to get to the bottom of this either way. Confirm or dispel this shit."

"I totally agree. I'll talk to you later."

In what felt like a brilliant flash, Pollard had gotten the information that he wanted. He got the phone pings on the right towers, phone calls to local restaurants and a possible host in Kennison for his fugitive. But he felt even less sure now than he was when the morning started, before all that information came to his attention. Had Washington just completely gone to radio silence on the cell phone and this new phone belonged to this guy named Hamel? He put it out of his mind and called Brown for a follow up briefing on the situation.

CHAPTER NINETEEN

Before anyone headed to check for Washington up in Kennison, Pollard had one more stop he wanted to make. He, Vatrano, and Brown rolled up to 28A Depot Street in Stanton in a fairly casual manner, at least compared to the last time they had been there. This trip was void of any large ballistic vests, long rifles, or shields. Only plain, casual, low-profile law enforcement attire.

It was late morning and bright and sunny. The time of day and lack of fresh snow made the duplex look slightly different but still familiar to the men making their second house call. Bixby answered the doorbell after the second ring, no loud knocking was required on this day.

"Hi Tia, do you mind if we come in and have a talk with you and Ms. Walsh?" Pollard asked, playing things in an overly cordial manner that probably bordered on patronizing, at least from the perspective of the young woman who answered the door.

"Sure, he still ain't here though, you know." She could probably tell by the different approach that morning in comparison to the reception they got at the door the previous week, that the three men weren't of the belief that Washington was present.

"Well, that's actually what we wanted to talk to you about," Brown stated as if she had brought up the subject of Washington's whereabouts and not them.

The crew entered the home while Walsh was coming down from upstairs. She seemed a little concerned about the presence of the deputies in the house again, but that initial alarm seemed to fade as Pollard started talking.

"Have you ladies had any contact with John?" Pollard knew what the phone records had already told him and unlike human beings, those records were incapable of telling a lie. He would have been shocked if either woman told him the truth at that point.

Both frowned their lips and shook their heads side to side as though they were surprised anyone would even inquire about the man. Pollard was tempted to ask to look at their incoming and outgoing phone messages, to call them on their lies, but that wasn't why they were there that morning. He knew that if the two women were to find out that he suspected Washington was using this new number, the new phone might also end up in a river. And there was always the chance that the number wasn't Washington at all. The decision to let it alone was a calculated gamble.

"Well, we've been told by a few of the neighbors that he's been in and out of here on more than one occasion. After we left the other day, we showed his picture around the neighborhood.

Why would we be getting these calls, from more than one person, if that wasn't the case?" The entire statement and question lacked even a shred of truth. Pollard was doing some of his own fishing and fibbing.

The women were quiet. Walsh spoke up with an assertiveness they didn't see the last time they were in her living room. "He hasn't been here. I know that's for sure." Maybe that's what the truth sounded like coming from her, Vatrano thought.

"Anyone that might look like him, fit his description been here?" Vatrano asked with eyebrows raised. "Maybe some of the neighbors on the street were mistaken." He wanted to follow up on Pollard's initial claim, like a poker player raising a bet just to see how his opponent would react for the next hand.

"No one I can think of," Bixby was quick to respond. "We haven't even had any men here at all."

"Me neither," Walsh confirmed, both women looking at each other and then back at Vatrano and then Pollard with a look of confusion. "It's only been the two of us and Lucas." She motioned over her shoulder at the four-year-old watching a movie in the living room.

Pollard and the rest of the group wrapped up their little meet and greet and left without asking any more serious questions about Washington. They never brought up the phone records and it was never their intention to do so. Pollard had accomplished the goal of this meeting perfectly and Brown and Vatrano knew it too. They got back into Brown's vehicle and cleared from the area all together.

"Well, that went well. If he's in Kennison, he's not leaving to come here, with us showing up again and letting them know the neighborhood is on watch. He's probably getting a call right now letting him know that we have no clue where the fuck he is. That should get him to settle right in." Now that Brown knew their brief mission was accomplished, his thoughts went to the city of Kennison.

"Kennison in the morning. I'll put out the email," Pollard stated before Brown had the chance. "And just to be clear, we do have a clue where he is. We have a couple clues, but this is no ground ball."

With nothing left to do with his day after the short conversation with the women on Depot Street, and just waiting to head to Kennison early the following morning, Pollard took the opportunity to get home at a normal hour. The February afternoon sun had produced a day with the temperatures in the mid-forties. It was one of those rare days during the second half of winter in New Hampshire to remind everyone that the season wasn't permanent.

Pollard pulled into the driveway of his house and parked like he always did. When he did so, he could see the garage door under the house opening, so he immediately looked up to the street from the bottom of the driveway. Kelly was pulling in too, pressing the remote opener attached to the sun visor above the steering wheel, now done with her workday as well. After she parked in the garage, Pollard greeted her with a kiss and followed her into the house, shutting the garage door behind them with a smack of the doorbell style button mounted on the wall.

"Any chance you want to go with Boomer and I for a run?" she asked with an expecting smile, hoping to take advantage of the temperatures approaching a comfortable feel, relatively speaking.

"Sounds good to me," Pollard replied, with his own desire to get out in the fresh air as well. Outdoor exercise would be a welcome change compared to the treadmill in the basement that made him feel like a pet gerbil or hamster.

As they walked into the house together, they were greeted by the bounding jumps of their little Jack Russell Terrier. Up in the bedroom, Pollard stripped off his gear and with it, the problems of the workday, at least for now. He got right into shorts that he hadn't put on since the abnormally warm day between Christmas Day and New Year's Eve. He smiled remembering how they went for a long run hoping to burn some holiday dinner calories and get a healthy jump on the new year.

It was cool out, but he would keep his extremities warm for the run. That's all he really needed, as the general thought of wearing shorts did him good psychologically in the middle of a long winter. Though not that much different than the temperatures of October and November, the feel of the sun in February was always warmer. They got in a quick warm up and stretch and provided the dog an opportunity to do his business so he wouldn't stop mid-run. Then they were off, Pollard gripping the leash in his right hand.

The first few hundred yards were enjoyed only by Boomer, happy to be with his family and out in the weather after a long, lonely day indoors. The roads were damp from the snowmelt on the sides, dripping onto the sun-warmed asphalt. The water kicked up from all eight paws, human and canine, giving a quick, cool, shot to Pollard's bare shins with each stride. It took a short while to get in a groove where the breathing became easier, and the run felt less like a chore and more like the stress relief that it was intended for.

As the miles went on, the breathing eventually got harder. Although the air felt good on their skin, it still filled up their lungs with the dryness of winter, creating a bit more resistance. It was Pollard's second favorite activity that involved heavy breathing with his wife.

When they completed their loop in front of the house, they eventually came to a walking pace. It took a few minutes to get to a point of enough comfort in the burning lungs to start a conversation. After Pollard presented an exhausted, half-hearted wave to a neighbor driving by, he was confronted with the same question Kelly asked him almost every day.

"How was work today?" she inquired, now fully capable of bringing her breathing back to a normal rhythm. To her credit,

Kelly always asked in a sincere tone, but really the question had become a simple formality over the years.

He decided against bringing up Kennison with her even though she would have probably been thrilled to hear that Pollard was headed to her alma mater. She spent four years at Kennison State College getting her teaching degree and she shared a lot of fond memories through her stories and friendships that had lasted from those times.

He just wasn't sure enough about the whole thing yet. Pollard genuinely cared that his wife thought highly of him and didn't want to embarrass himself if the phone data turned out to be someone else and he was way off from finding his target. If he told her about it now, she would certainly want to know about it after he went there to get his fugitive. Better to surprise her with the good result than disappoint with a poor follow up. Right or wrong, it was how Pollard's logic led him to the decision to keep quiet about it, at least for now. It was the same logic that had led him to keep quiet about so many of the other previous cases.

He mumbled some nondescriptive answer to her and posed the question back. She would no doubt have a story to tell him about the adventures in first grade that day and the conversation would move along.

High on the endorphins from the run, they made dinner, had a cocktail, and showered. Pollard knew he needed to get to bed early with the knowledge that the next workday would arrive quickly and could be a long one. He told Kelly about his earlier than normal expected departure time. She decided that she would go to bed early with him, mostly to keep the time spent on a rare afternoon and evening with her husband from coming to an end sooner than it had to.

CHAPTER TWENTY

The map on his dash mounted phone indicated that it was just under 100 miles to the Kennison Police Department headquarters from Pollard's house and would take about two hours to get there. He hoped the time of day and limited traffic would reduce that estimated time of arrival in the lower left corner of the screen, part wishful thinking, and as always, partly an internal challenge. Becoming more and more common those days, it was another zero dark thirty departure in a wind chilled mid-winter morning in New Hampshire. The whistling gusts that were cutting through his jacket and wool hat didn't prevent him from being able to see the stars at that clear and dark time of day, when the rest of the neighborhood was still deep in slumber. While walking up to the frozen truck, he took a minute and gave a quick thought to the morning that was also starting up in Kennison. His truck cranked over and started up. He saw that the temperature was reading just four degrees on the digital dash but had a feel to it that was more than a bit colder with the bustling breeze. Pollard was eager to get going as there were only about 20 miles of interstate highway with the rest being two lane state roads on this journey. It would be an excursion to a part of the state where he didn't often find himself, and the uncommon destination had him excited.

A few miles into the trip and the ring of a phone call rattled through the speakers of the truck like a breaking update cutting into the morning news going out on the local radio broadcast. His house was kind of on the way for Pollard, so Dorsey had been waiting to get picked up as part of the plan. He had apparently grown impatient with Pollard's perceived tardiness.

"Where the hell are ya?" Dorsey, a morning person, was always chipper and full of energy, probably a cup of coffee or two deep already.

"Five minutes out, can't wait to see your face first thing this morning."

"Well, I just wanted to make sure you woke up, didn't want you to be late to your own party north of the notch."

"Did you give everyone else a fuckin' wake-up call too?" Pollard feigned offense as though he had been singled out.

"No, just you. You're my ride." Dorsey knew that he didn't want to be late while leaning on Pollard for transport. It was his own tardiness with the group he was worried about. Pollard knew it too.

"In all these years, have I ever not shown up? See you in a few." Pollard wasn't interested in small talk over the phone knowing that they would have about an hour and a half in the car to talk about any and every subject that they wanted to. Dorsey didn't need to reply to the question anyway, they both already knew the answer. Pollard had, in fact, always shown up for him.

Pollard pulled into Dorsey's driveway almost exactly five minutes after the conclusion of their phone conversation. He could see the rear hatch on Dorsey's parked, government-issued vehicle was opened wide. After retrieving his necessary gear from the back end of his SUV and dumping it in the rear of Pollard's extended cab pick-up truck, Dorsey hopped into the passenger seat with a lack of grace that one would expect of a man his size, a "holder." He was also showing off his standard grin from just the left half of his mouth.

"I knew I couldn't wait to see that face," Pollard jabbed, figuring the one throwing the first punch had the advantage.

"At my age, it looks best this time of day." Dorsey's coffee, no doubt brewed in his kitchen a few minutes prior, filled the front of the truck with a fresh, rich aroma from the confines of his thermos.

"I think you are confusing early with dark, where it can't be seen quite as well." Pollard had missed some of the banter over the past few days as he had placed his head deep into records and search warrants. It was a nice change of pace since both men knew what they had already been through on this hunt, and what could be waiting for them halfway across the state later that day. After all the arrests, foot chases and take downs, it was still the small and often playful human interactions among his teammates that Pollard enjoyed the most, not the hunting of armed men that Ernest Hemingway had referenced on the canvas in his office. Dorsey put his fist out to Pollard, Pollard pounded his fist right back. It was really the only way they knew how to properly say good morning to one another now. After Dorsey got settled in his seat and slugged a few large sips of hot coffee from his stainless-steel mug, the back and forth started back up.

"Some weather," Pollard offered up generically, referencing the obvious biting wind chill.

Without missing a beat, Dorsey replied with a straight face, "Yeah, but it's a dry heat." Pollard should have known better than to try and get a hardy New Englander like Dorsey to admit that it was cold out. It was a tradition of northerners to pretend that it really isn't all that cold out even when the climate had clearly reached the edges of uninhabitable. Dorsey planned to honor that tradition and moved on from the comment as though he got one over on his partner, because he had. Pollard looked at the temperature on the dashboard thermometer that had now dropped to just three degrees in the darkest hours well before dawn in Dorsey's driveway.

Dorsey hadn't been present for much of the search warrant applications and phone record analyzing. As Pollard was getting him up to speed on the highlights of going before the judge with Vatrano, they talked a little about the case. Pollard was always happy to bounce the details off Dorsey, feeling that his experience mattered when things got complicated.

"So, you couldn't get the content of the text messages from the phones then?" Dorsey asked, a bit confused, wondering why it couldn't be determined that Washington was on the other end of the phone they suspected he was using by simply reading what was texted.

"I could, but that would have required a Grand Jury subpoena and an alleged crime. Because we haven't alleged a crime on either woman, and the State of New Hampshire is not alleging a homicide for Washington, it would have taken a lot longer and we would have had to be a lot more creative. It also would have taken a lot longer for the wireless companies to get that sort of information back to us. Either way, I don't believe there has been a single text message that came from that new phone, just calls. We could still go that route if we need to, but right now we only have the numbers it has called and cell tower information. And Matthews may have figured out our link to Kennison too."

"Well, there's no script for this shit, so I guess we'll see. Hey, my girl at the State benefits office is still keeping the card flagged. It will be a few days until there's more money placed on it, but we still have that too, and we know he's been using that. If it shows up that it's being used in Kennison, we'd know we have the right number." They both knew that a couple of secondary plans in the back pocket would reduce the pressure on what results may or may not come when they got to their early morning destination.

"Interesting that you would have brought her up. No offense, I know you want to talk to her again and everything, but I hope we don't need that or a subpoena." Pollard flashed Dorsey a knowing smile. Dorsey didn't need any explanation for why he was receiving it and sent back his own signature half-grin.

The familiar American-made trucks and sport utility vehicles began pulling into the parking lot at the Kennison Police Department before the sun made its first appearance of the day. Brown had been the first of the team members to arrive, as he often was. He had made his way into the building to speak with the lieutenant in charge of the overnight shift that was soon to turn into the dayshift. The lieutenant and his squad were about to go off duty at seven, so he suggested that the team should meet up with a couple of the detectives who would be coming into the office in less than an hour for the day shift.

The sun had just begun to come up as Vatrano and then Matthews arrived from their respective counties. The dawn was clear with a deep orange sunrise shining upon the few clouds stretching over the sky. There was still a biting breeze keeping things frigid, but no winter precipitation was predicted for the day.

The trip to Kennison was what the fugitive team referred to as an "away game," when they were looking for a suspect in a county that did not have representation by a deputy sheriff of that county on the team. Kennison was somewhat foreign to most of the members, a nice change of scenery from some of their more traditional haunts. None of them had a problem getting there but getting around town efficiently might be a different story later that day as things got going.

After piling through the employee door of the Kennison Police Headquarters, each member of the team went around the table and introduced himself to Detective Noyes. Matthews abstained, having spent sixteen weeks with him day and night nearly a decade before, so no introduction was needed. There were a handful of early morning chuckles from the crew regarding Detective Noyes and Matthews having showered together at the police academy back in the day, as all academy recruits did. Pollard interrupted the middle school atmosphere to give the detective the shortened version of why they were in town.

"So basically, we're looking in the radius from the cell phone pings from the unknown owner of the phone that I continue to get as recently as last night. We also have this guy named Hamel that we thought your department might have some information on. It looks like he has a Kennison football sweatshirt on in some of his recent photos on social media." Pollard passed a print-out of the Instagram page over to Detective Noyes for review. "We don't have a date of birth or anything. He doesn't have a New Hampshire license and has not registered any cars in the state. Nothing on his social media says where he's from and there aren't a lot of clues in the photos to help figure out if he's even in Kennison. If you guys have any information on this Hamel guy, that would certainly help us out a lot as far as locking down a place to start looking here."

"Let me look into it and see what I can do." The detective took the printout and sat down at his computer. He was eager to help, as a murderer in Kennison was certainly a big deal to him. After a brief pause, the detective looked up at Pollard. "Our department hasn't had any contact with him. But our records are merged with the records of the college public safety department. There is one kid with that name that they have a record of, looks like he's twenty-one years old. KSC public safety had contact with him earlier this winter, actually just a few weeks ago. I can make a call over to their office to find out more if that's what you guys want. They are usually really good about working with us with whatever we need from them." Detective Noyes was providing the type of accommodation they were hoping for when they came to town.

"Great, but please don't tell them about who we are actually looking for and why. Nothing against the college public safety folks, but I know how fast news of a murderer might get across a small campus." Pollard grimaced after envisioning his hard work going down the drain and having to start over due to the excitement and loose lips of a college public safety employee. He also worked to hide his excitement that there was some confirmation that Hamel was in town, to make it appear to the outside that he knew it all along.

"No problem at all, I'll get it." The detective gave a quick nod of acknowledgement and picked up the phone. It was clear how he dialed that he had the phone number to the Kennison State College Office of Public Safety committed to memory. As he began his conversation with whoever was on the other end of the phone call, the notes that Detective Noyes scribbled down on a yellow legal pad weren't initially legible to Pollard. But the fact that he was writing at all gave the entire team some hope. After a few moments and several more scribbles on the paper, the detective hung up the phone.

"So, the Hamel kid is from Utica, New York. He was identified by a New York driver's license at a party they broke up on campus in early January right when they all came back from winter break. He's twenty-one so he was not ticketed, and they wouldn't have called us, so he doesn't have any pending court dates or anything." They could see Detective Noyes was trying to find an angle to hold something over the kid in exchange for some information. Pollard took the same concept in a different direction.

"Is he a student? Because it looks like he is from what we've seen so far."

"Just started here in January according to the school's records," the detective said while looking at his scratch notes.

"What about a local address? Can we get a dorm hall or room assigned by the school?"

"Each student has a mailbox on campus to get their mail. Public Safety says the school records show that he lives off campus, so they wouldn't have a physical address in town for him. They aren't required to furnish off campus addresses to the school, usually only mom and dad's place where they send the bill for tuition. They have just the Lansing Street in Utica address and the mailbox number over at the student hall on campus, and so far, their only contact with him here was this winter." The detective said it almost apologetically. He knew when he got the information from the public safety officer that it wasn't what the team was going to want to hear.

"What about a phone number, would they have that?"

"Yeah, I wrote it right here." Noyes showed him the ten-digit number. Pollard noticed it didn't start with the 6-0-3 he was so familiar with in New Hampshire. "Three. One. Five. I think that's an upstate New York area code," the detective offered, indicating that it might match with Hamel's hometown. "But I'm not sure, we deal with people from a lot of states being a college town."

Pollard ran his fingers through his hair, rubbing his head a little as he considered the implications. If the kid just arrived at the college from New York in January, what were the odds he picked up a new phone around that same time? Maybe a phone with a New

Hampshire area code to make things easier. Maybe Bixby and Walsh were his only family or friends in New Hampshire, and he had called on them for support or to plan a meet up. Pollard had to cut this line of thinking off and get back to work on the positive possibilities that could be found in this. At least the public safety officer was able to confirm that he should be around, and if Hamel had his own phone, it could be even more likely that Washington was using this new one. Pollard took just a little solace in that. He had now confirmed that Washington's potential link to Kennison was in fact in Kennison. Whether Washington himself was around was to be determined.

"Is the address where he was identified at the party within the radius that we talked about earlier with the cell pings?" Pollard pointed on his printed-out map with the red circle drawn in the middle of it as a reminder of the neighborhood he was referring to. The tip of his index finger bounced off the encircled area like the beak of a woodpecker on a tree trunk.

"Yeah," the detective replied slowly. He could see that Pollard was wanting an explanation on behalf of that initial hesitation. "Half of the student body probably lives both on campus and off campus in and around that radius. It could have been a party at any one of a bunch of houses. Sometimes the parties are at multiple houses on the block and the college kids are all over the street." Pollard nodded his head slightly in agreement while he pulled up some of his own college memories of such monstrous gatherings.

"Are there any known off campus houses that are full of football players from the college? The kid looks pretty athletic, maybe he plays," Vatrano chimed in with his own question as he had been following the conversation intently. "I mean, he's got the sweatshirt on and it isn't like Kennison State is a national football powerhouse. What is it, Division III?"

"There's more than a few that I know of. How many guys are there on a football team, eighty or so? A good deal of them, especially the upper classmen, live off campus here in town. But usually pretty close to campus." Detective Noyes knew he was bringing down the buzz with what felt like every word he had to offer.

"And let me guess," Pollard sarcastically offered, "All the off-campus football houses are located in that radius too?"

"I would say that most of the football houses I can think of are, yes." More of the same let down from the detective, but it wasn't his fault. The honesty was appreciated more than the information.

Pollard was losing his grip on the human intelligence he had gathered even as he seemed to gain more of it. Instead, he found it spiraling the wrong way as the possibilities were growing, not narrowing. The next few volleys of pings he received would now be a glaring reminder of all the possibilities.

"Let's go take a ride through the neighborhoods in the radius that we're looking at here. It's not even 8 a.m., no way there's going to be much foot traffic at this hour in a college town. We can get a look at it without sticking out. Where's Matthews?" Pollard didn't know what else to do at that time but take a ride through town. It wasn't like looking for a lost dog, they were trying to find a murderer.

Matthews emerged from behind the huddle around the detective's desk like a pinch hitter out of the dugout in the late innings.

"You're driving, you look about the right fuckin' age. Vatrano and I will jump in back." This time it wasn't an age joke, Matthews' youthfulness could go a long way to prevent suspicion from anyone hiding a murderer in the house. Matthews could pass as a college kid without a problem. Without knowing who or where they would be surveilling, Pollard didn't want to risk it with any of the older faces of the team sticking out in public, on and near the college campus.

Brown looked over to the still seated detective and gave him a light elbow to the shoulder. "Usually, it's me they want driving in certain neighborhoods, you know?" The detective gave him an uncomfortable smile, figuring it was a statement on Brown's race but not wanting to add his own comment. "We can't be having two, big, dumb, white guys driving through some neighborhoods, might as well put a sign on the roof telling everyone it's the police."

Brown laughed in his deep tone, wanting to let the detective know that it was alright to laugh as well. The rest of the team didn't need such permission, they were already chuckling, as the joke contained the requisite amount of truth and a certain level of impropriety to be funny. Brown looked over at Matthews and stated semi-seriously, "Now you know how it feels. Get out there and drive while young. See if you're as good as me driving while black!" Brown faked some sort of offense, but no one was buying it from his current audience.

Vatrano, Matthews, and Pollard headed out to the parking area to jump into Matthews' vehicle. Like he was transporting some executives in a limo, Matthews sat alone in the front seat. Pollard and Vatrano in back, behind the façade of the tinted windows, to keep from view of the students who would be starting out for their morning classes soon.

Pollard had been around Kennison a few times with his wife for some college reunion weekends. He also had been a few times when he was in high school to play sports against Kennison High School. Although it was a small city, it had changed a little bit. He still hadn't been all that familiar with it other than some major landmarks and how to get in and out of town on the state roads. As Matthews started driving into the area that Pollard had plotted out in the potential radius, it became much clearer than it had been looking at the overhead view of the map. There were literally hundreds of residential buildings that Washington could be holed up in, if indeed, he was on the other end of that phone number.

Pollard checked his phone and saw another phone ping had just come through on his email a few minutes earlier. This most recent ping came from inside the radius as he expected. It almost made it harder to swallow when they went street by street through the area, thinking, but not knowing if Washington was inside one of the houses or dorms that they were passing by. Each street brought a new possibility while at the same time it felt as though each possible building lowered their overall statistical probabilities. It was like brushing past strangers in a growing crowd looking for someone specific, but without seeing anyone's face.

Matthews made a right turn onto Tremont Street and pulled up to an intersection of two main roads. Diagonally across the street from them sat the Brother's Burgers. Noticing the large orange sign out front, Pollard sat up a little in the back seat and grabbed at his file folder, thumbing through the records.

"Hey, pull over into the Brother's Burgers parking lot." Pollard broke a few minutes of silence among the three in the vehicle with a fairly sharp order.

"Okay," Matthews replied, feeling as though he actually was the limo driver and Pollard, the aristocrat barking directions in the back seat.

"That was one of the calls from the phone. Brother's Burgers." Pollard felt the need to soften his order with a better explanation, a move that accomplished its intent.

"Well, I'm guessing they won't be open for a few hours," Matthews stated, as though the trip into the parking lot might not be worth their time.

"No, they do breakfast, I think." Pollard didn't want to be a know it all, but he knew they were open for the first meal of the day as the chain had begun serving breakfast about a year prior. He had even stopped at one closer to home for breakfast during his travels on a different case recently.

"You would know." Vatrano, the third man in on the disagreement, knew Pollard was right, but he wasn't going to just agree with him. He didn't let the stress of the moment suppress the undying need he had to bust balls. Pollard and Matthews both smiled at Vatrano's delivery, though they couldn't see each other's faces with Pollard sitting behind the driver's seat that Matthews was occupying.

There were only two other cars in the lot at that early hour, early at least for a late rising college town. Pollard figured that wasn't evidence against his assertion that they were open as they probably got a lot more foot traffic than vehicles, being just off campus.

Matthews brought the vehicle to a stop in the parking spots nearer to the road than the front door. Pollard scribbled down a few notes on a piece of paper from his file and grabbed a printed photo of Washington. He clutched his heavy winter coat from the vacant middle seat next to him and threw it on to make sure no one would see the gear around his waist. As he hopped out of the car while slapping Matthews on the shoulder, he grabbed the driver's seat to unfold his large frame from the back seat and get out the door. Vatrano and Matthews were told to sit tight, as if there was another option.

"No need to draw attention with a crowd in there," Pollard explained as he headed for the entrance on his own.

"Riiggghhtt," Vatrano said slowly. "Get me a number two with hash browns and a black coffee." Vatrano was only half joking. Pollard continued to walk away while choosing not to acknowledge the request seriously or with a joke, either of which would have been acceptable to Vatrano.

Pollard took a deep breath of chilly February air to steady himself before he flung the out-swinging door open and strutted into the lobby. He could tell it was breakfast, as the pork products coming from the skillets out back smelled different than the beefy aroma of the lunch menu. The wonderful odor of cooking bacon distracted Pollard, nearly tripping over the wet-floor sign set up in a triangle on an area that had clearly already dried. Matthews and Vatrano would do their best to follow along from the parking lot, having to watch the body language of those inside through the glass to see how this would unfold.

The burger joint wasn't busy, just a set of four college kids at the front table occupied by their greasy food and cell phones. The assistant manager came out swiftly and introduced himself after Pollard asked the clerk to get the person in charge.

"Hi, I'm Mike, the assistant manager of this Brother's Burgers. What can I help you with?" Pollard was initially impressed with the young man's demeanor and customer service acumen. He brushed his hand on the side of his pants and extended it out.

"Hi Mike, I'm Mark Pollard, with the US Marshals Service," he greeted back as their right hands met in the middle with a smack. Not wanting to confuse him by identifying with his home county so far away, Pollard pulled his United States Marshal credentials from the zippered breast pocket of his over-sized winter coat. Holding his shiny badge and picture identification out just long enough for Mike to see it, he placed it back in his pocket, avoiding the attention of anyone else inside. It looked like there were only two other employees out back in the kitchen. The kid who retrieved the manager for Pollard disappeared, probably to the back as well, maybe looking to avoid the angry customer confrontation that he thought was unfolding.

"Okay," the young manager replied, almost a little confused and looking for some type of follow up from the marshal. Pollard enjoyed doing interviews of people who had no connection to his fugitives. Most of the time they were eager to help, a stark contrast to the interviews he had with people like Bixby and Walsh back in Stanton. They had their own reasons for lying, but the assistant manager of this place shouldn't have any.

"We're looking for some information on a guy that may have gotten food here. Do you guys do deliveries?"

"No. No deliveries, we mostly just serve hangover food to the college kids in the morning, and drunk munchies to them again in the evening. We're open until 11p.m. and back again at 7a.m." Mike had a smile on his face as though he was being clever. Pollard understood exactly what he was talking about, having sat down for the same meals plenty of times back in his days. He brought his thoughts back to the phone call in question that he knew was recently placed to that establishment.

"So, if someone was to call the restaurant here, they would be placing an order for pick up or trying to talk to an employee then?" It was a statement phrased as a question. Pollard intentionally gave him only two options, as they were the only two reasons he cared about. He also couldn't think of any other legitimate reasons to make a call to such an establishment.

"Yeah, most likely. We don't really do a lot of orders ahead for pick up. It usually doesn't take long for us to fire out a meal or two, so people usually just order when they come in and wait a few minutes for their food to come out. Or they order online."

"What about employees getting calls on the phone here, any of that?" Pollard wanted to eliminate the unlikely idea that his fugitive had a contact working there and might even be present while he was in discussion with the manager. It was even possible that manager Mike was Washington's associate.

"No, we allow our employees access to their cell phones during some of our quieter hours of operation and on their breaks. I don't think anyone has ever called the landline here to speak with one of us." The young man chuckled a little, sensing a generational divide in communication customs. It made sense to Pollard, but he had to be sure before moving along with his line of questioning. The banter also gave him a sense of how the young manager answered questions that were not real provocative, to get a base line sense of his mannerisms and facial expressions when questioned.

"Do you recall any orders for pick up in the past two weeks or so? It sounds like it's pretty rare." Pollard gently threw the manager's own assessment of the call frequency back at him to frame both the question, and hopefully his answer to it.

"Yeah, we've probably had a couple, why?" Pollard took note that it was the first time the young manager had answered a question with one of his own. The amount of information that he had already provided before his own inquisitive nature took over gave Pollard a good deal of confidence in his truthfulness.

Pollard had the exact date and time of the phone call to the restaurant from the phone in question. He had written it down on the back side of the folded-up booking photo of Washington he had brought into the restaurant with him.

"How about for lunch time? Around 1 p.m. in the last few weeks."

"The last one I remember was at least a week or ten days ago or so, maybe more. I was working the breakfast and lunch shift that day. There may have been others too, but I only remember that one."

"Would you have access to any video of that purchase?" Pollard asked while looking up at the cameras over the cash registers and looking back over his shoulder at an area above the exit door that he assumed would have a camera. His eyes caught the sphere mounted on the wall exactly where he had expected it would be. With his assumptions confirmed, he motioned his head toward that camera. His body language indicated to the manager that Pollard was hopeful that more than one angle might be available.

"Our cameras are on a one-week rotation. Basically, every new weekday replaces the same day from the previous week. So, Tuesday this week will record, and Tuesday last week will erase simultaneously. If it was more than a week ago, we don't have it. We don't have the digital storage to keep all the video from all the cameras for too long. Unless something noteworthy happens, like a slip and fall or a robbery or something, it doesn't get saved. We record twenty-four hours a day from multiple cameras, it's too much footage and data." Pollard was hoping to identify Washington on video himself. He knew it had been more than a week since the phone call to the restaurant. His second, but also less attractive option, was a close witness to the purchase, and he was hoping he had already found him.

"What do you remember about the person that picked up that lunch order?" Pollard was intentionally vague. He even excluded his use of the male pronoun with the hope of getting an unbiased answer regarding the details of the individual making the purchase.

"Nothing really stands out. Young guy, maybe a student here. He was wearing a hooded coat and he paid cash. That's about all I remember." Pollard felt as though he had jogged the assistant manager's memory well enough to that day and time. If the kid was going to have a mental image of that customer and it was Washington, it would be in his mind at this exact moment. It was the most opportune time to put a picture in front of him and get an accurate answer. Pollard didn't even want to get off topic by confirming the date and time of the purchase to make sure they were talking about the same food pick up order.

"Is this the guy?" Pollard asked while gently placing the folded photo on the counter like a car salesman sliding a price across a salesfloor desk of an auto dealership. All of the interviews, search warrants, talks with detectives and parole officers. The long drives for everyone that morning and all of the other mornings. All of the time spent pouring over reports and records was either worth it or not based on this kid's answer. It agitated Pollard that it had come to this, but the next step in the investigation hinged on the young man's answer. But more importantly to Pollard, the next step hinged on how the young man answered it.

"Yeah, that's him," Mike said with a touch of surprise as though Pollard had done some sort of magic trick and asked,

"Is this your card?" Instead of the nine of diamonds, it was a picture of his customer from more than a week ago pulled from thin air. The answer sounded confident, but Pollard needed to confirm.

"Are you sure?" Washington was an average looking dude, at least from Pollard's point of view. He was of average size and had no real discernable facial features. Could this kid have really picked out one of his thousands of customers over the past few weeks and matched him to a booking photo taken more than two years ago when Washington had first arrived at the prison? Pollard was afraid the young man was telling him what he wanted to hear. It may have been out of fear or a desire to impress, or to be part of the action like in the movies. Either way, Pollard needed more from the kid than simply saying it was him. He quickly got the reassurance that he needed without so much as a follow up question.

"Yeah, like I said before, we really don't get a lot of calls ahead for takeout food here, I remember this guy coming in," he said with a matter-of-fact tone while pointing towards the photo. It was convincing enough. For the first time in his investigation

Pollard had true confirmation that Washington was in Kennison, confirmation that the phone number he had been tracking was at the very least related to Washington's activity. It was the first solid sign that they were closing in on the fugitive and not chasing a made-up ghost that they simply hoped was him.

The chime on the main door caught both Pollard and the manager's attention as a new customer walked in and stood behind them by the counter. It was a young co-ed looking up at the menu board. Pollard didn't want any unneeded attention. He grabbed the photo off the counter, folded it and placed it in his breast pocket next to his credentials. He couldn't possibly know who might have a connection to Washington in this town.

The manager called to the rear kitchen area so that another employee could come and take the order of the young lady standing there patiently.

"Mike, can you step outside with me for a quick minute?"

Mike hung his apron, with "Brother's Burgers" emblazoned on the front and smeared with grease, on the hook next to the counter. He obediently walked outside without answering while Pollard followed close behind.

Matthews and Vatrano took notice from the vehicle across the parking lot that Pollard was coming out. They figured if he was still talking that it was a good sign, that there was still some hope.

"So, did he come here in a car that day?" Pollard picked right back up once they found a good spot on the curb outside the door. He raised his voice slightly to overcome the background hum of the traffic on the main road.

"What'd this guy do anyway?" Pollard noted the second question that the manager asked was a big one and was a little surprised it hadn't come earlier. That detail always seemed to be the one everyone wanted to know at some point.

"Nothing crazy, we just need to talk to him about someone in his family." Pollard was quick with a fib, especially when the interview was turning on him. The speed with which he rattled off the response gave Mike no reason to question further. "So, on foot or in a car?" The rewording of his previous question further moved the young man away from inquiring about the crime that had been committed.

"Oh, yeah, I'm not really sure. I don't remember him leaving. I probably turned away as he left." The assistant manager had placed his hands under his armpits, not a sign of nerves, but a self-preserving act on such a cold morning.

"Was he by himself that day?"

"Yeah, I think. He left the store alone, I believe. He didn't come in with anyone else anyways. Not that I can remember."

"How much food did he get, just for him do you think?" Pollard was flashing back to Bixby getting two sodas at the McDonalds back in Stanton.

"Yeah, it was just one meal, which made it a little weird that he called ahead. A lot of our calls ahead, and like I said, we don't

217

get a lot, are larger orders that take us a bit longer to make up. You know, sometimes the whole floor of a dorm will put in an order it seems like."

"Do you think he's been back since that day, you know, without calling ahead and just grabbing some food off the menu?" Pollard was getting greedy with the kid's memory and was flirting with getting unsure answers. He couldn't help himself though.

"That I don't know. I don't remember seeing him since then, but him calling ahead was really what was different. Otherwise, I don't think I would have remembered him just ordering from the line in the store." Pollard was hoping to get at some sort of pattern where Washington could show up to get his food and they could grab him right there. It was a long shot, but his fortunes were good right now and worth a try.

"Listen, if you see him back in here, give me a call. My cell phone number is on the back," Pollard said while jotting the number he had just referenced on the reverse side of the card. He held the business card between his ring and middle finger straight in front of the kid's face. Mike took his hand from his armpit and grabbed it, looked at it, and then placed it in his back pocket. "And thanks for your help. I need you to do something for me though." Pollard paused intentionally, assuring that he had the required attention from the young man.

"What's that?" Mike could feel Pollard had stopped talking as though he wanted him to acknowledge the importance of what was about to be said.

"Keep this quiet. Please. We need you to keep this whole thing quiet so that we can do our job safely. You wouldn't want one of us to get hurt out here, right?" It was a little dramatic but also true and effective. Pollard was paranoid about word spreading on the campus. If something got back to Washington, or the people he might be with, before they could locate him, all might be lost.

"Of course not. I won't tell anyone."

"Thanks, Mike. Make sure you know what you are going to tell your coworkers in there before you go back in, because they might ask what you're doing out here with me." He motioned to the front door with a head nod referencing the crew inside. It was a short lesson from Pollard on being a better liar. Anticipate the questions and have an answer ready before people start asking.

Pollard looked to his left and then his right before stepping off the curb and down to the roadside area of the parking lot. He walked briskly back to the car. Vatrano and Matthews looked like a couple of friends at a bar waiting to see if the girl had given their buddy her phone number. They could tell by Pollard's walk that he had scored, he didn't even need to say it, but as he opened the door to the truck he did anyways.

"It's him." It was all he needed to say.

A little out of sorts after driving around the radius of the cell phone pings while getting the lay of the land, Vatrano, Matthews, and Pollard found their way back to Kennison Police Headquarters. They decided not to call ahead to the others, waiting instead to deliver the big news in person. While driving, the chime of an incoming email caught Pollard a little off guard. It was another ping of the phone in his inbox. Same towers. Similar direction. Same radius. For the first time Pollard knew that the ping was now Washington. If a phone ping could take on a persona, this one was a killer, but Pollard still couldn't say exactly where he was.

It was now a little past 9:30 in the morning. Pulling into the Kennison Police Department parking lot armed with new information, Pollard saw Brown and Dorsey sitting together in the front of Brown's vehicle. He was a little surprised that Brown hadn't called while they were out looking around town. As far as Dorsey and Brown knew, that's where the others had been the whole time. They were unaware of the information gleaned from the assistant manager at the Brother's Burgers just down the road.

When the three returned, Dorsey, assuming there was no new information, started with the small talk, most notably describing how Brown had "blown up" the Kennison Police locker room toilet. Dorsey made it clear that there was a possibility that their invitation to go back into the building again may have been rescinded. Pollard broke up the laughter with the message that

Vatrano and Matthews were waiting for, that they knew was Pollard's to give.

"It's him," he said intentionally quietly and quickly. He guessed Brown would be the first to respond over Dorsey and he was right.

"Who is?" asked Brown.

"Washington, on the phone ping. It's him!" The intensity of his voice had picked up considerably. Pollard went on to tell the story of the Brother's Burgers interview with the assistant manager and the confirmation that it was Washington in town. Vatrano and Matthews were hearing it for the second time, but the tale had the effect of a mood changer with the entire crew now updated and on the same page.

"Well, to go along with that, Matthews' shower buddy gave us a list of a few places that he thinks are housing mostly college football players. One of them might be where the guy from New York is staying, we don't know. But they're all in the radius you have for the pings. He just got it from the College Liaison Officer who came into work about twenty minutes ago." Brown compounded Pollard's good news with some of his own. It could at least limit some of the possibilities that they might be able to take some sort of action on.

"That's great. It's still a little risky trying to sit on all these houses at once though," Pollard said while looking down at the list of residences he now held in his hand. "I have another idea." He was on a roll, and with food as the theme he was going to stick with it, "We need Chinese food."

"What? It's not even ten yet." Vatrano was so shocked even he didn't have a wise crack lined up for Pollard's suggestion of Chinese food at such a ridiculous hour, even though such a statement lent itself so easily to the jesting ridicule he loved to sling.

"King's Garden here in Kennison. Now that I know the phone belongs to Washington, or at least he's using it, the only other call he made, in addition to his mother and girl, was to King's Garden Chinese. We need to start that way," Pollard said, as though it shouldn't even be questioned. Matthews didn't get the same sense.

"We already confirmed it's his phone. And they wouldn't be open for a little bit anyways. What are we going to do, reconfirm it?" Matthews seemed a little confused about the plan especially given that they now had a list of houses they could be watching instead.

"Hear me out." Pollard was speaking directly to Matthews but was addressing the whole group. "Brother's Burgers falls well within the phone ping radius that we've drawn. It's most likely a walkable destination for our man. I'm doubting someone from Camden gave Washington a car to keep up here in New Hampshire. My guess is he doesn't have any wheels of his own right now." Pollard wouldn't just come out and say it, he had to be asked, as though it was some kind of production.

"So, what's your point, Pollard?" Vatrano stepped in as though speaking on behalf of the whole group.

"King's Garden is just under two miles away from Brother's Burgers. What are the odds that he had the Chinese food delivered last Thursday night when the call was placed?" Pollard phrased it as a question, but he had a good idea that he already knew. "If we can get the address that the delivery went to, and especially if he was the one who took delivery of the food, we got 'em." Pollard made it sound simple, but it was no sure thing. "What else do we have at this point? We can't just drive around Kennison looking for football team houses, shouting his name like he's a lost dog, hoping he jumps in the car with us. We don't even know that Hamel is on the team, he just had the fuckin' sweatshirt on in a picture."

"And if it was delivered to one of the houses that the Liaison Officer just gave us to look at, I would feel pretty strong that he's staying with Hamel." Brown was solidifying the probabilities in his head and out loud, no doubt making his own case for smashing in a door or two in his near future.

It was a solid plan if the information played out the way they hoped, but they were definitely getting ahead of themselves. Although well before opening time, Vatrano and Pollard started over to King's Garden while the rest of the team decided they would at least go put eyes on each of the houses on the list.

CHAPTER TWENTY-ONE

"Hey, listen man, we've got a meeting tonight at seven o'clock. We all have to be there, so no one else should be around the house." The statement caught Washington off guard as he wasn't quite sure what his host was implying or telling him this for. He had spent time in the house alone by himself during his brief stay on a few occasions already, and this would be nothing new.

"That's fine, I'll be in the basement most of the night anyway," Washington replied, hoping to put his host at ease and avoid any sort of confrontation. He had been with them for a while now and felt like he had gained some trust. Washington had stopped looking for loans from the guys when confronted and hadn't brought it up again even though he only had a few dollars left. Meetings weren't uncommon for the group of men.

"What's your plan here anyways?" A blunt question from the one who had already done so much to help him. It seemed out of nowhere given the small talk that led up to it, but Washington felt something like this coming when the conversation started. Really, he felt like it had been coming for a few days. Not having thought it all the way through himself either, he really didn't know how to answer. Each time he tried he had reached a dead end of ideas. It wasn't like he could go apply for a job or just take up permanent residency in the basement of the house. He had heard from his mother and Tia that they had a couple of recent visits from the law looking for him, so he couldn't go to them for fear of getting caught in Stanton. They were really the only other people he could go to. None of his friends from high school or the old neighborhood had even seen him before he had been to prison.

"I just need some time to pass, you know, for things to blow over." It was a lie. It was mostly just a lie to himself, and he knew it. Things like this don't just blow over. But this was the sort of lie he needed to keep telling to stay away from the law, to stay out of jail, and although a little dramatic, to stay alive. "And I really need your help right now to do it. I'll be gone soon enough, don't worry."

"It's not that I want you to leave." Washington knew by that first statement that his tactic to gain sympathy was working. "You know that. It's just, one of the guys was telling me that we can get in trouble having you live in the basement. It could get us evicted from here if some people found out about you staying here." It was a reasonable explanation. One that he knew deflected some of the emotion of the situation along with some of the pressure off him. It would be transferred onto the shoulders of some of his housemates and nameless, faceless, other people.

"Tell you what, after your meeting tonight, you and I can talk it over. I'm sure we can come up with a plan." Washington was adept at kicking the can down the road to buy time, and it worked again.

"Sounds good, I'll see you in a bit. Be cool." And with that, the situation had been successfully procrastinated.

"Have a good meeting."

CHAPTER TWENTY-TWO

Getting past the language barrier was going to be the most challenging part, at least that was what they had thought initially. Pollard and Vatrano were able to contact an employee at the rear of the building loading food boxes from an exterior refrigeration trailer. The best they could get out of him, in a frustrating exchange for all involved, was that the boss was going to be coming in soon. At least that was how they interpreted the broken communication that took place, but they couldn't be sure.

It was about 10:30 a.m. In his lifetime of vast eating experiences, Pollard had come to believe that Chinese restaurant proprietors were often the most present owners in the entire food service industry. That was probably true for most of the ethnic eating establishments that he patronized, but especially the Chinese places. Not wanting to get in the way, Pollard and Vatrano left the employee to do his duties and waited in the truck on the side of the completely empty parking lot.

Shortly before 11a.m. an older model, white Mercedes pulled into the parking lot at a speed that drew their attention to the vehicle immediately. The car came to a quick stop at the side door and a slim, middle-aged Asian man got out and walked into the

227

building with a pace that matched, or even exceeded his driving. Vatrano and Pollard were in immediate agreement that he was going to be the owner of the place. They followed to the side door where the employee they tried to speak with earlier made eye contact with them. The man nodded his head emphatically with a big smile on his face as he pointed to where the slender man had just walked in. The employee then opened the door for them as though he was inviting them graciously into his own home. It was even more clear now that he would be the owner, and that the broken conversation that they had earlier, though painstaking, was effective.

The employee yelled something down the hallway in his native language and the newly arrived man poked his head around the corner by the cash register. His eyebrows went up and his mouth remained open for a few seconds, clearly a little bit surprised by the presence of Vatrano and Pollard. He came to greet them appearing rather nervous.

It took a good deal of convincing, after showing the owner their credentials and identifying themselves, that they were not agents from Immigration and Customs Enforcement. They were also not Border Patrol, they assured the owner. Being in close proximity to the international boundary with Quebec, that wouldn't have been out of the question in that area of the state. The owner spoke fluent English, though with a heavy Mandarin accent. That fact was certainly going to make this a lot easier than they initially thought.

Vatrano and Pollard had made the effort to provide sufficient assurances to the owner that they were not interested in the immigration or visa status of any of his employees. Once successful with that convincing, Pollard was able to get down to the reason they were there. "We need some information on a call that was placed here a little over a week ago," Pollard started somewhat specifically. "I have the day and time that the call was made if that helps you at all," Pollard added. He knew that his specific request might be made easier by the extra information.

"If you give me phone number, I can tell you. We keep order by phone number and put address in computer, so when person call again from same number, we already have address for them." The owner sounded a little like he was boasting, like he had some pride in the operational system he had set up.

"What if the order was for pick up?" Pollard was immediately curious if an address would be available either way.

"We would not have address, but we would have order in computer with phone number." He pointed to the computer screen by the cash drawer and credit card reader on the counter. "But if we made delivery at any time with that phone number, address would be there." He looked at each man with a big toothy smile. Pollard and Vatrano returned the gesture though each man knew that the phone number had only been used to call just the one time.

229

"That's perfect, it's right here written down for you." Pollard slipped him a hand-written phone number on an otherwise blank piece of yellow paper from the legal pad he always kept with his fugitive files.

"Give me one minute, I have to turn computer on, I get here just now." He told them what they had already observed in the parking lot. The owner had clearly not taken note of them sitting in the truck as he blew past them in his car.

"No problem, take your time." Pollard was trying to be as patient as possible even though he had the feeling he was on the verge of putting the last piece of the puzzle together.

"So, this order go to one two nine Tremont Street last Wednesday night. From this phone number you give me." He smiled at Pollard as though he wanted recognition that his system had worked while holding up the note with the numbers scribbled on it.

"Perfect." Pollard obliged, picking that word carefully. The timeline was correct. The phone call was placed late in the evening of the previous Wednesday night. "Did you make the delivery on this order yourself?" Pollard was hoping to make a quick identification of Washington. He still possessed a lingering fear that Washington may have been borrowing a phone from someone else to make his calls, irrational as that feeling may have been given the evidence he had so far. The quick identification, and the allay of that feeling just wasn't meant to be.

"No, I have delivery driver, he from the college. He not come into work until dinner time hours when we get more busy." While Pollard continued talking with the owner, Vatrano, listening to the exchange between the two men, was texting Matthews the address on Tremont Street so he and Dorsey could go check the place out. He didn't have the list in front of him with some of the houses that had football players provided to Brown by the Liaison Officer, but he thought he remembered a place on Tremont Street in the mix.

"Is there a way we can talk to your delivery driver, maybe have him come speak to us here?" Pollard asked.

"I call him right now if that what you need." At this point, the owner appeared enamored with his own helpfulness. Pollard was going to let that emotion ride.

"Could you? Please tell him it is a bit of an emergency and that he is not in any trouble at all, but that the police need to speak with him as soon as he can." Pollard knew he was pushing it, but not too far.

"Ok, you hold on one minute please." It was a fair request from the owner and Pollard was more than grateful for the cooperation. Vatrano walked over to Pollard and held his phone towards Pollard's face showing him the text message that he had just sent out to Matthews regarding the Tremont Street address.

"We definitely drove past that address this morning before we got to the burger place, because the burger place is on Tremont,"

Pollard said to Vatrano quietly. He placed his attention back on the owner of the restaurant, not wanting to be rude to him and also checking to make sure he didn't overhear.

The owner had stepped back into his office between the kitchen and the main doors where he looked intently at a piece of paper thumbtacked to the wall. The sheet had a list of names and phone numbers on it, a hand-made employee roster, Pollard figured. He then began to punch in the numbers for one of his drivers on the restaurant phone. After completing the dial, he walked back over to Vatrano and Pollard. It was his proof that he was fully cooperating and not trying to hide anything from them by having this conversation with his driver anywhere else but in the presence of the deputies.

"Hello, Brian? Hi. I have something. You need to come down here now to talk to police. You not in trouble, but they want to talk with you." Pollard was happy that his initial greeting included the fact that the driver was not in any trouble. He was hopeful that it would invite cooperation from the delivery driver right off the bat.

"What?"

They could hear the young guy on the other end of the call express his surprise with a raised volume. Vatrano and Pollard could only imagine the young man mentally going through anything illegal he had done recently and in his past. They knew that it was not uncommon for delivery drivers to be making deliveries of goods other than food, especially in a college town. Pollard asked for the phone from the owner hoping to cut to the chase and avoid potential confusion.   He handed it to him obediently.

"Brian?" Pollard asked, hoping the change in accent and tone would lead the young man to understand that someone else was obviously talking.

"Yes? What is going on? Who is this?" It was certainly a fair cluster of questions for a college kid who just got blindsided on the phone by his boss at Pollard's direction.

"My name is Mark Pollard with the sheriff's office. We just need to talk to you. You really are in no trouble at all, I promise you that. We just want to talk to you about an address you delivered to last week and show you a picture. Not a big deal, but can you come on down here and do that for us this morning?" Pollard downplayed the issue for the sake of the man on the other end of the phone still trying to comprehend what exactly was happening.

"Yea, sure. It's no problem at all. I just got out of class a few minutes ago though. I have to go and grab my car. I'll be there in like twenty minutes or so, okay?" Pollard detected the cooperation and compliance he was hoping for. He needed to extend the most amount of understanding back to him as he could.

"Sure thing, we really do appreciate it." Brian hung up first after confirming he was on his way. Pollard handed the phone back to the owner and thanked him for taking that initiative.

"What was the order for that night anyways?" Pollard was back to his usual questions with a nod to the recollection of Bixby's order at the drive through in Stanton several days prior.

"It was number twenty-one dinner, the General Gao chicken with white rice, egg roll and wonton soup." The owner read it off as though he was taking a new order over the phone now.

"That's it, just dinner for one?" Pollard confirmed.

"Yes, probably for one person, right?" The owner didn't want to speculate for fear of appearing as though he might be lying, but any objective person would believe that to be for one person.

"Paid cash?" Pollard followed up quickly, remembering the order at Brother's Burgers and hoping to find similarities to this order for delivery.

"Yes, cash. When he deliver. No credit card." The owner was unsure why he was even being asked such a question, but he answered quickly and with confidence while looking at his computer screen.

It got Pollard thinking. Both meals ordered by that phone number were fit for just one person to consume. That detail led him to wonder about the connection Washington might have with whomever he was staying with that they weren't ordering food together in pairs or more. It was going to remain a mystery since he had no one, at that point, that could tell him why.

Matthews and Dorsey were on their way over to 129 Tremont Street to take a drive by. They strategically left Brown behind at Kennison PD to coordinate with the local police as needed with new information coming in. Matthews and Dorsey followed the numbers down from the 300 block of Tremont Street, near the Brother's Burgers where they had turned on from a side road.

As they approached number 129, Dorsey was able to see the house in full view. It was a medium sized two-story home with a dormer on the second floor coming from each side of the angled roof. The structure appeared as though it was a perfect square, in the middle of the densely populated area of the city next to campus. It did not take on a look as though it was a multifamily unit, with one main door on the first floor and a slider door on the backside leading to a small deck that was uncovered. The lack of any fire escapes furthered his suspicion that it was just one unit.

Matthews was the first to point it out, but Dorsey had also seen it just before being prompted to look. Matthews hit Dorsey's shoulder with a medium amount of force and pointed quickly at a car with New York plates. The street in the college town was freckled with plenty of out of state plates, but they knew Hamel was specifically from the Empire State. Matthews read the plate number aloud as they passed the vehicle parked on the street directly in front of number 129. Dorsey, without a pen in his hand, continued to repeat the plate number over and over again, out loud, until they were out of sight of the house, and he could write it down without being noticed.

Matthews dialed his home sheriff's office to speak to one of the dispatchers to run the license plate that Dorsey had scribbled down.

"Hey Cheryl, it's Matthews, can you copy on a New York registration? I'm looking for information on the owner." The dispatcher gave him the go-ahead, recognizing his voice. She took down the plate number as he had read it off to him from Dorsey's handwritten scratch on the piece of paper.

"That should be on a Honda Civic, color black," Dorsey could hear the dispatcher saying through the phone while Matthews was writing somewhat frantically to keep up with the pace of the readback. He then heard, "Lansing Street, Utica, New York," in the address portion of the conversation and knew that they had stumbled upon something big.

"What's the date of birth on the registered owner of the car?" Matthews inquired, doubling down on his request for information on the owner of the vehicle. "So, he's 46 years old then?" Shaky on his completed math, Matthews felt sure that it was accurate to within a year, more or less. "Hey, listen, thanks a lot Cheryl. Bye." Matthews hung up.

They had pulled to the side of an adjacent street at this point so that they could write without the jarring of a February frost heave on a secondary New Hampshire road. Matthews began scrolling his phone with a great deal of diligence. Dorsey was still catching up and wanting to turn the vehicle around to genuinely believe what he thought he had seen.

"Here he is. He's friends on Facebook with Washington and Washington's mother," Matthews said, looking at the phone as though he didn't believe it himself. "Looks like from the pictures that maybe that's the father of the kid from Utica that we were hoping to find earlier. You know, Hamel, in the football sweatshirt? Different last name though, maybe a stepfather or something."

"The registered owner of that Civic?" Dorsey needed to clarify for himself, trying to grasp the information that was evolving at a rapid pace.

"Yup. The owner."

Dorsey grabbed at his phone to call Vatrano while checking his own notes about the address for the kid from Utica. He figured Pollard might be mid-interview but wanted to get the information to him about the vehicle in front of the house. Dorsey confirmed in his notes that the registered address for the vehicle with the New York license plates in front of 129 Tremont Street was one he had seen before. It matched the address of the driver's license that the Public Safety Office at the college had from their interaction with Hamel at the party in January. There were two different last names, but the same address had to confirm it was the guy they were looking for, and the house that they were looking for.

Vatrano's incoming call came in on Dorsey's cell phone. He answered it with a shared excitement that he knew Vatrano would have. Dorsey placed the call on speaker phone so that Matthews was in on whatever information was coming.

"Hey man, that car?" Vatrano was setting up the suspense as though he needed Dorsey and Matthews' full attention for the unveiling.

"What about it?" Dorsey played along.

"That's got to be the one that picked him up down at the bus station in New Jersey. A small black car with a yellow license plate, right?" Vatrano was the first to make the alternate connection with the car.

"It sure is," Dorsey said as though he was slamming down the gavel on a closed case. Every possible sign was now pointing to 129 Tremont Street. The food was delivered to that address from the phone number in question. It appeared to be the off-campus home of Adam Hamel, social media associate to Washington's immediate family. And to top it off, a small black Civic with yellow plates, like the one described picking up their fugitive in New Jersey was parked out front. It was time for action.

CHAPTER TWENTY-THREE

Brown had stayed back at the Kennison Police Department to confer with Kennison Detective Noyes. The hope was that any information gained by the rest of the team while out on the town or at the Chinese restaurant would be quickly relayed back. Brown tried to gather whatever he could about the address in question after Dorsey and Matthews had sent him the information about the car out in front of the house, and the known connections to their fugitive. The address was confirmed as one of the addresses that the Liaison Officer for the college had provided earlier in the morning as a house with some members of the football team living in it. The detective provided Brown with an aerial view of the house they were looking at on Tremont Street from a mapping website on the screen of his computer.

By this time, the likely presence of a murderer in the small college town had drawn the attention of the officer in charge of the detectives in Kennison, Lieutenant Maloney. Brown and Lieutenant Maloney were standing around Noyes while he was sitting at his desk starting a serious discussion about the matter that was in front of them. The lieutenant offered to Brown whatever resources the fugitive team might need from the local police department. Brown, the supervisor of the group, had already begun to formulate a plan and knew it would take the efforts of the agencies working together to do what needed to be done. He made a phone call down to his office in Concord to get two of the other marshals started towards Kennison. From headquarters at the Federal Court, they would have just under a two-hour ride to get on scene. Deputy United States Marshals Lord and Phillips were on their way from the state capital immediately after Brown put out the call to them for assistance.

"It looks like a fence right here going between the backyards." The detective pointed at the screen with his pen like a local television weatherman in the foreground of a green screen, drawing the attention of the viewers to an incoming storm front. "A lot of the landlords and year-round residents have been putting up fencing to prevent the students that live in and visit the neighborhoods from cutting through backyards headed back to campus late at night. Usually, it's an issue after the parties and bar closings. The city regulates the number of people living in a two-story house like this, but chances are there are six or eight dudes sharing a three or four-bedroom house similar to the one here at 129 Tremont Street." The detective concluded his assessment, confident in his knowledge of what had been going on in that neighborhood over the past few years. He certainly had been around Kennison long enough to know.

Brown was progressing further in his planning mode. He inquired with Lieutenant Maloney about the availability of officers from Kennison Police to assist in an operation at the house on Tremont Street.

"We can give you whatever we have. The State Police K-9 is usually on duty around 1 p.m. for a ten-hour tour into the evening. The local troop barracks is right here in Kennison, so I can call over and ask if she's available. They are usually really good with assisting us whenever we need them to. We have a couple of detectives and me if you need us, and we can certainly free up the patrol officer working the sector around Tremont Street to help you out. I need to go run this up my chain of command sooner rather than later though." Lieutenant Maloney's cooperation and concern regarding this matter was obviously trumping whatever else he had thought he would be working on that day when he had arrived at his office. He left in haste with a page full of notes he had just written down, presumably to talk to the department commanders on the second floor.

Brown was especially adept at avoiding a turf war and facilitating the politics of playing nice in everyone's sandbox, a necessity when every town they went to as a team usually had a local police agency. Kennison Police had already shown themselves to be a valuable partner in the team's endeavors.

While Dorsey and Matthews were checking the house on Tremont Street and Brown had started organizing the plan at the local police station, Brian, the young delivery driver, had arrived in the parking lot of King's Garden. Vatrano and Pollard watched him come in the front lobby of the restaurant with some extra hustle, and they appreciated it. They also took note of his eagerness and were therefore somewhat cautious of his willingness to help. Like most skeptical investigators, they had to pick a time to trust someone, and this was that time.

"Hey Brian, Mark Pollard. I just spoke with you on the phone," Pollard introduced himself with his hand extended.

"Hey," Brian responded reaching for Pollard's outstretched hand, with some evident uncertainty.

"This is Deputy Vatrano," Pollard said cranking his head to his left to indicate who he was talking about, even though the marshals were the only two people in the room that the kid didn't know. Right after Vatrano shook Brian's hand, his phone rang. It was Dorsey looking to tell him about what they had found at 129 Tremont Street. Vatrano broke off from the conversation in the lobby and spoke on his phone outside, leaving Pollard alone with the young delivery man.

"We heard that you made a delivery over at 129 Tremont Street last week. Do you remember that one at all? It was late on that Wednesday night." Pollard wasn't going to waste too much time dancing around the important question, he was just looking for a confirmation of what he already believed to be true.

"Yeah, I remember that." The kid wasn't overly enthusiastic with his answer, most likely just a function of his personality, Pollard surmised. He was going to have to make the kid prove his memory with some detail.

"Have you made a lot of deliveries to that address before or not?" Pollard deliberately backed off of the big questions hoping to get a baseline idea about the driver's activities and how reliable his answers would be. There was no real hurry anyway, other than the pressure of the anticipation that Pollard was trying to play down.

"Yeah, it's a bunch of football guys that live there. They usually have a big order, but the one last week was just for one guy. You know, a smaller order." Pollard was happy with his ability to recall the details of the delivery without a lot of prodding, a known detail that Pollard had already learned from the owner. He was also pleased to get further confirmation of the football players living there.

"Would you remember the guy you delivered to that night if you saw a picture of him?" The questions were starting to narrow.

"I would think that I probably could," the young man replied with a slight shrug of his shoulders, still not exuding the energy in his answers that Pollard thought he might have, given his pace into the lobby.

The folded picture in his pocket had, by this time of the day, been creased and scratched up. Pollard wanted to get a clear photo for the young man to look at, so he took out his cell phone and pulled up the digital booking photo. He held the cell phone screen out in front of Brian's face a little more than a foot away. Pollard figured that looking at a digital photo on a screen was a more familiar medium for the young college kid anyway.

"Yeah, that's the guy. He was a little light on the tip too. Paid me the cash and left me just the coins." Pollard sensed a little justified annoyance in Brian's tone.

Confident in Brian's answer, especially as he added the detail about the tip, Pollard got ready to collect up Vatrano and get moving. Pollard began counting his blessings. He now had the address and an eye-witness visual of his suspect at that address nearly a week ago. To make things even better, it was an eyewitness with nothing to gain or lose by lying. Even without having the information that Vatrano was getting outside from Dorsey yet, Pollard was sky high. He thanked Brian and his boss. After providing the same warning to keep things quiet he had given the manager at Brother's Burgers, he scooted back to the truck in the still nearly empty parking lot.

A drive by 129 Tremont Street was definitely in order. While on the way over, Vatrano filled Pollard in on the details about the vehicle and information about the owner that Matthews and Dorsey had found. "That's the car that picked him up in New

Jersey, it has to be!" Pollard said before Vatrano finished describing it. Although Pollard explicitly trusted Dorsey and Matthews' report to Vatrano, he still had to see the car parked out in front of the house for himself.

A few minutes after leaving the Chinese restaurant and not quite to the house, Pollard pulled up his email on his phone. Two more pings with similar towers, direction and radius were on his email. It didn't appear to Pollard that Washington was on the move anywhere.

The phone was still on and in the area. Pollard was now flush with human intelligence about who had the phone, the address the phone should be at, and who the person was that may be with the suspect. Washington was probably inside 129 Tremont Street right now, and the curiosity of it all was killing Pollard. He regained his composure and reminded himself to take it slow. At this point he needed to act like a predator who had cornered his prey, with measured action and without mistakes. He knew Brown would be working on getting some other badges to help out.

After seeing the car in front of the house with his own two eyes, and then taking a minute to let it sink in, Pollard and Vatrano went right to Kennison Police headquarters to meet up with Brown. They passed by Dorsey and Matthews sitting on the side of Tremont Street, patiently watching the house and waiting.

Brown pressed the red button on the cracked screen of his overused cell phone, ending what had turned into a long string of coordinated telephone calls, text messages and hurried conversations. With all the information now shared with each of the members of the team, including the marshals coming from headquarters and Kennison Police, everyone appeared to be in complete agreement that they had the right house to act on. No one felt one hundred percent positive that Washington was in the house at this exact moment, but every possible sign was now leading them to Tremont Street.

Brown began to institute a surveillance rotation as a first act since Dorsey and Matthews had never left the area. They had good sightlines in the direction of the house and the newly discovered Honda Civic parked out in front. With its passenger side wheels to a granite curb that was encrusted in day's old snow smattered with road sand, anybody getting in the driver's seat would be easily seen traversing the front of the car to get to the door. The team had done this exact same thing hundreds of times before, just like they had done watching the house on Depot Street in Stanton. Deputies would rotate in and out to get food, gear up, and take a quick leak all the while maintaining a visual on the house and car.

Vatrano had broken off from Pollard and hopped in a fully marked cruiser with the Kennison patrol officer assigned to work that sector of the city. An added bonus of such a pairing of a local officer and a member of the team would be the greatly enhanced communications between the agencies. The plan was for the marked car with Vatrano in it to remain out of sight, but to be available should someone need to be stopped or identified in a more discreet or common way. A patrol officer from the town instead of the heavily armed men in tactical gear tended to prevent a big commotion or attention-grabbing scene. Avoiding an action sure to provide the spark in this college town that could get word back to Washington was paramount. Vatrano went with light gear in case he was needed to conduct an interview of someone coming or leaving from the house without drawing that unwanted attention.

Brown, with a scribbled list of cell phone numbers for the members of the Kennison Police Department that might be joining in at some point, jumped in the passenger seat of the truck with Pollard so he could continue to coordinate and not have driving responsibilities. Knowing Pollard had all the case information made the pairing even more advantageous for the man in the position of responsibility. They made their way out to the Tremont Street neighborhood where Matthews and Dorsey were reporting no activity from their perch on the street just up from the suspected address.

The idle hands and anticipation had become somewhat overbearing for most of the group. They all knew to a man that the correct thing to do was to ascertain confirmation beyond a phone ping with a three hundred yard or larger radius of confidence. That fact didn't make it any easier to sit and watch a house, especially when they thought a murderer was inside. It was a shared feeling, but one that went unsaid.

The late February daylight had already begun to fade. There had been some light activity in the area of the residence with minimal foot traffic and cars driving on the streets nearby, but nothing directly associated with the property at 129 Tremont Street. A few cars from up and down the street had come and gone, parking and leaving again, or not coming back at all. No one, it had appeared, took any notice of the team members or their vehicles in the quiet neighborhood.

"It's a good thing we're sitting in a college campus neighborhood. I don't think a single person has even looked at us. Almost everyone that has walked by has had headphones in and was looking at their phone." Dorsey's message pierced through the radio catching Pollard off guard as he was getting used to the lack of chatter. Another young female walked past with a lack of situational awareness of her surroundings almost on Dorsey's cue, surroundings that included vehicles foreign to the neighborhood full of heavily armed men. There was still no sign of Washington in the area. There was also no sign of his friend, Hamel, other than the car still parked on the street where it had been since Dorsey and Matthews first laid eyes on it in late morning.

"Don't any of these guys go to class?" Brown, following Dorsey's invitation for chatter, was growing more impatient with the situation with nothing going on at the home they were all staring at so intently.

"I'm sure we'll get some sort of activity out here soon enough," Pollard stated while making eye contact with Brown sitting in the next seat over. It was the best he could do to pacify Brown's instincts and desire for action. As soon as Pollard got the last word out of his mouth, the radio cracked.

"Movement on the back deck, movement on the back deck!" It was Matthews calling out the motion he could see from his view of the back side of the residence. "It looks like someone's ripping a cigarette and talking on the phone. He just came out from the slider door!"

"Is it our guy?" Someone had to ask the obvious question and Brown had beaten everyone to it as he was still holding his radio from his previous transmission.

"It's a possible for our guy... same build. He has a winter hat and heavy coat on though. Not real sure." Matthews knew he couldn't be cavalier in throwing out a positive identification that wasn't certain, especially with Brown's penchant for action. Dorsey, from the driver's seat next to Matthews, was trying to get a better view with his binoculars before making his own assessment.

The clear day and sky at dusk had deceived the crew into thinking that they could see without any difficulty. They couldn't approach the male on the deck, even though it was possibly

Washington, for fear of tipping him off if it wasn't him and he wasn't home. They couldn't lose him now, knowing full well that if he wasn't there at present, he would be sooner or later.

The male eventually retreated inside the house. Matthews called that out over the radio too, a little disappointed that he was never able to make a positive identification of what was essentially nothing more than a silhouette in the distance. Dorsey's inability to make an identification with the binoculars gave Matthews a little bit of solace. He was only outside long enough for a smoke, he figured. It wasn't really a nice night to hang out on the deck during a northern New Hampshire February evening.

A few minutes later and the team could now see the glow of the interior lights of the house as they were coming on, highlighting the motion of the people within. By their best guess, there were at least a couple of people in the house based on that activity, having seen two separate individuals moving at the same time. There were some windows that didn't have shades drawn that allowed vision right into the kitchen area, the only windows in the house with such a view inside. Dorsey tried to get a good look in with the binoculars but was unable to see anyone. They then decided to send Matthews, in plain clothes and with a younger look, on a walk past the house a few times, to make an attempt to see inside on each passing trip. He was unable to confirm any sighting of Washington through the windows on any of his passes by. As Matthews got back to the vehicle, he and Dorsey observed another male walking towards their position on the street from the rear of their parked vehicle.

"Brownie, are you able to get a look at the guy coming up behind us? He fits the description, and it looks like he's headed in the direction of the house." Dorsey was grasping at straws, hoping that Washington would just be out on the street. That was an easy and safer grab than entering the house, though more likely to result in a foot pursuit.

"That guy has got to be at least sixty pounds heavier than our guy," Brown responded. They watched as the larger man continued walking past the house without going in. It wasn't Washington, they confirmed as he strolled past Pollard and Brown from just a few feet away on the sidewalk. There was almost no activity in the whole neighborhood for about an hour after that. It must be dinner time, they figured.

The sun was now completely down over the horizon. The night had gone to total darkness except for the streetlights and the occasional passing headlights. Pollard began thinking back to some of his overnight shifts in Windsor and how he could tell when certain lights in the neighborhoods and business districts weren't illuminated in their normal manner. His bladder was telling him that it had now been a few hours sitting in the truck, watching, anticipating, and preparing. Pollard also couldn't help but miss the ancillary benefit of having a place to piss nearly anywhere in town in the middle of the night, all while remaining undetected.

This workday had started long before the sun came up when he and the members of the team left their respective houses, and it was now pressing past dinner time. The sun's shift was about to end for the day, while theirs would continue.

TWENTY-FOUR

Pollard's daydreaming, or more accurately, evening dreaming, was cut short in an instant as a male appeared from the front door of 129 Tremont Street. Brown, with the best view of that door, immediately called the action out over the radio with a precise play-by-play.

"He's coming down the walkway. Looks like he's getting in the Civic. Unsure if it's our guy. He has a hooded sweatshirt on!" Brown did his best to control his urge to pounce, an act of disciplined restraint he didn't know he had in him. "Vatrano, you still with Kennison PD?" he asked knowingly over the airwaves. For the same reason the team didn't want to roll up on the male smoking the cigarette on the porch, they didn't want to tip off Washington if this wasn't him leaving the house now. There was always the possibility of a heat run.

"Affirmative Brownie, we're right around the corner. Let us know on the direction of travel when the Civic pulls out." Vatrano was excited to get in on the act as he hadn't even had a house to stare at. His entire afternoon and evening had been spent staying out of sight in the marked cruiser with a local patrol officer he didn't even know. He knew what Brown was asking for him to do without having to give the order to do it.

"He's got the car started up, and he's pulling ahead." The vehicle rolled down Tremont Street right towards Brown and Pollard's truck where they had been sitting about one hundred and fifty feet from where the car was initially parked. They were hoping to get a good look at the driver as he passed by them, driver's side door to driver's side door. The driver's window of Pollard's truck had begun to fog up a little bit due to the body heat contrasting with the cold outside air. Each member of the team had shut off their engines when it got dark out to avoid detection. After dark, light shining on the fumes from a running vehicle could give away their positions and compromise the surveillance.

Pollard wiped the condensation clear with his left sweatshirt sleeve as the black Honda Civic approached them getting up to cruising speed. The yellow coloring of the front, New York license plate was a shimmering contrast with the dark car and darker night as a backdrop. The glare of the oncoming headlights, finding a path directly to their eyes, made it difficult to see the interior of the small car.

"He still has his hood on. I can't make him either way," a frustrated Pollard said to Brown. Brown then relayed the message to the other units on his handheld radio. It was still unknown who was driving the car other than the fact that it was a male with a hood on. It could be Washington or Hamel, or anyone else with access to the car.

"Vatrano, you guys follow that for a little bit, he's coming towards you. Dorsey, you guys go back him up. Everyone else stay in position near the house!" Brown was now taking firm control of the movements of the team he was charged with leading.

Dorsey confirmed they were on their way as they drove past Brown and Pollard's location about ten seconds after the Civic had passed. A murder suspect might be driving the car they would be trying stop once out of sight of the house, which meant also out of sight of the rest of the team members. The murder suspect could, in theory, still be in the house, a Schrodinger's cat situation that required both dangerous possibilities to be treated as true.

"We see him coming right at us over by the traffic light next to Brother's Burgers. We see you coming too, Dorsey." Vatrano let everyone know the exact driving route the vehicle was taking via radio. The fully marked cruiser slid out into the light traffic behind the Civic while leaving some space to prevent the appearance that they were going to pull him over immediately. When Dorsey and Matthews had caught up behind the marked cruiser and confirmed they were ready to take action, the blue strobe lights of the Kennison Police car brilliantly lit up the darkness around them. The Civic didn't immediately pull over as required. Vatrano thought for sure this would end in a pursuit, something no one wanted, a murder suspect driving a deadly weapon. A quick bleep of the siren pierced through the anxious silence between Vatrano and the Kennison officer driving the cruiser. That auditory invasion was far more effective than the visual strobes. Either way, the crew was happy that it got the driver's attention.

The Civic pulled into the parking lot of the strip mall to his immediate right, slowing and then coming to a complete stop under a lamp post perfectly illuminating the area around it. The vehicles of the lawmen who had been behind him followed. Dorsey did not put his lights on for fear of making too much commotion after the vehicle had come to a stop already, but he did pull into the lot with the marked cruiser. He brought his vehicle to a parked position directly to the right of the black and white patrol car, but still behind the Civic. The actions of the operator to immediately comply with pulling over at the sound of a siren and then the sight of blue lights had the team members believing that it was not Washington. They weren't ready to bet on it yet though, certainly not with their own safety as their ante.

Dorsey and Matthews unholstered their weapons and came up between the passenger side of the marked cruiser and the driver's side of their own truck. The Kennison officer got out on his driver's side, drew his pistol, and crouched behind his now open cruiser door while able to keep a visual on both sides of the car. Vatrano went around the backside of the cruiser and then approached the driver's door of the Civic. Matthews and Dorsey went towards the passenger side of the suspect's vehicle, careful to stay on an imaginary line with Vatrano so that neither group got too close too fast.

"Police, put your hands on the steering wheel where I can see them!" Vatrano shouted as he got closer to the rear, driver's side, fender of the Civic. Dorsey and Matthews could see into the car as the vehicle was spotlighted from the cruiser and the ambient glow of the overhead lamp post lights casting around them. It was only clear to them that the driver's right hand was on the wheel, they couldn't see his left from their side of the vehicle. It also did not appear as though anyone else was in the vehicle, a detail that they didn't take for granted even though they had watched only one person get in the car. After making brief eye contact, they both nodded to Vatrano to let him know that the driver had complied.

Dorsey yelled out to Vatrano, who was now joined by the Kennison officer, "We got a right hand, do you have the left?" Vatrano could clearly see the driver's left hand on the wheel through the open driver's window where the operator was expecting the approach of an officer.

He replied back, "Got left!" It was the confirmation needed to move forward. In unison, Vatrano from the driver's side and Dorsey and Matthews from the passenger side, approached. They were careful to keep the driver positioned in front of them and not to either side to avoid a crossfire situation, should it come to that.

The driver had pulled his hood off earlier as he was being pulled over, so the deputies could now clearly see his head, though just the back of it and a little bit of a side profile. Vatrano approached with a few careful steps, briefly taking his focus off the hands of the driver positioned at ten and two on the steering wheel. He was quickly able to recognize the driver as Hamel, from the social media photos. Vatrano, looking down into the vehicle, observed the license and registration in the hands of the driver maintaining the requisite grip on the steering wheel. The documents were immaterial to the deputy, the only thing that really mattered was that nothing in the driver's hands were a threat.

The young man was initially confused by the low-profile attire of Vatrano coming from the marked cruiser. Further perplexing the young driver was the thought of a minor traffic offense that he was unsure he had even committed. As Vatrano saw the documents coming to him from the shaking left hand of the driver, over the roof of the car he made eye contact with Dorsey and shook his head "no" in an exaggerated manner to make sure it was clear. Dorsey knew exactly what it meant, and it was what he expected. He went out over the radio to Brown and the other members keeping a watchful eye on the house.

"We've got the car stopped, not our guy, not our guy, not our guy." He repeated it three times and added some emphasis to let everyone know that the actual suspect could still be in the house. The remaining members on Tremont Street needed to stay vigilant around that house, as their cover may have been blown by current activities taking place so publicly at the strip mall near the main drag in town. It put each of the deputies still near the house at an even higher state of alertness, sensing that things were about to get real. "Vatrano's going to start on an interview." He knew he had to keep Brown apprised to prevent the constant request for more information, and he was hoping to alleviate distractions.

"Copy, not our guy. Copy," Brown replied while getting ready to strive toward another great personal effort in patience.

Pollard's focus on the house was now laser like. With one less male in the house, the odds had improved as though a dealer playing three card monte had just slashed it to two. They had all come to a consensus earlier in the evening that there were two, maybe three people in the house, before the one leaving in the car was accounted for.

Pollard had complete trust in Vatrano's ability to get the information that was required from the driver of the Civic. Vatrano had been prepping this case all along, and he knew the players and places involved as well as anyone else. He had a firm grasp on what had gotten the team to this time and moment and what was about to happen next. Furthermore, he was an excellent interviewer, with his legal experience as a training ground for just this type of moment. Though even Vatrano would admit, this was no deposition at some conference table in the offices of a cushy law firm and different tactics may be necessary.

Brown was now on the phone with Detective Lieutenant Maloney from the Kennison Police Department. That conversation was just background noise to Pollard who was still focused on the house. It sounded to him like Charlie Brown's parents were talking on both sides of the phone.

"If we can get the K-9 over to the area of Tremont and a couple of your detectives or patrol officers, that would be perfect." Brown knew that with a car stop taking up some of his resources he would need more staffing to lockdown the perimeter of the house to prevent any attempted flight of the suspect.

"I already got the heads up from our guy with your guys over at the car stop at the mall. Trooper Charron and her K-9 are on the way from the barracks. Detective Noyes and I are on the way over as well. We'll be there in less than five minutes, we just got in the car." Brown could hear that they were on the move by the shortness of breath and speed of his answers, while the engine of the Ford Crown Victoria revved in the background. It was certainly a distinct sound to most cops, especially those who might be calling for assistance. The pieces were moving that Brown needed, now he would just have to wait, along with everyone else, to see what Vatrano could get out of the kid in the Civic.

"You're from Utica, huh?" Vatrano was holding the man's driver's license in his left hand with his right hand on his now holstered weapon. Dorsey and Matthews, on the other side of the vehicle, still had guns drawn and pointed to the pavement, but they could not be seen by the driver who had turned over his left shoulder toward Vatrano to speak with him. Vatrano began his conversation like he had so many others, with an easy question that both he and the recipient of that question knew the answer to and would therefore be difficult to lie about. He could see the young man's hands on the steering wheel gripping tight, which was often a sign of tension and nervousness. Vatrano knew the signs well but was put at ease as the hand placement, no matter how tight, implied a certain lack of potential threat to him. It was also now obvious that the kid was all alone in the vehicle, making the safety of the four officers on scene that much more definite.

"Yes, sir. Utica." An honest answer as it had to be, given Vatrano had clearly just looked at his driver's license. He recognized Adam Hamel's name from the printout that he still had in his pocket; the final positive identification needed.

"Listen, I'm Tony Vatrano from the United States Marshals Service," he started. "We didn't pull you over for any vehicle infraction tonight, so take a second and relax. I do need to talk to you about a pretty serious issue that you might have some information about though." Vatrano was intentionally vague to see if the young man might utter something about his suspected house guest. It didn't work out that way.

"Okay, but I feel like this is some kind of joke. Am I being pranked? I'm new here, is this like a hazing ritual?" He didn't say it in a rude way, but in more of a manner of disbelief.

"This is absolutely not a joke. Can you step out of the car for me and place your hands on the roof?" The simple request was the first step in the ask, order, demand trilogy that would give some indication as to the young man's anticipated level of cooperation. It was a tactic similar to a parent counting out loud to three for a child.

Vatrano took a step back as the kid swung open his door with a high-pitched squeak from the cold and under-lubricated hinges, clearly choosing to comply at step one. The group of deputies in the strip mall parking lot were anticipating that it was a sign of more cooperation to come.

Matthews had rotated around to the driver's side of the car to offer support to Vatrano as the young man had stepped out. Hamel rotated and placed his hands flat on the still cold roof of the car, now facing the passenger side of the vehicle. He made eye contact with Dorsey who had held his position on that side of the Civic for the duration of the interaction. Dorsey offered half of a smile to him as though he knew what was going to happen next because Dorsey, of course, did know what was going to happen next. The sight of Dorsey and Matthews in full tactical gear let the young man gauge the seriousness of the matter without a further word being spoken.

After Vatrano patted the man down and was given verbal assurance that there were no weapons on his person, it was time to get some much-needed information about their man. Up to this point, Hamel had been completely cooperative, and Vatrano was hoping to keep that momentum going throughout his questioning. He asked Hamel to take his hands off the roof and turn and face him.

"So, I'm going to be straight with you and I need you to do the same with me. We just saw you coming out of 129 Tremont Street. We followed you here to stop and have a chat about that." Vatrano wanted to lay a baseline with the kid. He knew that someone who felt as though he was being watched would have reason to believe the person asking the questions knew certain other things that he couldn't lie about. "Is that where you are living right now?" It was another easy question, and one that he would have no reason to lie about.

"Yeah, that's where I live. I just moved here at the start of the semester. I transferred here to Kennison State from my old college in Buffalo."

"In January, right?" Vatrano didn't really know when the kid had actually moved there, but he figured the winter semester probably started in January and wanted to reinforce the idea again that he knew a great deal about the young man and his activities.

"Yeah, I did, right after Christmas. Why?" the young man asked, starting to believe that the stranger inquiring might not be a stranger to him at all. That impression was creating an unbalanced relationship between the two men.

Vatrano ignored the question that had been asked back at him and continued down his path, showcasing his knowledge about the individual in front of him. The kid was now shaking, partly from being questioned by law enforcement, but also from the cold February temperatures that seemed to plummet immediately after the sun went down. It was turning into what the team jokingly referred to as a north country waterboarding, except instead of water and a fear of drowning, it was cold temperatures and a fear of freezing that got them answers.

"You're on the football team, right?" Another question they both knew the answer to, asked with a purpose.

"Yeah man, just transferred here like I said. We've got a team meeting tonight over at the athletics complex. I'm on the way over there now. How'd you know that?" His concern for why Vatrano knew such things was rising.

Vatrano again ignored the question and followed up quickly with his own. "Is it all football players over there living with you on Tremont Street, or are there others?"

"Yeah, there's five of us. We're all on the football team," he said without hesitation.

Vatrano had given the young man enough softball questions and he was hoping to keep the momentum going with a few more direct questions, but not the big one yet. "Anyone new recently move in with you guys? You know, since you moved over here in January?"

"Nah, man, no one new. I am the new guy."

It was the kid's first trip up. Vatrano thought Hamel might be a little dishonest as he was confident Washington would be in the house, but he wanted to make sure it wasn't just a minor miscommunication. Having someone stay on the couch or in the basement for a few days or even a couple of weeks doesn't necessarily mean by everyone's definition that they've moved in.

Vatrano was going to give the kid a chance to clarify. He figured now was the time for the visual portion of the interview, as it might have a memory jogging effect. It also might be a more effective way to show that he knew one more thing about the kid.

Without saying a word, Vatrano pulled out his phone, tapped on the photo of Washington and enhanced it out to full screen. He turned the phone and held it up toward Hamel's face. Vatrano then asked the exact same question, in the exact same manner and tone, while looking directly into the kid's eyes as he waited for the answer. "Anyone new recently move in with you guys? You know, since you moved over here in January?" Vatrano wasn't waiting to hear the answer, but rather, was intent on watching the young man's facial reactions and body language when he saw the photo. Hamel looked at the phone screen, looked at the ground, and lowered his head even a bit further. It was all Vatrano needed to see.

"How do you know Mr. Washington?" Vatrano skipped to the next question without giving him a chance to answer the previous one that he had to ask twice. It was implied by Vatrano that he knew the answer, just like he knew about the football team and what house he left from and when he had moved into that house last month. It put the young man in a position where he knew it was pointless to lie.

"That's my cousin, John. He said that people were trying to kill him down in Jersey and he needed to hide out. He's been here for a few days now. Man, his kid is my godson, his mom is my favorite aunt. I grew up with him in New Hampshire before I moved to New York with my mom and stepdad when I was like twelve years old. John is like a brother to me. Is he in trouble with you guys too?" Hamel knew all too well about Washington's previous time in prison. It was an obvious question with an obvious answer, but to continue with the rapport he had developed, Vatrano humored him with an answer instead of ignoring this one. To reinforce the seriousness of the situation, he provided a very blunt answer.

"He's wanted on a homicide." The answer fired out of Vatrano's pursed and tightened lips. There was no smile, no frown, just facts. The plain answer appeared to have stunned the young man.

"Holy shit man. Are you serious?" It looked to Vatrano as though the young man's shock was sincere, and not some act. He had already told them without actually saying the words, where Washington could be found. There was no further need for dishonesty or unnecessary theatrics.

"I wouldn't make something like that up," Vatrano said with almost no emotion in his voice. "But here's the thing. You've got a guy wanted for murder in your house. I know you care about him and all, but he's going to get arrested in this little college town that you just moved to. That's probably not going to be good for you, or your status on this new football team of yours, especially if you don't fully cooperate with us on this." Although Hamel had been cooperative, Vatrano didn't want the magnitude of a murder charge to get in the way of continued compliance that was morphing into assistance. A reminder of what he might have to lose for not continuing the help would do the trick. The young man just nodded with tears starting to form in the corner of his eyes, no doubt from the emotion of the situation he found himself in, but also encouraged by the cold breeze whipping across the mall parking lot.

"He's in that house right now," Vatrano stated while raising his dark eyebrows. He was only somewhat sure of it, but he started his preamble with conviction anyway. "And we know you just left there. What room is he staying in?" Vatrano was going for the final knockout blow.

"He's been staying in the basement. He's got a mattress set up down there. He's been trying to stay out of everyone's way because I'm new here." Hamel was now shaking his head side to side with disbelief as each phrase he blurted out reached a new level of frustration. "My housemates and teammates are going to fuckin' kill me, man. My new coach is going to kill me!" Just as Vatrano had hoped, the seriousness of the matter was beginning to register even in such a short time.

Vatrano, having attained his main goal of the interaction, asked a few more follow up questions about possible weapons that Washington might have access to, the layout of the house, and how many people should be home. He felt confident that he got honest answers to those inquires as the point to lie about something had long since passed.

"So. You are going to stay here with this officer from Kennison PD." Vatrano motioned to the patrol officer just to make sure the kid knew which of the lawmen he was referring to, though it would have become obvious after three of the four had left. "You can have a seat in your car to stay warm, but you are not to get on the phone at all. Do you understand me?" Vatrano waited for a confirmation of understanding knowing he didn't have a legal right to take the device.

"I got you man." He replied in a dejected but serious tone.

"You are in no trouble right now. If you tip your cousin off and someone gets hurt, you will definitely be charged with several serious crimes. The house is already surrounded so he's not getting away. A call wouldn't help him anyway, it would only create a situation that would get him and you into more trouble, or worse." It was clear to the young man what the expectation was for everyone involved, but most importantly himself.

Matthews, Dorsey, and Vatrano jumped in the car and started towards Tremont Street while letting the entire crew know over the radio that the target of their investigation over the last couple weeks was indeed at the house they were all staring at. Waiting at the stop light to make the left toward Tremont Street, the New Hampshire State Police K-9 passed them at a quick pace, making the turn in front of them at a cross street. They made radio contact with Brown specifically to verify that all three of them were on their way back to the area of the house to join in.

CHAPTER TWENTY-FIVE

An operational plan rarely survives the initial contact with an adversary. That is a paraphrased, timeless, age old, standard law enforcement adage, probably stolen from the military. Put in movie industry terms, the actions and results of the team could be directed, but not produced. Everything up to this point in the investigation into the whereabouts of John Washington was part of a plan that had continuously evolved, with parts getting thrown out and new pieces added as the information changed. Brown and Dorsey started discussing the plan of how to extract the wanted murderer from the house on Tremont Street. The new intelligence that Vatrano had gathered from the interview of Washington's cousin factored heavily into how that initial contact would be made. Unlike the attempt to locate Washington back in Stanton where the team had to finesse consent from the women living there, getting him out of the house on Tremont Street was markedly different.

Washington's cousin had confirmed that the wanted man was inside the house at that exact moment in time. Furthermore, he confirmed that for the past several weeks or more, that was where Washington had been residing and would therefore be considered his residence in the eyes of the applicable, constitutionally settled case law. The information provided could not have been any more contemporaneous as the cousin had left the house just a few minutes before, and the team members had eyes fixed on all sides of the house to confirm no one else had exited. They now had probable cause that this was the suspect's residence and probable cause to believe that he was in there at that exact time. No type of search warrant was necessary, and none would be applied for. No one needed to grant them access to the home or give their consent to search it. Dorsey made it clear to everyone over the radio where they stood on entry.

"We're going in on train tracks, boys," he said over the radio with what Pollard could only assume was a twinkle in Dorsey's eye that he couldn't confirm from distant vehicles. For some of the members of the team, putting the clues together to find a suspect were the more challenging and interesting parts of the job. For others, like Dorsey, knocking on and smashing through a door, screaming "US Marshal!" and grabbing up the suspect after tactically searching a house was the best part, even more fun if the suspect was hiding. Pollard had always been undecided as to which aspect he preferred since both could be a great mental and physical challenge. At this point, Pollard felt he had done his best as an investigator, with quite a bit of help, to get the team outside of a house that they knew their suspect was in. He was happy to leave the tactics of the approach to Brown, the team leader, and Dorsey, the tactical master, while he waited on the word to go get the object of his efforts over the past several days.

All involved parties on the fugitive team and from the local law enforcement agencies confirmed they were ready to deploy to their respective positions. Dorsey led the entry team on the way up the walkway to the house with Matthews, Brown, Vatrano, Pollard and the two other marshals who had arrived from headquarters right behind him. Kennison Police personnel, including a couple of detectives, the lieutenant, and the K-9 Trooper Charron from the State Police, accompanied by her four-legged German Shepard, Arkel, took up positions on each corner of the house. They each approached the perimeter posts with footsteps quiet as possible with the crunch of days old snow coming from under their feet and paws. This created a ring around the house with sightlines where each officer could see two other corners and the silhouettes of the other officers standing there.

The only streetlight in the area was about seventy-five feet from the house casting its light downward, and only really backlighting the area and not the structure itself. The ambient glow of interior lights from the neighborhood was just enough so that the motion of the men approaching the door could be seen, but their movements were like shadows and tough to clearly make out. The darkness had created a reliable cover that would allow them to get to the edge of the property undetected by seemingly anyone in the area and most importantly, from inside the house.

The group of seven deputies responsible for entering the home got closer to the house, preparing to dominate the inside. They stacked up in line with their left shoulders making contact to the exterior wall and the main door in front of them on that same left side. Dorsey had assurances from Hamel that the house would be unlocked. Never willing to take chances when unnecessary, he lugged the fifty-pound battering ram with him anyway. He did not want to approach a closed door without the tool he affectionately referred to as his key to any city.

Dorsey looked back towards the formation of men behind him. He felt like the lead guy on the toboggan and needed to confirm everyone was ready to do some serious sledding. To the Kennison and State Police personnel on perimeter duty, it looked like all seven guys could be riding the same motorcycle, they had strategically grouped so tightly.

Dorsey crouched down like a catcher behind home plate, just below window level on the front door and checked, ever so slightly, to see if the doorknob would turn. Getting confirmation through that brief action that the door was unlocked, he gently placed the ram in the snowbank to avoid any loud thuds, knowing he wasn't going to need it. He removed his handgun from his holster and placed it in his dominant left hand and made three separate fist pumps with his closed right hand like a referee counting off seconds. The cadence put the team into a rhythmic unison before they would enter on the third first pump, like the sticks of a drummer setting the beat for the whole band to start the next song.

Dorsey, noting that the front door was out-swinging to his right, opened the door, held it ajar and then got out of the door opening while holding it in place as Matthews entered first with a ballistic shield. They flowed into the house like water breaking through the first crack in a dam. Brown, the assigned initial vocalist to keep announcements clear and not muddled, was yelling "Police with a warrant!" and "US Marshals!" several times in succession both before and after passing the threshold of the main door. When Pollard traversed from outside into the home, the familiar scent of stale beer and sweaty athletic clothes hit him in the face, a quick reminder of his own college residences back in the day.

The first floor was cleared in what felt like mere moments with seven deputies. It consisted of just the kitchen, a half bath and a large open dining and living room area. The main floor was deemed void of any humans other than the group of deputies that had just entered.

As directed in the plan, Matthews took the shield and two others to what Washington's cousin had described to be the basement door. Vatrano and Pollard held a position at the bottom of the stairs going up to the bedrooms. It would be insurance that Washington couldn't surprise them coming down if he was up there, as the others were headed into the basement. Matthews was about to open the basement door when the officers from Kennison near the back deck and stockade fenced-in yard began shouting with urgency. The barks of the K-9 overpowered and drowned out what his human partners were screaming at, making it impossible for the group inside the house to understand exactly what was happening. Brown and the two other marshals that had arrived from headquarters turned from their position behind Matthews at the top of the basement steps and went back outside via the main front door that they had all just entered from. Making their way around to the other side of the exterior of the house, they found the K-9, the trooper handling him, and a Kennison detective yelling up towards the roof.

John Washington, making his first actual appearance to the team that had been hunting him, had come out on the roof through an open dormer window. It appeared his initial plan was to hang over the edge and drop down to the ground in a desperate attempt to evade the men coming through the house. Seeing that the drop put him just a few short yards from becoming dinner for the police dog making powerful leaps toward his dangling feet, he made the choice to hoist himself back through the open dormer window.

"He's on the roof, he's on the roof!" Brown radioed back to the remaining deputies inside.

In the time it took for Washington to get off the roof and crawl back through the still open window, Matthews, with the shield in front, Vatrano, Dorsey, and Pollard had gotten to the top of the stairway leading to the second floor. Hearing the sounds and feeling the cool breeze of an open window, they made a direct route to the bedroom where Washington was coming back in through the opening. A left leg and foot appeared from the night sky on the other side. As Washington was put his second foot on the carpeted bedroom floor below the window, he looked up at the screaming deputies.

Brown's role as sole communicator had dissolved. All four deputies began to shout at Washington, "Get on the ground!" and "Show your hands, show your hands!" Washington heard the voices from the other side of the small window in the black shield, with Matthews' blue eyes staring intently at him. Matthews didn't give Washington time to comply with the orders. He didn't really give him time to react at all, as the ask, order, demand sequence went from zero to its abrupt end in less than a second.

Lunging forward, the top edge and side of the shield struck Washington in the chest sending him back. Matthews, pushing hard into the murder suspect, lost his footing when the counter resistance of Washington's weight had evaporated as he stumbled backward and down to the ground.

The hand-held shield was now the filling of the sandwich between Washington and Matthews as they went from vertical to horizontal. The holders did their job, as 900 pounds of "man meat" landed on top of Matthews, who was on top of his shield, that was on top of Washington, morphing the sandwich into something more closely resembling a lasagna.

Even if he wanted to, Washington was not going to be able to resist and break free. He didn't offer up much resistance, either due to his respect for the laws of man or from his inability to overcome the laws of physics. No one could really tell which in the moment. Pollard was able to get his weapon holstered, his own hands free and get a handcuff on Washington's left hand. Dorsey and Vatrano were then able roll Washington over, marrying the right hand behind his back with the left in the set of chain-linked cuffs.

With Washington in custody and checked to make sure he was unarmed, Dorsey looked out the still open dormer window down to the ground at Brown and the rest of the crew with a thumbs up to let them know that Washington was in cuffs. And for the sake of safety, he also stated over the radio, to make sure everyone had the news, his two favorite words in a fugitive hunt, "in custody!"

Matthews had rolled Washington onto his hip and then into the seated position. Pollard glanced quickly at Dorsey hanging his head out of the window. The sense of relief that Pollard started to experience was like a near miss on a high-speed car accident. He was calmed knowing they didn't end up on the roof with the suspect for the same reason he never became a firefighter, because he just might have pissed his pants a little. It was a thought he could only address with the luxury of having his target located, and now safely under control.

That moment was the first time anyone on the team had met the man they had been looking to find for so long. Pollard briefly returned back to his thoughts of the relationship that they shared as the hunter and the hunted. The fugitive track had come to an end, with the relationship soon to follow that same fate. Pollard chuckled as he thought about the fact that Washington's version went from having no idea who might be looking for him, to having almost all of those people on top of him in a split second at his first encounter. No introductions, no background information. Just a pile up of law enforcing humanity in that second-floor bedroom on this chilly February night in Kennison, New Hampshire.

"Got him, coming down." Dorsey let the other team members know over the radio, a little winded from the short, but intense skirmish that had just ensued. No other occupants were located within the house, and it was now safe to move Washington out. The joyous and high-pitched praises of the K-9 handler coming through the open window caught Pollard's attention. He felt as though the praise for the dog was justified. He also felt it might have been a symbolic praise for the local, state, and federal law enforcement officers that were able to get Washington into custody safely. They all deserved a nice pat on the head and a tasty treat, Pollard surmised, if not a little bit selfishly.

Matthews pulled a chair out from underneath the kitchen table so that Washington could sit while they figured out transport arrangements. It was one part of the plan that was rarely discussed before an operation because it implied that the suspect would be caught, and they didn't want to tempt the gods of superstition. Washington had sat down on the chair at the kitchen table with his hands restrained behind his back under the watchful guard of several heavily armed men. The mood had lightened for the team as it often did with a successful capture. Their suspect was in custody, no one was hurt or worse, and the long day that started well before sun-up nearly a hundred miles away had an end in sight as the clock neared 8 p.m.

"Just like we planned," Brown said with a deep chuckle as he walked back into the house to find the group around the table. The statement was a nod to the old adage, and a chance for everyone to smile about the few seconds it took for the operational plan to evolve, or devolve, on first contact.

They were now awaiting the arrival of one of the marked Kennison Police vehicles with a proper barrier to contain Washington in the back seat so he could be brought in.

Brown, with the thought of his own dark skin and Washington's white supremacist connections now on the front of his mind, took the liberty of breaking the ice with the fugitive as he sat at the table awaiting his ride.

"So, Mr. Washington, you'll be headed over to the Kennison Police Department right now and then held over at the county jail to await your return to NH State Prison on this parole warrant we have here for you." It was an unintentional oversight by Brown because the New Hampshire State Prison was just the next step. But the look on Washington's face had everyone more than a little confused. A wry smile crossed his tense lips and Washington spoke out loud for the first time that anyone on the team had heard in the few minutes that they had been in his company.

"All of this for a god-damn parole warrant?" he asked, looking at the several heavily armored men staring back at him, though this time not in a large pile on top of him. It was a question they had heard before from one of the women on that morning in Stanton, and they never did correct her. He hadn't given Brown a chance to finish explaining what was next, most notably his charges from and eventual return to New Jersey. It was an overly optimistic and incorrect assumption that this whole event was all over the armed robbery from several years ago that he had been paroled on and absconded from. A few more months back in the prison in New Hampshire with his old gang would be a cakewalk, Washington was no doubt thinking. The smug facial expression was about to change as quickly as it had appeared.

As the whole team had been chasing him for murder, the question didn't quite fit, or worse, it was just some silly, almost snarky, way for Washington to maintain his innocence on the murder charge. Vatrano always had the last word for anyone showing an inappropriate attitude for the seriousness of any situation. He leaned over the table and said in a low, whispering tone, "And you killed a guy," as if it was obvious to everyone else in the room, because it was. After a brief pause, he finished his statement, "Allegedly, of course," in his own snarky way. Vatrano didn't wait for a response and just walked away, mostly for effect, but also because he didn't have it in him to listen to the bullshit after all the work they had put in over the past weeks.

The comment had the effect he intended because Washington appeared to be in quiet reflection almost immediately. It was the first time he learned that the man he had shot had been killed in the incident, not something processed quickly. His meditation on the matter was interrupted by Brown, in his baritone voice, making a basic inquiry regarding Washington's sock covered feet.

"Got any kicks my man?" The game was over for Brown, there was no need to deprive Washington of something as basic as footwear. With hands still cuffed behind his back and unable to point, he motioned with his head toward the door where a pile of sneakers, sandals and boots sat waiting for the feet of the residents of the house.

"The blue Nikes," he mumbled in a subdued and defeated manner.

Brown quietly placed each sneaker in front of the corresponding foot like a parent would for a toddler. He didn't provide any direction and Washington didn't ask. Sliding each foot into a sneaker, he failed to make eye contact with Brown, or any of the others in the room. It remained quiet for a few more minutes until the marked cruiser arrived to start him on the first leg of a trip that would eventually get him back to the Garden State.

As Pollard and Brown placed Washington in the rear of the Kennison cruiser, Washington looked up at Brown hoping for a last-ditch way out. "They're going to kill me down there in Camden. Man, I can't go back!" he pleaded, almost begging, as though he wanted to say something the whole time sitting at the kitchen table but didn't. No sympathy leaked out of Brown or Pollard. After all, this was all business to them, a warrant for the arrest of the body of John Washington. With confirmation that Washington's legs were out of the way, Brown gave the back door of the cruiser a nudge causing it to close.

The team swept their way through the house one more time, checking for any gear they may have lost in the tussle or left behind. After accounting for all the team members, Dorsey scooped up the battering ram that he didn't have the opportunity to use on his way past the still open front door.

A small group of concerned and curious college students were on the sidewalk across the street and on some of the front porches of the neighborhood houses. None seemed familiar with the man carted away in the cruiser, as the whispers and rumors were no doubt flying. Dorsey smiled and waved with his empty hand not carrying the battering ram as one student was holding up his phone clearly taking video of the scene.

The deputies went back to their vehicles and began the parade of sorts towards the Kennison Police headquarters. Vatrano placed a call over to the officer still with Hamel in the parking lot of the shopping mall. He was advised of the successful resolution and told to notify Hamel about his cousin's extradition hearing the following morning in the local court in town.

With his arms pinned behind his back and a seatbelt holding him from moving too far forward, Washington couldn't really do anything but look to the front, to his left or to his right. It wasn't a long ride from 129 Tremont Street to the Kennison Police Headquarters, but there was enough time for Washington to start thinking about the events leading up to him being in that caged seat behind the uniformed officer driving.

He spent the most time trying to figure out how the fugitive team had found him. Suspicion arose in his head around his mother or maybe Tia. But they had told him that the police had been to the house in Stanton. Maybe they were trying to warn him he thought. He never actually came out and told his mother or Tia that he was with his cousin, but he had called his mother from the bus station looking for his phone number. She could have relayed that information to the investigators.

Then he thought about his cousin. Just prior to his arrest Hamel was asking Washington when he was going to be moving out of the house. Maybe he tipped off the authorities as a way to avoid the awkward confrontation of him moving out. He knew that his cousin sort of idolized him, so it would be unlikely that he would have gotten him hooked up. But maybe that same idolization was the inspiration for his avoidance of the responsibility of kicking Washington out. At the end of all that reasoning though, Washington had never actually told his cousin about the murder, so had he turned him in because of the violation of parole?

"Can you open the sally port please?" the officer driving spoke into the microphone of the radio mounted on his console. Washington's streaming thoughts came back to the reality of the situation as the garage door began to open as requested.

By the time Washington was escorted into the booking area, the lieutenant and Brown were having a brief conversation. Washington watched as Brown handed over some documents. Not wanting to wait much longer in the booking area and needing a photo for his own records, Brown walked in and asked Washington to look at him for a quick picture. Brown pulled out his cell phone and snapped a shot to attach to the report he would be sending back to Philadelphia the next day. After Brown placed his phone back in his pocket, Washington spoke up, but in a less desperate manner than their last interaction.

"How'd you guys find me, anyway?" It wasn't the first time Brown, or any of the team members, had been asked that exact question in his years of fugitive hunting. Though tempted to tell Washington that some of his fellow white-power friends sold him out, he balked. His answer to that common question had been refined to a standard reply, and using his better judgement, he stuck with the normal answer.

"We don't reveal any of our sources." He turned and left the room, not wanting to engage with Washington any further, and not wishing to delay the process that the Kennison Police had to undertake before Washington could be brought to the county jail. Brown shook a couple of the officers' hands, extended his gratitude to all of them for the help, and made his way out to the parking lot.

CHAPTER TWENTY-SIX

The sound of Velcro straps being torn apart cascaded through the chilly night, as large tactical vests were taken off tired shoulders. It sounded like a million consecutive record scratches until the last vest was shorn. As he was removing his, Pollard had noticed his neck was a little sore, some from the weight of the vest, with a little extra ache from the stress of the whole investigation. The back slaps and handshakes continued as the team members streamed in and back out of the lobby of the police department to use the bathrooms before starting the long trek back to their homes. The "good nights" and "great jobs" were tossed around with a certain casual freedom but also with earnest sincerity.

After taking what felt like the longest piss of his life, Pollard washed his hands, pushed the swinging bathroom door open using just his right shoulder and pivoted slowly into the lobby. Brown had just come out of the police department and into the lobby when he had finished dropping off copies of warrants and other documents to the booking officers, and obtained his own mug shot of their target.

He beckoned Pollard over to him with an exaggerated hand wave. Before making it all the way to his location across the tiled floor, Pollard watched as Brown pulled out his phone, scrolled his contacts and hit dial without saying a word. On the receiving end, a voice answered, clearly familiar with the man calling on him.

"Brownie! What's the good word?" It was the team leader down in Philadelphia, Supervisory Deputy Marshal McKay.

"We got 'em. In custody right now up in the town of Kennison, New Hampshire." It was Brown's mission accomplished moment, supervisor to supervisor. Not exactly the same, but a close relative to celebratory drinks.

"No shit. It worked like you planned huh?"

"Yup." Brown would fill him in with all the details later, probably with his written report on the case.

"Well, I'll let Detective Luce over at Camden County know the good news. I'm sure he'll be eager to make notification to the victim's family and get some closure on this case. I know we're pretty happy with that result for our team down here. We were all still thinking we'd missed him in Camden, and he might still be around, and we were sending you all on a shit mission." It was a concern that the teams on both ends of the collateral lead had shared but was just now put out in the open.

"No man, you were right. He wasn't where you thought he was going to be in New Hampshire, but he was in New Hampshire none the less."

"Listen, thanks so much, man. I owe you a beer next time we're together." McKay wasn't sure when that would be, but it was a customary offer.

"You sure do."

Brown touched the end call button on the phone. He wanted Pollard to hear the gratitude and excitement of the other team. Pollard himself had been on the other side of those conversations, showing his appreciation to a team in another part of the country grabbing up one his fugitives from Stanton and the surrounding towns of the county. It was also nice to remind everyone about the victim's family being notified and what a relief that might be for them. Brown and Pollard said goodnight and shook hands one more time in the lobby before walking back out into the cold. Pollard left to go get warm in his truck and wait for Dorsey to finish up his latrine call to start towards home.

Vatrano and Matthews had just finished shaking hands and were getting ready to get in their cars as Pollard left the lobby. Knowing they might depart in the few seconds it would take him to traverse the parking spaces, Pollard put two fingers to his lips and let out a high-pitched whistle. He broke into a slow jog, hoping to avoid any icy patches on his route that would spell disaster for his tired body. Both Matthews and Vatrano looked up at the sound and saw him coming. They delayed entry to their vehicles for a moment to let Pollard catch up, partly out of respect, and also for the chance to possibly watch him slip and fall on the icy patches he was clearly trying to dodge.

"Hey guys, thanks again for everything." Pollard mustered the statement as though he was slightly out of breath from the extra effort. Vatrano and Matthews appreciated the hustle as their cars were both running and likely warm in the interior.

"Yeah, it all worked out great," Vatrano added.

Pollard didn't need to mention the work on the search warrants and the social media research that were instrumental in locating Washington. The mood indicated that no one was interested in waiting around for any prolonged speeches or toasts. A simple hug and a back slap from each man to the other signaled the end of the day and the end of this installment of hide-and-seek.

Pollard strolled to his own truck, in stark contrast to the hustle he had just displayed. Matthews and Vatrano pulled their vehicles out of the parking area and started toward the main road. Vatrano added a double tap on his horn on the way out, prompting Pollard to throw up a hand to acknowledge it without turning around to look.

As the clock ticked past 9 p.m., Pollard had calculated that he had been gone from home for about seventeen hours at that point in the day and was looking at another two hours behind the wheel before he got back. A quick text to Kelly, Pollard thought. It would be an opportune time to do so while he was waiting for Dorsey to come out of the lobby.

While Pollard readied himself to punch in the letters, he noticed that the last several exchanges were all him typing "going to be home late" and Kelly typing back a simple "OK." Pollard wasn't one to often communicate via text, or phone call either, even with Kelly. Unlike a lot of his co-workers, he was rarely on the phone at all, outside of the standard work correspondence that was required. He figured he should give her a call, it would be good to hear her voice if nothing else, and it wasn't that late yet.

It took about three rings and a cut off fourth before she picked up, a sign to Pollard that his estimation may have missed, and she was likely sleeping already.

"Hey, honey," she murmured, her sleepy voice masking her concern as she was receiving a phone call instead of the conventional going-to-be-home-late text. She hadn't seen or heard from her husband since she went to bed with him early the night before and was now preparing to head back to bed again, though this time, alone.

"So, I'm obviously going to be home late tonight. I just need to get Dorsey home first. It should probably take at least a couple of hours anyways," he said trying not to give an exact time of arrival that he would feel pressure to try and uphold.

"A couple hours! Where the heck are you guys?" It wasn't the normal travel distance on this night. He could hear in her voice that she was now fully awake while giving him a wedge in the conversation to broach the fun news he had been hoping to share with her but hadn't yet.

"Kennison State College, your old stomping grounds," he replied with a chuckle.

"What are you guys doing up there?" She knew what his job function was, but she was still a little stuck on the Kennison connection. Pollard answered her question literally and with more than a hint of sarcasm.

"Fugitive hunt," he said plainly.

"Any success?"

"Yeah, we got 'em. He was at one of the football team houses over on Tremont Street. You know it?"

Kelly perked up a bit, getting a rush of memories she wasn't expecting when the phone call began. "I used to party there all the time. That's crazy. Hahaha." It was actually laugh out loud funny to her. This strange circle of life, she figured.

"Well, the cops showed up and ruined it tonight. That ever happen to you there?"

Kelly just giggled on the other end of the phone knowing that the question was a rhetorical one and intended only to make her laugh. "Well, I'm glad it went well for you guys," she said redirecting the conversation away from her youthful indiscretions and back onto the here and now.

"You don't know the half of it. I'll tell you all about it when I get home." He meant it too, and she could clearly sense it.

"Well, I can't wait to hear about it," she said a little shocked about such an offer. "Love you," she said signaling a close to the conversation on her end.

"I love you too," Pollard replied calmly, while closing his eyes to picture her face as he hung up. Dorsey's voice caught Pollard by surprise as he walked up behind him from the opposite side of the truck bed.

"What are you doing, talking to the sheriff?" Dorsey joked, knowing full well the love was meant for Kelly. Pollard didn't answer.

"Let's get the hell out of here, we've got a long ride home," he stated with a smile.

Both men climbed up into the cab of the truck secure in their knowledge that there was a whole lot of two-lane road navigation ahead of them. They were both exhausted from the extremely long day, but now running on the adrenaline that could only come from a successful capture after a long chase like this one. The adrenaline boost was temporary, and the energy would begin to fade. Dorsey vowed to keep Pollard awake for the ride, both as a friendly gesture and for the sake of safety, mostly his own, he joked. Pollard returned the pledge. After they pulled away from the parking lot for the long journey home, Dorsey, still looking ahead through the windshield out into the cold night, broke the brief stretch of silence from his passenger seat.

"Well, that was something, huh?" Dorsey said, mostly to acknowledge the events of the day and not really asking a question. "I'm guessing Washington is wondering right now if the K-9 might have been the better poison to pick tonight instead of getting popped by the shield and having the entire fuckin' offensive line land on top of him." As a holder, it was acceptable for Dorsey to make such weight jokes with another member of the club.

"You're probably right, but I'm guessing he's got bigger things on his mind," Pollard said knowing he certainly would if he was facing Washington's fate.

"Yeah, probably. Hey, I'm starving, we haven't had dinner and it's a long ride home. Want to get some grub somewhere on the way out of town?" Dorsey asked, peeking over at Pollard with a smile from half of his mouth, already knowing what the answer would be. Pollard, of course, did not disappoint.

"It's Tuesday. Time for some tacos."

Fortunately for Pollard and Dorsey, most college towns often have good food available late at night and Kennison was no exception to that rule. Before heading out of town, Pollard and Dorsey found a Mexican place that made them up some spicy street tacos to go in short order.

Dorsey came out of the restaurant with a plastic bag filled with Styrofoam containers of tacos, rice, and refried beans. The precious package was visibly steaming from the open top like a chimney in the February New Hampshire night. They sat in their respective front seats in the truck and snacked at a rapid pace in the parking lot. Pollard braced his container up against the steering wheel and Dorsey placed napkins on the center of the dashboard, so they were easily accessible to both men. Per usual, there was little discussion while eating, as the job at hand was food consumption. The wrappers, containers and napkins were squished up, thrown back in the to-go bag, and tucked away in the rear of the truck to be disposed of on another day. Pollard let out a belch, put the truck in gear and started out of the parking lot of the Mexican joint back toward the main road out of town.

A few miles into the drive, the adrenaline from the night's activities and the digestion of tacos battled for control of the energy level of the two men going forward. With another several dozen miles to go, there was ample time for either one to dominate. Dorsey was apparently first to let the tacos win out, or at least the first to say so.

"How the hell did I let you talk my old ass in to eating tacos at this hour before a long drive home?" he asked while holding his gut with his right hand. The chuckle that had followed the ridiculous question was enough evidence to prove that Dorsey had faked at least some of that outrage, with nobody to blame but himself.

"You could have gotten a salad Rick, don't let me pressure you now." Pollard gave him a big smile because he knew a salad was never really an option. "You took D.A.R.E. class back in the day, right? You should know how to handle peer pressure situations!" Pollard joked.

Dorsey's face went from smiling to a little bit flat after making eye contact with Pollard while catching his smile. His tone went serious as Pollard looked forward out the windshield to navigate the turns of a winding two-lane country road.

"Man, I'm proud of you. That was a really good fuckin' hunt. You could have tapped out after they weren't at momma's house over in Stanton and sent it back to Philly, but you stuck to it. Really, man. Great fuckin' job on this one." Dorsey, like many of the alpha, type A personality men in their line of work, was more likely to joke than give an actual compliment that came from the heart. Pollard was a little shocked at first but took the praise in stride. He had a great deal of respect for Dorsey and his vast experience in the field, so it meant something more to him than just the words. He chose not to return the compliment with a joke as his initial instinct was telling him to do.

"It was a team effort, just like it always is. The best hunts are always the ones when everyone contributes, and we come to a successful and safe ending." As he finished saying it, he felt as though the answer sounded like a politician, or something someone might say in an interview with the media. He convinced himself that he meant it while shaking off the idea that such a statement was corny. Pollard took a quick moment to reflect on all the efforts that so many had made to track a murderer from southern New Jersey all the way to the snow country of northern New Hampshire. It was humbling to think of the number of people and law enforcement organizations it took.

A few miles further and the tacos had dominated the true battle of the night. Pollard and Dorsey were well into their eighteenth hour of work that day and it was showing. Opening the window a little, Pollard hoped the fresh and freezing air would keep him astute behind the wheel and provide the ancillary benefit of combating the effects of digesting tacos and beans.

Looking to double-down on his efforts to remain awake, he reached for the dial on the console and turned up the stereo. It was 90's alternative rock, something Dorsey always poked fun at him about, having graduated from high school exactly one decade before Pollard.

"You know, in the 80's when I was running the streets and the high school, the songs were all about beautiful chicks and having fun. Then your little generation shows up in the 90's and it's all sad shit and angst. What the hell?" The conversation had returned to a less serious and familiar baseline for the two men, a nice follow up to put the complimenting and praise behind them.

"Good thing we're almost to your house so you don't have to endure another minute. I don't think I can take another back-in-my-day lecture from you anyways." Pollard chose his words carefully, painting Dorsey as an old man. He wasn't going to take the intended slight lying down. After all, Pollard had an entire generation to defend.

Sitting in Dorsey's driveway, Pollard looked in the rear of the truck to make sure Dorsey hadn't left anything behind other than the garbage from the taco dinner. A fist bump and a head nod were their way of saying good night, much like it was their good morning greeting so many hours before. Pollard even sat and watched to make sure Dorsey got into his house without any difficulties before leaving, as though he was dropping off a date at the end of the night. Sometimes, Pollard thought, the desire to provide security for one another isn't just something that can be shut off, even in the safety of their own yards.

With Dorsey successfully dropped, he had a little less than a half hour of driving remaining to get home. To be in his warm bed for the night. To be back with Kelly.

That last half hour made time stand still. For Pollard, it easily felt like the longest leg of the trip home. Not so much in time, but in thought. With no distractions, he was left to himself to digest exactly what had happened over the past days, and even weeks. As the intentionally loud music faded to the background without having to adjust the volume, his brain wandered from event to event. His thoughts flowed freely, first contemplating Washington sitting in a county jail cell over in Kennison waiting for his court hearing the next morning. He questioned to himself if

Bixby and Walsh had even been made aware of what had happened yet or if Washington's young son, Lucas, could even comprehend it if they had.

His mind turned to the people in New Jersey. Had the victim's family been notified yet and how fast had that word traveled in his circles of friends? They were all questions that he could not answer, that he would have to leave for someone else to take care of. Much like an assembly line worker, Pollard and his team had to send it down the line as their task was done until the next fugitive. Just like this case had been sent up to them in a collateral lead, this investigation for them was over now. There was no more information to dig. It was part of fugitive hunting; the next step was to hand the whole ball back to the Camden County officials and the prosecutors who would try the case or come to a plea agreement.

Murder cases always took months, if not years, in court. Pollard wouldn't know the outcome of all of this unless he stumbled upon the press clippings on the internet months or years from now, maybe having his memory jogged seeing a Volkswagen with blue hubs riding around Stanton. He wondered if Washington would confess to it all and cooperate.

As he searched for that final summation of all the recent events, he failed to find the single emotion that he could point to as the end. While searching for that emotion, his thoughts started to drift toward Kelly. He owed her the full story. The whole thing ended up at a college house that she used to party at, it was the least he could do. He vowed then and there to skip the summary and give her that glimpse into his working world that he had so many times avoided, when the timing didn't seem right, or he just didn't have the energy or desire to get into it.

Tired from the extremely long day, he pulled into the driveway at his house and slugged his way up to the porch and entered the side door. Mexican food bag in hand, he was going to make certain that he would avoid starting the next shift with a car smelling like refried beans. He knew in his head he would be going to work late the following morning as that decision was made before he even left Kennison. When he looked at the spot on the wall just above the stove, he could see on the clock that it had just passed midnight. The following morning had become the present, and he had been at it since about 4 a.m. the previous day.

CHAPTER TWENTY-SEVEN

Pollard had always held some jealousy toward Kelly's ability to sleep so soundly. It was a seldom occasion that she woke up when he would arrive home late or leave really early in the morning. She might make a light sound or roll over onto her side, but rarely did she sit up or have a cogent conversation when she was in that state of slumber. This night, now early morning, was no different. It had now been just under three hours since he had talked to her on the phone from the parking lot of the Kennison Police Department, further reassuring his decision to avoid giving her an exact time of arrival.

The dog, however, did not possess Kelly's deeper sleeping abilities. Pollard walked into the bedroom to see the outline of Kelly's body, shaped underneath the heavy winter blankets, from what looked like the ears down. He was navigating in the bedroom by the secondary illuminations coming in from the hallway, trying hard not to jar his wife awake with any bright lights. Pollard accidently bumped the frame of the bed with his left leg while having difficulty in the nearly dark room, getting to a closet he had been to hundreds of times before in similar situations. It was a clear indication of Pollard's fatigue.

Though Kelly lay motionless through Pollard's clumsy act, the rapid motion of a docked tail waving frantically back from under a blanket caught Pollard's eye. Soon, the face of man's best friend appeared out from beneath the soft covering. It was as if Boomer's eyes needed to verify and confirm it was his master that had entered the room and no barking was warranted, along with confirmation that his tail wagging instinct was appropriate. Pollard gave the dog a quick pat on the head to acknowledge the excited greeting and then began shedding clothes, tossing each piece quietly into the hamper.

Leaving just the hallway light on for navigational aid, Pollard closed the bathroom door behind him as he entered and flipped the switch, hoping to prevent the light from casting into the bedroom. The hot water handle in the tub squeaked a little as he turned it to the left to get the shower started. He quickly brushed his teeth to get the taco taste from his mouth while waiting for the water to obtain a reasonable temperature before immersing himself on that cold winter night.

Pollard took a quick shower. He always did. The unfortunate side effect was that it gave him little time to rehearse what he was going to say to Kelly. At this point he didn't have the mental energy to script any plans, and the plans would no doubt be thrown out after first contact with his wife just like all the other plans had, he thought. He made himself chuckle out loud, though somewhat muted, with the comparison of plans that needed revision or even discarding from that day. Before stepping from the shower, he looked down at the shampoo and body wash bottles lined up nicely against the wall. He smirked in remembrance of how that line-up was a break in this now successful case.

Clean and ready to get into bed, Pollard felt a sudden burst of energy that he would so often get when first lying down to sleep at the end of a marathon day. After having struggled to stay awake while driving just thirty minutes prior, it was frustrating, but he worked through it.

He was careful not to lay down on top of the dog and gently shook Kelly's shoulder to wake her. It took a few jostles and he gently spoke her name a few times. She mumbled at first but then acknowledged her husband. Wiping the sleep from her eyes, she turned away from him to click on the small lamp on her nightstand, taking the majority of the blankets with her as she rotated. She then turned back wanting to see his face much like Boomer had moments before. If she had a tail, it no doubt would have been wagging too.

"Glad you're home," she said softly while propping herself up on her elbow. The cold and dry winter air was clearly a contributing factor to the static, causing the ends of her hair to stay in contact with the pillow as she created distance from it.

"Glad to be home," Pollard replied. For several reasons, he thought to himself.

She leaned across the space between the pillows and gave him a quick kiss. "So, what were you guys doing over in Kennison?" She clearly hadn't forgotten about the promise he had given to her on the phone several hours earlier.

"Looking for a murderer," he replied, playing it cool as though it was an everyday occurrence for him. Kelly's eyebrows perked up as that was a new one to her, though unconvinced by his nonchalant act. "It started a couple weeks ago now, when Brown got a lead from down in New Jersey about this guy whose mom and baby momma live in Stanton." Pollard went on to tell her in detail the events that had taken place leading up to the capture of the fugitive, even her own unintentional contribution by placing the shampoo bottles just so. She was both intrigued as he continued and appreciative of his full account.

After he was finished narrating the story for his wife, Pollard fell into a deep sleep. So deep that he didn't wake up before Kelly had already left for work the next morning, a role reversal in sound sleeping for the couple. The dog was still there in the bed though, waiting for Pollard to make the first move to get up before Boomer felt obligated to.

It felt good to sleep later and start the morning a bit more casually than he was used to. He went to the kitchen to grab his cell phone from the charger and found a small note from Kelly on a piece of scrap paper. It just said "Thanks" in a big heart. He folded it in half, closing the writing on the inside, and placed it in his pocket. He called for the dog to come downstairs for their morning routine, a bit delayed from the normal schedule by a couple of hours.

At the same time Pollard was standing in his kitchen, Washington was transported by two of the Kennison detectives from the local county jail into the dark basement that was the Kennison District Court holding area. His extradition hearing was set for 10 a.m.

On the ride over, he caught a glimpse of the presidential mountain range. The peaks were covered in a new, overnight layer of brilliant white snow, made more striking by the clear blue morning sky as a backdrop. The natural beauty of his home state brought him to think about the contrast to his last few months living just outside Camden. He didn't even want to think about what the jail would be like there. He could only go on the stories he had heard from his old cellmate, and they painted a picture that was less than flattering. The crime he had committed and who the victim was only added to Washington's anxiety.

The hearing was expected to be straightforward and without a lot of content. New Hampshire state laws required that Washington be held without any opportunity for bail on a homicide charge from another state while awaiting rendition. His parole violation would have prevented his release even if he could produce bail on the charge. The judge wouldn't even require that

Washington address the court in any way, only that he acknowledge that he understood the process that was taking place, and that it was going to take him back to New Jersey at the end of all of it.

Shackled in cuffs and chains at his hands and feet, he was led into the courtroom by two gray haired bailiffs, no doubt retired cops that had seen and done plenty in their days. Washington was seated at the defendant's table next to his court appointed public attorney that he had only spoken to briefly in the holding area of the court building.

He turned toward the gallery of people in the courtroom, all present there for their own reasons that day. He could see the faces of a whole host of people, most having no idea there would be a murder case on the docket. Many of those congregated had just appeared in court that day to address traffic tickets and other minor offenses. Even some of the police officers from the local surrounding towns, waiting to testify on the other matters, looked surprised at the charges they were reading in the usually mundane docket of a local district court in northern New Hampshire.

Washington was able to catch the eye of his cousin through the sea of heads in the gallery. Adam Hamel was sitting with his back against the side wall with his head cranked to the left, watching the activities of the courtroom, waiting patiently for Washington's extradition hearing to begin.

As they first made eye contact, Hamel just gave him a knowing head nod. One of understanding, maybe one of support.

It was possible that his cousin thought that with a few twists of fate, it could just as easily have been him sitting in that defendant's chair that morning. Instead, he had driven the used car that his stepfather had purchased and registered for him, from his house at the college he was privileged enough to attend to get to court that morning for the hearing. He had been instructed by his aunt, Walsh, after he spoke to her following the arrest, to call her and report exactly what had happened during the hearing. The promise would later be fulfilled for his favorite aunt as soon as Washington left the room, one short, shackled step at a time.

Washington, having spent the overnight in the county lock-up awaiting this hearing, had plenty of time to try and answer the question he had posed to Brown in the booking room at the Kennison Police Department the night before. Who was the rat? He acknowledged the cold steel of the shackles on his extremities, sitting in a court room full of strangers. There was one man present that had always cared for him, and probably would have traded places with him. Washington's infatuation with who, changed to why, and then again to what might have been.

Staying with his cousin for a couple of weeks, and seeing him for the first time since his release from New Hampshire State Prison on parole, sent him on a trail of "what ifs?" He should have listened to his mother as he got into his late teen years. He should have been a better and more involved father for Lucas. He should have followed the example that the man who became Hamel's stepfather had set for both of the boys.

As the "should haves" piled up, he began to bargain with himself. If only that half of the family hadn't left for New York, Washington thought, things might have turned out differently. He wouldn't have been in prison for the armed robbery. He never would have met the man that begged him to come to New Jersey to make a few quick bucks. He never would have killed a man that he didn't even have any bad blood with.

The sequence of events racing through Washington's head led him to a place of deep regret, a lamenting of grand proportions. How could he have been active in another armed robbery hundreds of miles away from his home? The lesson was clearly not learned the first time, and worse, in this new case he was now the trigger man. His friend from the west side was still doing his prison bid for shooting the clerk that night in New Hampshire a few years ago. Washington knew his fate would be much the same.

He looked back over his shoulder one more time at his cousin as though wishing he could start over and be sixteen years old again, as though Hamel might be able to take him there. Somewhere, back in Stanton, he knew that his mother was wishing the same thing, waiting for a report from her nephew about what was transpiring in court that morning, knowing that there was no turning back time.

Washington's head snapped forward as the judge hit the gavel and called out, "State of New Hampshire versus John Washington." His publicly appointed defense attorney grabbed him by the sleeve to direct him to stand up, as the attorney was now upright next to Washington. The hypotheticals crashed back to the reality as Washington stood as erect as he could, the shackles determining the distance between his feet and his hands in the required position of attention before the court.

"This is a Fugitive from Justice case arising from a homicide charge in the state of New Jersey." The charge being read out in court sent a brief buzz from the unexpecting gallery, though not enough for the judge to call for order. From atop his bench, he started in on the case. Washington basically tuned him out, only hearing the prosecutor and his defense attorney exchanging words with the judge, but not actually comprehending what was said. It was merely a formality, and Washington knew it. There was no plea to give on the homicide charge, and if there was, it was not going to be to a judge in Kennison, New Hampshire that morning.

At nearly the exact same time that Washington was in court, Pollard was on his way to his office in Stanton, almost a hundred miles away from the extradition hearing. He was proud of what he was able to accomplish over the past couple of weeks. The volume on the music in the truck was up a shade louder than normal, though this time not because he needed to stay awake. The feeling was light. He felt like he had won, exactly what, he wasn't sure. There was even a general lack of concern regarding the reports he would have to catch up on that day when he got into the office. The daydreaming was cut short by the ring of his phone through the truck speakers. It was Brown on the other side.

"What's up Brownie?" He was expecting some continued congratulations from the team leader or an update on the extradition hearing he knew was happening in Kennison that morning. What he got was the dose of reality he really should have expected.

"We got one in the southern part of the state, over on the seacoast. It's the sex offender case I had been working up last week. Are you available to meet at Matthews' office?"

Pollard wanted to say no. He didn't want to lose that feeling but couldn't resist. Spurning the temptation to decline wasn't difficult knowing that he was needed on another case already.

"I'm spinning around right now, be there in an hour or so." The next hunt was on. Pollard thought about the canvas art with the quote on the wall of his office. Hemingway was right, he concluded, there is no hunting like the hunting of man.

Brown, unsurprised by Pollard's acceptance of his request for assistance, responded the only way he knew how.

"Great. We'll see you there. Love you."

If you enjoyed "Collateral Lead," the second novel in the Deputy Mark Pollard Fugitive Series, "Failure to Register" is available for purchase at StephenColcordBooks.com or at Amazon.com today.

ABOUT THE AUTHOR

Stephen Colcord graduated from Fairfield University with a degree in Sociology in the spring of 2001. Shortly after September 11th that fateful autumn, he took a job in law enforcement. Since that time, he has been behind a badge and on the streets for more than two decades as a Police Officer, Deputy Sheriff, and Special Deputy United States Marshal. Colcord's debut novel, "Collateral Lead," is the first installment in the fictional Deputy Mark Pollard Series. The second book in the series, "Failure to Register" is also available now on Amazon.com, with the third book in the series expected in 2023.

For information regarding the author and updates on the release of new books, visit:

StephenColcordBooks.com

SCB

StephenColcordBooks.com

SCB

Made in United States
North Haven, CT
29 June 2022

20757286R10200